William Franklin Gore Shanks

Personal Recollections of Distinguished Generals

William Franklin Gore Shanks

Personal Recollections of Distinguished Generals

ISBN/EAN: 9783337219017

Printed in Europe, USA, Canada, Australia, Japan

Cover: Foto ©Andreas Hilbeck / pixelio.de

More available books at **www.hansebooks.com**

SHERIDAN'S RIDE TO THE FRONT.

PERSONAL RECOLLECTIONS

OF

DISTINGUISHED GENERALS.

BY

WILLIAM F. G. SHANKS.

NEW YORK:

HARPER & BROTHERS, PUBLISHERS,

FRANKLIN SQUARE.

1866.

PREFACE.

THE purpose of this volume is to make more familiar to the general public the actual characters of some of our great military leaders during the late war. I have attempted to portray them not as on parade, but in undress uniform, and to illustrate not only their great military qualities, but more particularly their mental peculiarities and characteristics. These pages will be found to contain many facts about some of the great battles which official reports have left untold, with such recollections of our generals as history proper will not perhaps condescend to record, and to embrace singular facts about great campaigns and strange stories of great men. The portraits are freely drawn. They are made from actual studies, if not special sittings, and while taking care to give every beauty, I have omitted none of the deformities or blemishes of my subjects, though I have told in full detail their virtues, and have touched on their faults and vices lightly. I have avoided alike extreme extravagance in praise or censure. Still there is enough shadow to the pictures to give the necessary, if not agreeable contrast to the lights. The reader must not, however, mistake the stand-point from which I have written. Distance, unfortunately for truth, lends enchantment not only to objects, but to men. The atmosphere of Olympus produces many phantasmagoria, and the great at a distance exist to our eyes in a sort of mirage. The philosophy of perspective as applied to natural objects is reversed when applied to mankind, and there are very few men who do not grow smaller as one approaches them. Most men are pyramidal in shape only, not proportions. "No man is a hero to his valet." Even Jupiter was ridiculous at times to Homer. Very few generals have appeared great to the war correspondents; and though very few of the latter can claim to be descendants of Diogenes, they can assert, with equal positiveness, that very few of the generals have been Alexanders, and that "the very sun shines through them." I have written under the disadvantage of being too near the objects drawn; and those who do not know the subjects as well may imagine I have made them undeservedly Liliputian in dimensions.

Writing contemporaneous history is the most thankless of tasks, and I discover also one of the least independent of labors. Still I have not written with a goosequill, and there has been some gall in my ink, yet I do not think I have any thing in the ensuing chapters to blot. I do not think I have done any man injustice. I have written many sentences and made many assertions which will doubtless be termed strong, but in writing these I am only the amanuensis of truth; and I write with the firm belief that "historical truth should be only less sacred than religious truth."

I have no doubt, however, that others will think differently after perusing the book. When publishing in Harper's Magazine I was told that the language of some of these sketches offended the subjects, but I have been unable to find any fact that ought to be stated otherwise. I think it best to say, for the benefit of all who may choose to object or condemn the volume as now published, that I have written nothing that I do not believe to be true—I trust not one sentence that, dying, I would wish to blot, and certainly not one word that, living, I intend to retract.

New York, *Sept*, 1866.

CONTENTS.

CHAPTER I.

SHERMAN AS A STRATEGIST.

CHAPTER II.

THOMAS AS A TACTICIAN.

A 2

CHAPTER III.

GRANT AS A GENERAL.

CHAPTER IV.

SHERIDAN AS A CAVALRYMAN.

CHAPTER V.

FIGHTING JOE HOOKER.

CHAPTER VI.

RECOLLECTIONS OF ROUSSEAU.

CHAPTER VII.

PECULIARITIES OF VARIOUS GENERALS.

CHAPTER VIII.

SOME PECULIARITIES OF OUR VETERANS.

ILLUSTRATIONS.

WILLIAM TECUMSEH SHERMAN.

PERSONAL RECOLLECTIONS

OF

DISTINGUISHED GENERALS.

CHAPTER I.

SHERMAN AS A STRATEGIST.

OF the few really great men who have been developed by the late war in this country, and who will leave a lasting impression on the minds of the people, William Tecumseh Sherman may be regarded as the most original. His name has been made more widely prominent, and his character more universally popular, than that of any other of our heroes; but it has been less in consequence of his brilliant success as a leader than by reason of his strongly-marked characteristics of person and mind. He is, without doubt, the most original and eccentric, though not the most powerful—the most interesting, though not the most impressive character developed by the rebellion. He is by far our most brilliant general, but not by any means the most reliable; the most fascinating, but not the most elegant; the quickest, but not the safest; the first to resolve, but not the most resolute. As a man he is always generous, but not uniformly just;

affectionate by nature, but not at all times kind in demonstration; confiding, and yet suspicious; obstinate, yet vacillating; decided, but not tenacious—a mass of contradictions so loosely and yet so happily thrown together as to produce the most interesting combination imaginable. General Sherman's character has many beauties and virtues, but also many glaring defects and faults. His picture, as I have seen and studied it, possesses what the artists call "great breadth of light and shade," and is full of contrasts alternately pleasing and offensive, and which, in order to properly analyze the character, should be portrayed and described with equal force and impartiality. He is a character without a parallel among his contemporaries, though not without a contrast; and it is for the latter reason that I have chosen his character as the one upon which to base, as it were, the following estimates of the characters of his fellow-officers of the United States army, and not because I think, as may be supposed, that he deserves the first place in the rank of our great captains. The war lasted long enough to give the leaders, if not their proper places in popular estimation, at least their true linear rank in the army. General Sherman may be considered as first among the strategists of the war; General George H. Thomas as first among the tacticians; but Grant, combining the qualities of both tactician and strategist, must always be ranked as greatly the superior of both Thomas and Sherman.

General Sherman may be described as a bundle of nerves all strung to their greatest tension. No woman was ever more painfully nervous; but there is nothing of the woman's weakness in Sherman's restlessness. It

is not, as with others, a defect of the organization; it is
really Sherman's greatest strength, for from it results the
brilliancy of conception and design which has characterized his strategic movements, the originality which has
appeared in his views on political economy and the policy
of war, and the overwhelming energy which is "his all
in all," the secret and cause of his great success.   From
his extreme nervousness results the most striking feature
of his character—a peculiar nervous energy which knows
no cessation, and is resistless.   It is not merely that energy and quickness of movement which naturally belongs to nervous organizations, but intensified a hundred fold.   At the same time, it is energy without system,
and oftentimes without judgment, but nevertheless always effective.   General Sherman is the engine, but he
is not always the engineer.   He furnishes the motive
power, but he frequently requires some person or thing
to keep him to the track; in fact, he requires to be controlled and directed.   He is untiring in his efforts; you
can never dismay him with the amount or frighten him
with the dangers of a task; and he hesitates at nothing,
matters great and small receiving his attention.   He is
no believer in that too common fallacy that labor is a
wearisome waste of the physical and vital powers; a punishment, not a privilege; and degrading, not elevating.
Work is necessary to his existence, and hard, earnest
work at that.   Always a hard, earnest worker, he devoted, during the continuance of the war, but little time
to sleep, and that little sleep was never sound.   His active mind, I once heard him say to a fellow-officer, delights in preposterous dreams and impossible fancies,

and, waking or sleeping, continues ever active in planning and executing.

A few anecdotes will perhaps better illustrate the nature of this nervous energy. The most remarkable instance of this characteristic which I can now recall occurred at Nashville, Tennessee. When Sherman assumed command there in March, 1864, the great difficulty in the way of an advance from Chattanooga upon the enemy, then covering Atlanta and the Georgia railroads, was the lack of provisions at Chattanooga and Knoxville. The military agent of the railroads from Nashville to Chattanooga was running through to the army at the latter point about ninety car-loads of rations per day. This merely served to feed the army then gathered there; nothing was accumulating for the spring campaign. General Sherman demanded the cause of this insufficient supply of rations. The agent reported that he needed both cars and locomotives, and added it was impossible to obtain them. General Sherman answered that nothing was impossible, and immediately began to devise means by which to remedy the evil. After a short deliberation, he decided to seize a sufficiency of cars and locomotives in Indiana, Ohio, and Illinois, and at once went to work to do so. In an incredibly short space of time he extended the northern terminus of the Louisville and Nashville Railroad through the former city, a distance of three miles, to the Ohio River. On the levee, or wharf, he built an inclined plane to the water's edge. One of the ferry-boats which plied between Louisville and Jeffersonville was seized, and especially prepared by the laying of rails across its bow and stern to carry cars and locomotives. On the Indiana side of the river he extended the Jeffersonville Railroad through that town to the Ohio River, and built another inclined plane from the bluff on which the town is situated down the steep wharf to the water's edge. At the same time he ordered the impressment of the necessary cars and locomotives from the various northwestern railroads, taking them off routes as far north as Chicago, and rushed them off to Nashville, crossing the Ohio by the means he had provided. The effect was soon visible. In a month after this movement began the railroad agents reported that they were running two hundred and seventy cars per day through to Chattanooga. By the 20th of April, the day Sherman left Nashville to begin his Atlanta campaign, he had accumulated at Knoxville eighteen, and at Chattanooga thirteen days' rations for his whole army of 120,000 men. The energy which inspired the railroad agents was communicated to the quarter-masters located at Nashville, and the result was the increase of the laboring force of this department from four or five thousand to nearly sixteen thousand men. During the progress of this work General Sherman required the railroad agents and quarter-masters to report progress daily. I happened to be in his office one morning when assistant quarter-master General James L. Donnalson reported a small increase in the number of cars forwarded on that day over the supply of the day before. General Sherman received the announcement with more evidences of gratification than he would have shown on hearing of a heavy re-enforcement of his numbers, for at this time he had more men than he well knew what to do with. "That's good!" he exclaimed — "that's good, Donnalson; we'll be ready for the start;" and then he hastily resumed his seat, and made a rapid calculation of some sort, which he showed with much apparent delight to Generals Donnalson and Webster, the latter his chief of staff. He could not have been more delighted if he had heard the news of a great victory. A moment afterward he turned to me to deny, in a very gruff way—he was always gruff to newspaper correspondents — my application for a pass over the military railroad to Chattanooga. "You see," he said, "I have as much as I can do to feed my *soldiers*," with a very ungracious emphasis on the word soldiers. As I had Lieutenant General Grant's pass to any point and by any route in my pocket, and had only submitted the question to General Sherman through deference to him as the immediate commander of the department, I could afford to smile at the slur conveyed in his emphasis, and turned away enriched with a reminiscence, and with increased admiration of the man.

Some former experience with, or, rather, observation of the general, had given me somewhat of the same opinion of his energy and earnestness. When he first assumed command at Louisville, Kentucky, in 1861, the agents of the New York Associated Press throughout the country were employed by the government in transmitting its cipher or secret messages, and correspondence between the various military commanders, by telegraph. In consequence of this arrangement, General Sherman frequented the office of the Louisville agency, in which I was at the time employed. He was always at this office during the evening, often remaining until three o'clock in the morning, when the closing of the office would force him to retire to his rooms at the hotel. During these hours he would pace the floor of the room apparently absorbed in thought, and heedless of all that was going on around him. He would occasionally sit at the table to jot down a memorandum or compose a telegram. He would sometimes stop to listen to any remark addressed to him by other occupants of the room, but would seldom reply, even though the remark had been a direct question, and would appear and act as if the interruption had but momentarily disturbed his train of thought.

In July, 1864, while besieging the enemy's position at Kenesaw Mountain, an incident occurred which may be given as illustrative of Sherman's energy. When the campaign opened he had published an order informing the army, in terms which were laughed at at the time as rather bombastic and slightly egotistical, that "the commanding general intended making the campaign without a tent," and during the greater part of the march his head-quarters actually consisted of nothing more than a tent-fly for the use of his adjutant general. He generally slept under a tree during dry weather, and in very wet weather in any convenient house. When the army was concentrated in the gorge of Snake Creek Gap, in which there was not a house of any character, General Logan "raised the laugh" on Sherman by sending him a tent to protect him from the rain, and which, owing to the terrible state of the weather, Sherman was compelled to use. But the greater part of the campaign was actually passed by Sherman without any other quarters than I have described as for the convenience of his adjutant general. Early one morning a regiment of troops passed his bivouac near Kenesaw Mountain, Georgia, and saw him lying under a tree near the roadside. One of the men, not knowing the general, and supposing him, from his jaded, weary, and generally dilapidated appearance, to be drunk, remarked aloud, "That is the way we are commanded, officered by drunken generals." Sherman heard the remark and instantly arose. "Not drunk, my boy," he said good-humoredly, "but I was up all night looking after your rations, and am very tired and sleepy." He soon after broke up head-quarters, and, passing the same regiment on the march, was received with loud and hearty cheers.

He makes his subordinates work, too, with the same zeal. When the rebels, in evacuating Resaca, succeeded in burning the railroad bridge over the Oostenaula River, he turned to Colonel Wright, his engineer in charge of railroads, and asked him how long it would take him to replace that bridge. Colonel Wright replied after a short calculation, during which Sherman showed his impatience at the delay in the answer, that he could rebuild it in four days.

"Sir," exclaimed the general, hastily, "I give you forty-eight hours, or a position in the front ranks."

The bridge was forthcoming at the proper time.

This nervousness of Sherman's organization has naturally produced a peculiar restlessness of manner and admirable vigor of expression. He talks with great rapidity, often in his haste mingling his sentences in a most surprising manner, and accompanying his conversation by strange, quick, and ungraceful gestures, the most common of which is the knocking of the ashes from his cigar with the little finger of his left hand, frequently knocking at it until ashes and light too are gone.

In a conversation of importance, and particularly on a battle-field, he seldom gives a person time to finish his remarks or reports. He replies as soon as he has heard enough to convey the idea, never waiting its elaboration. In giving his instructions and orders, he will take a person by the shoulder and push him off as he talks, following him to the door, all the time talking and urging him away. His quick, restless manner almost invariably results in the confusion of the person whom he is thus instructing, but Sherman himself never gets confused. At the same time, he never gets composed. Under all circumstances, he is thus restlessly, never timidly nervous. In danger the restlessness is not so visible, and hence it is apparent that there is nothing of timidity in it. On the battle-field where he commands Sherman's nervous manner is toned down. He grates his teeth, and his lips are closed more firmly, giving an expression of greater determination to his countenance. His eyes are somewhat closed, as if endeavoring to see the furthermost limits of the battle-field, and, as it were, peer into the future and see the result. His cigar is always kept firmly between his lips, but he suffers its fire occasionally to die out. He is less restless of body; his arms are more confined to their proper limits; and he is content to stay in one spot. He talks less at such moments than at calmer ones. On light occasions, however, he is invariably ill at ease. His fingers nervously twitch his red whiskers—his coat buttons—play a tattoo on his table or chair, or run through his hair. One moment his legs are crossed, and the next both are on the floor. He sits a moment, and then rises and paces the floor. He *must* talk, quick, sharp, and yet not harshly, all the time making his odd gestures, which, no less than the intonation of his voice, serve to emphasize his language. He can not bear a clog upon his thoughts nor an interruption to his language. He admits of no opposition. He overrides every thing. He never hesitates at interrupting any one, but can not bear to be interrupted himself. He is very well aware, and candidly admits that his temper is uncommonly bad, and, what is worse, he makes no attempt to control or correct it. In speaking of the late General McPherson, of the Army of Tennessee, he once remarked, "He is as good an officer as I am—is younger, and has a better temper." Grant, once speaking of Sherman's peevishness, said, "Sherman is impetuous and faulty, but he sees his faults as soon as any man." The fact is, if Sherman's faults alone could be given to another, they would serve to distinguish him from the common herd.

The idea generally prevails that commanding generals are very didactic on the battle-field, and give their orders in precise language and stentorian voice. A little familiarity with actual war will soon dispel this false impression, particularly if you meet Sherman on the battle-field, for there is less of dignity, display, and grandiloquence in him than any other general whom I have met during the war. At the battle of Chattanooga he gave his orders for the advance of his troops against the enemy's strongly fortified position to his brother in law,

General Hugh Ewing, in the words uttered between two puffs at a bad cigar: "I guess, Ewing, if you are ready, you may as well go ahead." Ewing asked a few questions in regard to retaining the *echélon* formation of his command as then marshaled for the advance. Sherman replied, "I want you to keep the left well toward the river (the Chickamauga), and keep up the formation four hundred yards distance, until you get to the foot of the hill."

"And shall we keep it after that?" asked Ewing.

"Oh, you may go up the hill as you like," said Sherman; and then he added, *sotto voce*, with a smile and a wink to his aid, and General Ewing's brother, Charley Ewing, who stood near by, "if you can." As General Ewing was mounting his horse and about to leave, Sherman called out to him,

"I say, Ewing, don't call for help until you actually need it." General Frank Blair, and others of the Army of the Tennessee who were standing near Sherman, laughed at this in such a manner as left the impression on the minds of others, as well as myself, that on some former occasion General Ewing had called for help before General Sherman thought that he really needed it.

It is recorded of Sherman that, on witnessing from the top of a rice-mill on the Ogeechee River the capture of Fort McAllister by General Hazen's forces, and the successful termination by that capture of the "march to the sea," he exclaimed, imitating the voice of a negro, "Dis chile don't sleep dis night," and hurried off to meet General Foster and complete the junction of the two armies.

His nervousness is not less perceptible in his writings than in his conversation and manners. His writings lack

in elegance, but not in force. Some of his letters, remarkable for absence of grace and presence of vigor, are ·
already accepted as among the model documents of the
war, not only as to style, but as to argument. His
speeches, letters, and orders are seldom more than skeletons, framed of sharp, pointed, but disjointed sentences,
from which the ideas to be conveyed protrude so prominently as to be comprehensible when the sentence is but
half conveyed. His ideas are never elaborated in his letters, though given more fully than in his conversations,
but you never have to finish the sentence to discover
its meaning. There. are several specimens which every
reader will naturally think of in this connection. His
letter to the rebel General Hood on the proposed depopulation of Atlanta is a curious document, an impromptu
reply, thrown off-hand from his pen, and it reads as if it
were Sherman talking. He begins this letter by acknowledging the receipt of a communication at the hands
of "Messrs. Bull and *crew*." The bearers, who were designated by this undignified title, were members of the Common Council of Atlanta, for whom Sherman does not
appear to have entertained the most profound respect.
The letter ends by advising Hood to tell his tale of oppression "to the marines," as he (Sherman) is not to be
imposed upon. In the same correspondence he indicates
his action in depopulating Atlanta, and gives his peculiar
"theory of suppression." Sherman's whole theory, in
which, by the way, he has been consistent from the first,
is embraced in .the proposition to "fight the devil with
fire." He was for vigorous war all the time—hard blows
at the organized armies, frequent and oft repeated. He

has none of the elements of Fabian in him. He writes in defense of the action at Atlanta alluded to: "We must have peace, not only in Atlanta, but in all America. To secure this, we must stop the war that now desolates our once happy and favored country. To stop war, we must *defeat the rebel armies* that are arrayed against the laws and Constitution, which all must respect and obey. To defeat these armies, we must prepare the way to reach them in their recesses provided with the arms and instruments which enable us to accomplish our purpose." His expression in the same letter, "War is cruelty—you can not refine it," is a sharp, terse rendition of an undisputed truth, to the illustration of which whole chapters have been less successfully devoted by more distinguished writers.

While endeavoring to fill up his dépôts at Chattanooga and Knoxville preparatory to the campaign against Atlanta, Sherman was asked by members of the United States Christian Commission for transportation for their delegates, books, tracts, etc., for the army. His reply is very characteristic of the man: "Certainly not," he wrote; "crackers and oats are more necessary to my army than any moral or religious agency." As this incident shows, Sherman is not a very firm believer in the utility of Christian or Sanitary Commissions, or aid societies generally. He thinks female nurses about a hospital or an army a great nuisance. He once alluded contemptuously to the efforts of a large number of ladies at Louisville, Kentucky, to send clothing, lint, sweetmeats, etc., to his troops, but was induced, in lieu of discouraging their efforts, to take steps to properly direct them.

He met the ladies by agreement in one of the public halls at Louisville, now known as Wood's Theatre, and made an address to them. He went among the lambs with all the boldness and dignity of a lion; but the rough, uncouth manner of him who had frowned on thousands of men melted in the presence of a few hundred ladies. They found that, though "he was no orator as Brutus is," he could talk very tenderly of the soldier's wants, very graphically of the soldier's life and sufferings, and very gallantly of woman and her divine mission of soothing and comforting.

During the campaign of Atlanta communication with the rear was very much obstructed, the news correspondents found many difficulties in forwarding information, and telegrams to the press seldom reached New York. During the movement around Atlanta Sherman was applied to directly by the news agent at Louisville for the details of the movement. In reply the general telegraphed, "Atlanta is ours, and fairly won;" following up the expression, which has already passed into song, with a brief and graphic report of the flank movement around Atlanta and the battle of Jonesborough. This report is one of the most admirable narratives I remember to have ever read, and at the time of its publication I wrote for the Herald, of which I was then a correspondent, a long criticism of it. The letter never appeared, however, for the reason that I endeavored to show that, successful as he had been, Sherman had mistaken his vocation as a general, and ought to have been a war correspondent. I suppose Sherman would have been mortally offended at such language, particularly as he affected to hold correspondents and editors in contempt; but undoubtedly he would have been invaluable to the New York Herald or London Times in such a capacity, and could have made more money, if not more reputation, in that capacity than as a major general. He has lately declared that he does not believe he will ever have occasion to lead men again, and I advise him by all means to go into the newspaper business. Any of the principal papers of New York will be glad to give him double the pay 'of a major general to act in the capacity of war correspondent.

Until Sherman had developed his practicability, this peculiarity of expression and manner were accepted as evidences of a badly-balanced mind. It will be remembered that in his early career a report was widely circulated to the effect that he was a lunatic; but the origin of this story, if properly stated, will redound to his credit, as evincing admirable foresight and sagacity. The true origin of this report is as follows: Sherman succeeded General Robert Anderson in command of the Department of the Ohio on October 13, 1861. Up to that time about ten thousand United States troops had been pushed into Kentucky. The Western governors were under a promise to send as many more, but were slow in doing so. General A. Sidney Johnston, the rebel commander at Bowling Green, was endeavoring to create the impression that he had about seventy-five thousand men, when he really had only about twenty-eight thousand. In this he succeeded so far as to cause it to be supposed that his force largely exceeded Sherman's. Sherman urged upon the government the rapid re-enforcement of his army, but with lit-

tle effect. The troops did not come, for the reason that
the government did not credit the statements of the perilous condition of Sherman's army. So repeated and ur-
gent were Sherman's demands for re-enforcements, that
at last the Secretary of War, Mr. Cameron, visited Louisville in order to look into the situation of affairs. An interview took place at the Galt House at Louisville, Sherman, Cameron, and Adjutant General Thomas being present. Sherman briefly explained the situation of affairs,
stated his own force and that of the enemy, and argued
that re-enforcements were necessary to hold Kentucky,
to say nothing of an advance. "My forces are too small
for an advance," he said—"too small to hold the important positions in the state against an advance of the enemy, and altogether too large to be sacrificed in detail."
On being asked how many men were required to drive
the enemy out of the state, he answered, without hesitation, "Two hundred thousand." The answer was a surprise to the two officers, which they did not attempt to
conceal. They even ridiculed the idea, and laughed at
the calculation. It was declared impossible to furnish
the number of men named. Sherman then argued that
the positions in Kentucky ought to be abandoned, and
the army no longer endangered by being scattered. This
was treated more seriously, and vigorously opposed by
Cameron and Thomas. They declared the abandonment
of Kentucky was a step to which they could not consent.
Subsequently they broached a plan which had been de-
vised for dividing the Department and Army of the
Ohio into two; one column to operate under Mitchell
from Cincinnati as a base against Knoxville, and the

other from Louisville against Nashville. To this Sherman was strongly opposed. Satisfied by the persistence of Cameron on this point that the government was not disposed to second his views of conducting the affairs of the Department, Sherman asked to be relieved and ordered to duty in the field. Cameron gladly acquiesced in his wishes, and he was relieved by Buell, November 30, 1861.

On the same evening of the famous interview between Cameron and Sherman, the latter paid his customary visit to the Associated Press-rooms at Louisville. Here, while still in a bad humor over the result of the interview, he was approached by a man who introduced himself as an attache of a New York paper, and asked permission to pass through the lines to the South in the capacity of a correspondent. Sherman replied that he could not pass. The correspondent, with unwarrantable impertinence, replied that Secretary Cameron was in the city, and he would get a pass from him. Sherman at once ordered him out of his department, telling him that he would give him two hours to make his escape; if found in his lines after that hour he "would hang him as a spy." The fellow left the city immediately, and on reaching Cincinnati very freely expressed his opinion that the general was crazy. A paper published in that city, on learning the story of the interview between Cameron and Sherman, which soon became public, employed the fellow to write up the report which was thus first circulated of Sherman's lunacy. His opinion that two hundred thousand men were required to clear Kentucky of rebels was quoted as proof of it by this man, and thus the story came into existence.

Subsequent events revealed the fact that Sherman did not much exaggerate the force necessary to carry on the war in the central zone of the field of military operations. Although we have never had a single army numbering two hundred thousand men in the West, much larger armies have been necessary to the accomplishment of the campaign of the Mississippi and Tennessee Rivers than any person other than Sherman thus early in the war imagined. The army of Grant at Fort Donelson and Shiloh, combined with that of Buell, was not over eighty thousand men. That of Halleck before Corinth numbered exactly one hundred and two thousand. Sherman left Chattanooga in May, 1864, with one hundred and twenty thousand men, the largest army ever gathered in one body in the West. At the same time, he had under his command at different points on the Mississippi River and in Kentucky an additional force of about fifty thousand, while the forces operating under other commanders in the West would, if added to his, make a grand total of two hundred and fifty thousand men operating on the Mississippi River, every one of whom was necessary to the conquest and retention of the Mississippi Valley.

Sherman may have been at one time crazy, but his madness, like Hamlet's, certainly had marvelous method in it. Such lunatics as he have existed in all ages, and have, when as successful as himself, been designated by the distinctive title of "genius," in contradistinction to men of medium abilities. Not only Shakspeare, but Dryden, seems to have encountered such madness as Sherman's, and to have appreciated the truth that

> "Great wits are sure to madness near allied,
> And thin partitions do their bounds divide."

Doubtless the same author had such a genius or madman as Sherman in his mind when he described one of his characters as

> "A fiery soul, which, working out its way,
> Fretted the pigmy body to decay."

The peculiar formation of Sherman's head shows his great development of brain. His forehead is broad, high, and full, while the lower half of his face and head are of very diminutive proportions. In a person of less physical strength and vitality, this great preponderance of the mental over the physical powers would have produced perhaps actual lunacy. The head of Sherman is of the shape peculiar to lunatics predisposed to fanciful conceptions. There is too much brain, and in Sherman it is balanced and regulated only by his great physical development. Sherman's brain, combined with bad health, would have produced lunacy; his brain and sinewy strength combined produced his peculiar mental and physical nervousness. Had he been a sedentary student instead of an active soldier, the last line of Dryden's poem might also have applied to him, and we should know of him only as an "o'er informed tenement of clay."*

When this report of his lunacy was first circulated, Sherman was much chagrined at it, and often referred to

---

*
> "A fiery soul, which, working out its way,
> Fretted the pigmy body to decay,
> And o'er informed the tenement of clay."

it in bitter terms. ˙ Time and success have enabled him to frown it down, and justified him in laughing at it. He once laughingly referred to this report about himself, and the rumor which simultaneously prevailed regarding Grant's drunkenness during the battle of Shiloh as illustrative of the friendship existing between them. "You see," he said to a gentleman, "Grant stood by me when I was crazy, and I stood by him when he was drunk."

During the siege of Corinth he commanded the right wing of Thomas's corps, while T. W. Sherman, of Port Royal memory, commanded the left. The latter was very unpopular with his division on account of a painfully nervous manner and fretful disposition, and the officers of the command discussed him critically with great freedom, many condemning his manner as offensive. One day General W. T. Sherman was visiting General Steedman—then a brigade commander in T. W. Sherman's division—and the latter's name was brought up, Steedman giving a very ludicrous account of Sherman's conduct.

"Oh !" said William Tecumseh, "this is the crazy Sherman, is it ?"

Great difficulty was found during the operations before Corinth in distinguishing the two Shermans. The soldiers solved the problem by giving each Sherman a nickname. T. W. Sherman was called " Port Royal Sherman," in allusion to his services in South Carolina, while W. T. Sherman was known by the somewhat inappropriate title of " Steady-old-nerves," in contradistinction to the other, who, as before stated, was more timidly nervous. Mr. Lincoln, with some recollection of this coincidence of names on his mind, asked General Grant, on being introduced to General Sherman, if he was W. T. or T. W., and laughed with boyish glee at the "joke on Sherman."

As another natural result of Sherman's nervous energy, he has acquired the habit of decision in the most perfect degree, and his peculiar organization has tended to make him practical as well as petulant. He never seems to reason, but decides by intuition, and, in this respect, has something of the mental as well as bodily peculiarities of the gentler sex, who are said to decide intuitively. But Sherman is by no means a woman—he would have been a shrew had he been—and possesses not one particle of the sex's beauty or gentleness. Sherman jumps at conclusions with tremendous logical springs; and, though his decisions are not always final, they are in effect so, for, if he is forced to retire an inch, his next jump will probably carry him forward an ell. Facts are the only argument which prevail with him, and the best arguments of wise men are wasted in endeavoring to convince him without undeniable facts at hand. Obstinate, and vain, and opinionated as he is, and indisposed as he may be to listen to or heed the arguments of equals or inferiors, he never hesitates to sink all opposition before the orders of his superiors, and pay the strictest deference to their views when expressed authoritatively.

I have before said this nervousness of mental and bodily organization was the main-spring of Sherman's character. From it result not only his virtues, but his faults, and as man and commander he has many. He is as petulant as a dyspeptic; excessively gruff, and unreasonably passionate. His petulance does not, however, prevent his being pleasant when he is disposed; his gruffness does not destroy all his generosity, and his passionate moods are usually followed by penitence. His fits of passion are frequent but not persistent, and, though violent, are soon appeased.

His gruffness often amounts to positive rudeness. While in command at Louisville in 1861, the wife of the rebel commander Ingraham passed through the city *en route* to the South. The lady, who was rebelliously inclined, pleaded consumption as her excuse for wishing to inhale the Southern air. Sherman gruffly advised her to "shut herself up in a room and keep up a good fire— it would do her just as much good." He often replies in this petulant tone to both sexes, particularly if the person addressed has no business of importance.

He once took great offense at having his manners, and particularly this habit of gruffness, compared to the manners of a Pawnee Indian, and expressed his contempt for the author of the slur in a public manner. He was much chagrined shortly after to find that the correspondent who had been guilty of the offensive comparison had heard of his contemptuous criticism, and had amended it by publicly apologizing to the whole race of Pawnees!

During the battle of Bull Run, where General Sherman commanded a brigade, he was approached by a civilian, who, seeing him make some observations without the aid of a field-glass, proffered him the use of his own. Sherman turned to the gentleman and gruffly demanded,

"Who are you, sir?"

"My name is Owen Lovejoy, and I am a member of Congress."

" What are you doing here? Get out of my lines, sir —get out of my lines."

Nothing satisfied Sherman but the immediate retreat of the member of Congress to the rear.

I have heard that Sherman's bad temper was the cause of his leaving his chosen profession of the law. After resigning his commission in the army in 1853, he became, after several changes, a consulting lawyer in the firm of his brothers-in-law, the Ewings, at Leavenworth, Kansas. He had entered into the copartnership with the distinct understanding that he was not to be called upon to plead in the courts; for, though possessing a thorough knowledge of legal principles, a clear, logical perception of the equity involved in all cases, and though perfectly *au fait* in the authorities, he had no confidence in his oratorical powers. He was not then the orator he has latterly become, and utterly refused to take any part in legal debate or pleadings. One day a case came up in the Probate Court of Kansas requiring immediate attention. Tom and Hugh Ewing were busy; McCook was absent, and Sherman was forced, *nolens volens*, to go into court. He carefully mapped out his course until it looked like plain sailing; laid down his plan of procedure, as he used subsequently to do his plans of marches; but he was destined to be driven from his chosen route, not by a Joe Johnston or " foeman worthy of his steel," but by a contemptible, pettifogging lawyer, with more shrewdness than honesty, and more respect for the end to be attained than the means to be used. In the debate which the trial involved, Sherman lost his temper, and, consequently, his case. He returned to his office in a towering rage, dissolved the partnership with his broth-ers-in-law, and, without farther hesitation, accepted the presidency of the Louisiana Military Academy, the prof-fer of which he had received a day or two before.

General Sherman's violent temper greatly endangered his reputation toward the close of the war, and he came near sacrificing, in an evil hour of passion, all that he had won before. His passion was to him as the unar-mored heel was to Achilles, and the vulnerable point of his character came near costing him even more dearly than did the vulnerable part of the Grecian warrior's body. His diplomatic feat with Joe Johnston was gen-erally denounced as a blunder, but it was not the blun-der which came near costing him so dearly. That piece of diplomacy took the shape of a blunder in consequence of the unfortunate and unforeseen circumstances and dis-asters which occurred simultaneously with it. Had Mr. Lincoln lived, General Sherman would to-day have borne a brilliant reputation as a diplomatist, and his agreement with Johnston would have been at once, as it was eventu-ally, accepted as the basis for the political reconstruction of the country. That agreement was repudiated by the people and President Johnson in an hour of frenzied passion, though the latter has since modeled his plan upon it; and Sherman lost his chance for becoming a great diplomatist. But he, and he only, was to blame for the grave blunder which immediately afterward nearly cost him his fame and position as a soldier. Sullen at the repudiation of his agreement with Johnston, angry at the interference of General Halleck with the co-opera-tive movements of himself and Sheridan, and furious at the countermanding of his orders to his subordinates by the Secretary of War, Sherman forgot himself, and marched to Washington with his army, breathing vengeance upon Halleck, and hate and contempt for Stanton. Fortunately for Sherman, history will not record the scene. History never yet recorded—no nation ever before safely witnessed such a spectacle as that of a victorious general, at the head of eighty thousand men devoted to him and jealous of his fame as a part of their own, marching to the capital of the country with threats against his military superiors breathing from his lips and flowing from his pen. For days Sherman raved around Washington, expressing his contempt for Halleck and Stanton in his strongest terms, and denouncing them as "mere non-combatants" whom he despised. More than this, he wrote to his friends, and through them to the public, comparing Stanton and Halleck to "cowardly Falstaffs," seeking to win applause and honor for the deeds he had done; accusing the Secretary of War of suppressing his reports, and endeavoring to slander him before the American public in official bulletins. For days his army roamed the streets of the capital with the same freedom with which they had roamed through the fields of Georgia and the swamps of the Carolinas, and no man dared to raise his voice in condemnation of their leader, or approval of the superiors who had opposed him. No republic ever before survived such a condition of affairs; this republic never was in such danger before, and yet the danger was hardly suspected. The spectacle is one which Sherman will ever regret, but every true American, and every lover of republican liberty, can point to it with pride as a remarkable illustration of the stability of republican institutions. Powerful as Sherman was against Stanton and Halleck (and a word from him would have destroyed them), he was powerless against the nation,.and not one man of his mighty host would have followed him in an attempt upon its existence. It is, perhaps, a still greater proof of the power of republican principles that, in the midst of his furious rage, such a thought as the injury of the government never for a passing second entered the brain of the leader of these men. He has reason to be thankful that the nation was as generous as he was honest; and that the people made no record against him for the offense against discipline which in any other country would have cost him not merely his position, but his reputation, and in any other army his head. At the same time, the nation must and will cherish the honest man who, thus tried and tempted, never for a single second forgot his allegiance to the principles for which he had fought and the country which he had served.

General Sherman's reputation as a soldier must rest entirely on his strategic abilities. His successes were those of strategy only—not of tactics. His faults as a commander are glaring as his faults of character. As an organizer of armies for the field, and as a tactician in battle, he was an utter failure. He never commanded a well-organized army whose discipline did not become relax under his administration, and he was never commander-in-chief in any battle which was not a failure. Instead of being an organizer, Sherman was a disorganizer; he was always chief among the "Bummers" which he made his soldiers, and by which name they were eventually designated. His whole career shows him to have been solely a strategist, absolutely incapacitated by mental organization for disciplining and fighting an army. His attempt to organize the army in Kentucky in 1861 was a most egregious failure. He gave it up in despair to General Buell, who, on assuming command, found it a mob without head or front, or appropriate parts. Buell, in contradistinction to Sherman, was great as an organizer and disciplinarian, and he soon made a fine army out of Sherman's unorganized mob. General Sherman shortly afterward went into the battle of Shiloh with a division of troops who were also unorganized, and only escaped annihilation by the timely appearance of Buell and the now thoroughly disciplined troops which Sherman had originally commanded. When Buell's troops on this occasion made their appearance on the small plateau which is called Pittsburg Landing, the great numbers of Sherman's demoralized new recruits who were there huddled together welcomed them as veterans. "Buell! Buell!" was their cry; "here come Buell's veterans." One can not but smile when he remembers that the men thus hailed as veterans had never been engaged in even so much as a skirmish. Their conduct in the desperate battle which followed on the day after their arrival proved them to be worthy of the name. One year's thorough discipline had made them veterans without having fought a battle.

Throughout Sherman's career his troops were noted for their lack of discipline. When he assumed command of the Army of Tennessee on the promotion of General

Grant in 1863, he found it one of the best disciplined armies in the country, though not the best provided. I doubt if there was ever a division, brigade, or even regimental drill in that army after Sherman took command. He subsequently became indirectly in command of the Army of the Cumberland, which, though directly commanded by that strict disciplinarian, General George H. Thomas, soon felt the effect of Sherman's presence and control, and became very relaxed in discipline. Subsequently, on the march to the sea and through the Carolinas under Sherman, the discipline of the formerly model armies became still more relaxed, and gradually the whole army became regular "Bummers," a term which is not generally understood in its proper sense of reproach. The people to this day only half know what a "bummer" is, from having a general idea of the character of Sherman as the chief of bummers. The veil of romance which surrounded Sherman's army has never been entirely torn away. Its pilgrimages are still romances. It has always been viewed in that dim and distant perspective which adds a charm to beauty, and hides internal troubles and blemishes, and the evils it did and the outrages it committed have never been made public. But the friends of Sherman might reasonably claim even the want of this special tact for organizing and disciplining troops as a virtue. It can not really be said to have detracted from Sherman's ability as a soldier. What was lost thereby to the army in discipline was made up in mobility. If its morale was bad, the marching was good, and that satisfied Sherman. If he did not teach his soldiers how to fight, he gave them the mobility which the execution of his strategic designs required of them, and thus the end aimed at was gained, and the country was satisfied. He merely changed his men from heavy to light infantry. Success justifies all means, and thus Sherman became—and justly became—a great general without ever having won a battle.

It is very strong language, I admit, to say that Sherman never won a battle, but considerately so, for if the purely tactical operations of General Sherman be critically examined, it will be found that they were almost invariably failures. He was the chief in command, the central and controlling power, in the battles of Chickasaw Bayou, Resaca, Kenesaw Mountain, and Jonesboro, all of which, with the bare exception of the latter, where his overpowering force and strategic march of the night before insured victory, were tactically great failures. The failure of the co-operative movements of Grant at Chickasaw Bayou doubtless caused Sherman's defeat at that point—at least it has served to explain it away, and stands as the excuse for it; but all will remember how signal a failure it was. The battle of Resaca was a still greater failure. Doubt, delay, and inaction lost Sherman the great advantage which his strategic march through Snake Creek Gap had given him in placing him in the rear of the enemy's position, and he ought to have captured every gun and wagon of the enemy, and dispersed the army which subsequently retarded his advance in Atlanta; but the battle was begun too late and pushed too feebly. Sherman's strategy had at one time rendered a battle unnecessary, and it was forced on him through another's indecision (I believe that General McPherson admitted before his death that that fault was his), but certainly it was the fault of Sherman that the battle, when fought, was indecisive. Every body will remember the Kenesaw Mountain battle and its useless sacrifices, and every body will remember, too, the candor with which Sherman wrote that it was a failure, and that the fault was his. All the minor engagements of his great campaign against Atlanta were either positive defeats or negative advantages, and yet that wonderful campaign was won, and all the advantages which could have under any circumstances accrued from it were gained to us without the losses which a great battle would have caused. The strategic marches executed during that campaign are now chapters in the theory and history of war, and the close student of the art will see more to admire in the passage of the Chattahoochee River, the march through the gorge of Snake Creek Gap, and across the Alatoona Mountains, and the flank movements around Kenesaw and Atlanta, than in the more dashing but less skillful marches through Georgia and the Carolinas. The campaign of Atlanta was made in the face of the enemy commanded by their most skillful general, while during the other and more famous marches no enemy was met. The campaign through Georgia was merely extensive; that against Atlanta was both grand in conception and difficult in execution. One was accomplished at a stride, the other step by step. The campaign of Atlanta gave rise not only to a new system of warfare, but even to a new system of tactics. Never before in the history of war had an army been known to be constantly under fire for one hundred consecutive days. Men whom three years of service had made veterans learned during that campaign a system of fighting they had never heard of before. The whole army became at once from necessity pioneers and sharp-shooters. The opposing armies lay so close to each other that not only pickets, but whole corps were within musket-range of each other, and every camp had to be intrenched. As a singular fact, showing the impression made on the minds of the men by the changed tactics which this campaign rendered necessary, I may mention that the soldiers called each other "gophers" and "beavers;" and "gopher holes" were more common in the armies' track than were camp-fires. It used to be laughingly said of the men that, instead of "souring onto," *i.e.* taking without leave each other's rations, they were in the habit, during the Atlanta campaign, of purloining each other's pick-axes and spades with which to dig their "gopher holes" or trenches for their protection from the enemy's sharp-shooters. I imagine it is on this campaign and its results, rather than on that from Atlanta to the sea, and from thence to Goldsboro', that General Sherman would prefer to rest his reputation in the future.* We of to-day study the holiday marches from

---

* A more laborious campaign than that of Atlanta was never undertaken, and it is difficult to say which soldier deserves the most credit for the movements, Sherman or Joe Johnston. The retreats of the latter were not less admirable than the flank marches of the former, and Johnston showed as clean heels as Sherman did a fully guarded front. His camps were left barren ; Sherman found only Johnston's smoking camp-fires, but no spoils left behind him. It was looked upon by the officers of Sherman's army as the "cleanest retreat of the war," and it is very evident now that, had Johnston remained in command, and been allowed

a very different stand-point from that which the generations which follow. us will view them. When all things comé to be critically examined and carefully summed up, it will be decided and adjudged that the battles which made the campaign to the sea and through the Carolinas successes were fought on the hills around Nashville by General Thomas, not by General Sherman. Yet they are not without their great merit. Undertaken with deliberation and after elaborate preparation, they were not wanting in boldness and originality of design, but they do not serve to illustrate strategy: it is only the logistics which are so admirable.

A great deal has been said and written about General Sherman's dislike for the newspapers and for that class of necessary nuisances which were with every army, the war correspondents; but it was a dislike that was in a great measure affected. All men are egotists, Grant and Sherman among the rest, and both like to be well spoken of and written about; they would hardly be human if they did not. In fact, if Sherman can not find somebody to write about him, he does it himself. One of the instances in which he has complimented himself is destined to give every student of the art of war a knowledge of

to continue his Fabian policy, Sherman could never have made his march to the sea, and the capture of Atlanta would have been a Cadmean victory to him. Johnston proved himself a very superior soldier·—in fact, the superior general of the Southern armies. If it could be said of any of the rebels, it could be said of Johnston that, in fact, he was

> " The noblest Roman of them all :
> All the conspirators, save only he,
> Did that they did in envy of great Cæsar.
> He only, in a generous, honest thought,
> And common good to all, made one of them."

this weak point of his character. Shortly after the successful passage of the Chattahoochee River in the face of the enemy, an operation which was among the finest accomplishments of the campaign of Atlanta, Sherman published an address to his troops, in which he said, with pardonable egotism, " The crossing of the Chattahoochee and breaking of the Augusta Road was most handsomely executed by us, and will be studied as an example in the art of war." A still greater piece of egotism from his pen is not less amusing. It is that letter in which he refers to his having been a scourge to the South, and in which he adds, " Think how much better that it was I than Ben Butler or some other of that school." This, to say the least, must have been pleasant to " Ben" and " others of that school," if not modest in General Sherman.

This egotism led to an affectation of simplicity in style and carelessness in habits which produced a very pleasant incident at Nashville in 1864. Sherman was very fond of the theatre, and would go as often as he found time. When he first arrived in the " City of Rocks," the manager of the " New Nashville Theatre" waited on him with the tender of a private box. The general declined it, and instead of appearing in a private box, would be found very frequently sitting in the pit of the theatre surrounded by his " boys in blue," and laughing at the comicalities or applauding the "points" with as much gusto as any of the audience. This affectation of the republican in manners gained him more notice than if he had sat in a private box, and every body enjoyed seeing him there except the manager, who complained that it was injuring his business. No officer dared to sit in a private box with Sherman present in the pit, and these places became, during Sherman's stay, "a beggarly account of empty boxes" indeed.

I once had a long conversation with General Sherman on the subject of the press and war correspondents, from which I learned very little more than that he was very much disposed to underrate the advantages of the one and the abilities of the other, but very willing to accept, though with an affected ill grace, the praises of either. He declared in that conversation that the government could well afford to purchase all the printing-presses in the country at the price of diamonds, and then destroy them, and that all the war correspondents should be hung as spies. Sherman, with all his affected contempt for the press, is more indebted to it than any other officer in the army.

From time immemorial—at least from the days of Suwarrow and of "Old Fritz"—Frederick the Great—troops have always given nicknames to the commanders they adored. The veteran soldier is an affectionate creature, and he evinces his lovable disposition pretty much as the women do, by the use of pet names and expressive adjectives. The veterans had a slang of their own, as expressive to the initiated and as incomprehensible to the ignorant as the more systematically arranged jargon of the showman, gambler, or peddler. Increasing affection for a popular leader was evinced by an increase in the intensity of the adjective or pronoun applied to the person. A popular leader may have at one time been only "Colonel," but as his popularity increased and he won the affection of his men, he was called "*The* Colonel," "Our Colonel," and "Our Bully Colonel." At the height of M'Clellan's popularity his soldiers invariably called him "Little Mac." Sheridan was always "Little Phil," John A. Logan always "Black Jack," and Thomas has successively been known as "Old Slow Trot," "Uncle George," and "Old Pap," the latter being the superlative form of expression.

Sherman has not entirely escaped "nicknames," though he has been more fortunate in this respect than some other commanders. In 1861 the Home Guards of Louisville gave him a name which has never been used by any other body of troops. It was under the following circumstances: The Home Guard marched under Sherman's leadership from Louisville to meet the invasion of Buckner. While moving to Lebanon Junction the general spoke to the men, telling them of the necessity which had arisen for their services, and proposed to muster them into the United States service for thirty days. Few of them had blankets, none had haversacks, and no tents were at the time on hand. The men were really not prepared to remain long in the field, and some demurred at the length of time mentioned. Sherman grew very angry at this, and spoke very harshly, intimating that he considered the Home Guards a "paltry set of fellows." The men were chagrined at this, and much embittered against him, and on the spot voted him "a gruff old cock." They soon found, however, that they had to accept him as a commander, when one of them remarked, "It was a bitter pill." Out of this grew the title of "Old Pills," which was at once fastened upon the general. The men consented to be mustered for fifteen days. This put Sherman in an excellent humor again, and he promised them tents, blankets, etc., immediately. This, in turn, put the Guards in a high glee, and one of them suggesting that "Old Pills" was sugar-coated, the nickname was modified, and he was known ever after as "Old Sugar-coated Pill."

Later in the war his troops fixed upon one title of endearment for Sherman which will doubtless stick to him to the last. It expressed no peculiarity, was not properly a nickname, but simply an expression of affection. He will always be known to his veterans as "Old Billy." His veterans of 1861 and 1862 called him "Old Sherman," and few will forget it who heard General Rousseau's brigade hail him by that title during the battle of Shiloh. On the day of that battle, while hotly engaged near the log church which gave its name to the field, Sherman met a brigade of Buell's fresh troops moving forward to his support, and hastily asked whose troops they were. General Rousseau, who commanded the brigade, rode hastily through the line to meet Sherman, who had been dismounted for the third time by the fire of the enemy, and had one wounded arm in a sling, while his face was blackened by the fire of his own artillery.

"Rousseau's brigade," said that officer — "your old troops, General Sherman."

At the mention of Sherman's name, Rousseau's men, who had made their first campaign under Sherman, recognized him. "There's old Sherman," ran along their lines, and in an instant more there broke above the din of the battle three loud ringing cheers for "Old Sherman." Sherman took no notice of the cheers at the time, but his subsequent report of the battle showed that he was not oblivious to the compliment. At the moment he simply ordered the brigade forward. It was about the time the rebels began falling back, and soon the advance thus ordered became a pursuit of the foe.

Sherman is an inveterate smoker. He smokes, as he does every thing else, with an energy which it would be supposed would deprive him of all the pleasure of smoking. He is fully as great a smoker as Grant, whose propensity in that line is well known, but he is very unlike him in his style of smoking. Grant smokes as if he enjoyed his cigar. Sherman smokes as if it were a duty to be finished in the shortest imaginable time. Grant will smoke lying back in his chair, his body and mind evidently in repose, his countenance calm and settled. He blows the smoke slowly from his mouth, and builds his plans and thoughts in the clouds which are formed by it about his head. He smokes his tobacco as the Chinese do their opium, and with that certain sort of oblivious disregard for every thing else which it is said characterizes the opium smoker. He enjoys his mild Havana in quiet dignity, half-smoking, half-chewing it. Sherman puffs furiously, as if his cigar was of the worst character of " penny grabs" and would not " draw." He snatches it frequently, and, one might say, furiously, from his mouth, brushing the ashes off with his little finger. He continually paces the floor while smoking, generally deep in thought of important matters, doubtless; but a looker-on would imagine that he was endeavoring to solve the question of how to draw smoke through his cigar. He seldom or never finishes it, leaving at least one half of it a stump. When he used to frequent the Associated Press-rooms at Louisville in 1861, he would often accumulate and leave upon the agent's table as many as eight or ten of these stumps, which the porter of the rooms used to call "Sherman's old soldiers." Even until long after Anderson's assumption of command at Louisville the agent of the New Orleans papers continued sending his telegrams for the rebel papers to New Orleans. This man was a rabid secessionist, and disliked Sherman exceedingly. He used to say of him that he smoked as some men whistled—"for want of thought." This is undoubtedly a mistake; for close observers say that, while smoking, Sherman is deepest absorbed in thought.

He is certainly, when smoking, almost totally oblivious to what is going on around him. This peculiar absence of mind had an excellent illustration in a circumstance which occurred at Lebanon Junction, Kentucky, when first occupied by Sherman and the Home Guards. While walking up and down the railroad platform at that place, awaiting the repair of the telegraph line to Louisville, Sherman's cigar gave out. He immediately took another from his pocket, and, approaching the orderly-sergeant of the "Marion Zouaves"—one of the Home Guard companies—asked for a light. The sergeant had only a moment before lighted his cigar, and, taking a puff or two to improve the fire, he handed it, with a bow, to the general. Sherman carefully lighted his weed, took a puff or two to assure himself, and, having again lapsed into his train of thought, abstractedly threw away the sergeant's cigar. General Rousseau and several other officers were standing by at the time, and laughed heartily at the incident; but Sherman was too deeply buried in thought to notice the laughter or mishap. Three years subsequently, at his head-quarters in Nashville, Rousseau endeavored to recall this occurrence to Sherman's mind. He could not recollect it, and replied, " I was thinking of something else. It won't do to let to-morrow take care of itself. Your good merchant don't think of the ships that are in, but those that are to come in. The evil of to-day is irreparable. Look ahead to avoid breakers. You can't when your ship is on them. All you can then do is to save yourself and retrieve disaster. I was thinking of something else when I threw the sergeant's cigar away." And then he added, laughing, " Did I do that, really ?"

With the personal appearance of General Sherman the public are but little acquainted. Very few full-length pictures of him have been made. Of the numerous engravings and photographs which have been published since he became famous very few are good likenesses, and none convey a proper idea of his general appearance. The best picture which I have seen is the one from which the accompanying engraving is made. The outlines of the features are given with great accuracy, and any one familiar with the general's physiognomy will pronounce it a faithful likeness, though the position in which the subject sat serves to conceal the extreme Romanism of his nose. There is a scowl on the face, and yet the expression is that of Sherman in a good humor. He seldom has such a self-satisfied air. A critical observer of the picture in question would remark that Sherman has done in this case what he seldom takes time or has inclination to do, and has given the artist a special sitting. He has "made himself up" for the occasion. If the critic were one of Sherman's soldiers, he would notice the absence from his lips of the inevitable cigar. The coat, it will be observed, is buttoned across the breast, and is the chief fault of the engraving, for Sherman seldom or never buttons his coat either across his breast or around his waist. His vest is always buttoned by the lower button only, and, fitting close around his waist, adds to his appearance of leanness. It is doubtful if at this time any one can be found, except the general's tailor, who can tell when his coat was new. He appears to have an aversion to new clothes, and has never been seen in a complete new suit or heard in creaking boots. It may be said that he never conforms to the regulations in respect to the color of his suit; for the uniform he generally wears has lost its original color, and is of that dusty and rusty tinge, and with that lack of gloss which follows constant use. One would readily imagine, judging by its appearance, that he purchased his uniform second-hand. The hat which he generally wears is of the same order of faded "regulation," with the crown invariably puffed out instead of being pushed in, in the "Burnside style." The regulation cord and tassel he does not recognize at all.

With the exception of his eyes, none of the features of Sherman's countenance are indicative of his character. Altogether he is commonplace in appearance, neither excessively handsome nor painfully repulsive. At the same time, divest him of his regulations, and in a crowd his face would attract attention and afford a study. His eyes, conforming to his general character, are as restless as his body or mind. They are rather of a dull though light color, their restlessness giving them whatever they possess of brilliancy and animation. His lips close firmly and closely, and with the deep lines running from his nostrils to either corner of his mouth, give to the lower half of his face an air of decision indicative of his character. His hands are long, slender, and tapering, like those of a woman, and are in admirable keeping with his figure. His short, crisp whiskers, which grow unshaven, and which appear to be stunted in growth, are of a dingy red, or what is commonly called "sandy" color. He takes very little care of his whiskers and hair, each having to be content with one careless brushing a day. He has, perhaps, as great a disregard for his personal appearance as he pretends to have for what others may say or think of him.

C 2

CHAPTER II.

THOMAS AS A TACTICIAN.

WHILE General Sherman was pursuing Hood, when that gallant but not very sagacious rebel was making his ill-judged and ill-advised but bold march northward, leaving Atlanta and our armies in his rear, some exigency arose which made General Sherman regret the absence of General George H. Thomas, who had been sent to Nashville. I do not now distinctly remember what the exigency was other than that it related to some important movement — perhaps the movement to the sea — but, at any rate, so undecided and troubled was Sherman in coming to a decision, that he suddenly broke a long silence, during which he had been seriously meditative, by exclaiming to one of his aids,

"I wish old Thom was here! He's my off-wheel-horse, and knows how to pull with me, though he don't pull in the same way."

There was never a truer word uttered in jest, and describing Thomas as the "match horse" of Sherman is a comparison by no means as inaccurate as it is rude. In the chapter which precedes this I have endeavored to show that the distinctive feature of Sherman's character is a certain nervousness of thought and action, inspiring a restless and resistless energy. The best idea of Gen-

GEORGE H. THOMAS.

eral Thomas is obtained by contrasting him with Sherman, and illustrating Sherman as a great strategist, Thomas as a great tactician. Sherman is not merely a theoretical strategist as Halleck is, as McPherson was, but one of great practicability, and an energy which has given practical solutions to his strategic problems. Thomas is not merely a theoretical tactician, with a thorough knowledge of the rules, but one who has illustrated the art on extensive battle-fields, and always with success. The two appear in every respect in contrast, and possess no similarities. One may be called a nervous man, and the other a man of nerve. Sherman derives his strength from the momentum resulting from the rapidity with which he moves; Thomas moves slowly, but with equally resistless power, and accomplishes his purposes by sheer strength. Sherman is naturally the dashing leader of light, flying battalions; Thomas the director of heavily-massed columns. He may be called heavy ordnance in contradistinction to Sherman, who may be likened to a whole battery of light rifle-guns; or, in the language of the prize-ring, Sherman is a light-weight and quick fighter, while Thomas is a heavy, ponderous pugilist, whose every blow is deadly. Sherman's plans are odd, if not original. Though I have heard learned military critics deny that they embraced new rules of war, still it can not be denied that his campaigns have been out of the general order of military exploits. Thomas, on the other hand, originates nothing, but most skillfully directs his army on well-defined principles of the art. Sherman jumps at conclusions; Thomas's mind and body act with equal deliberation, his conclusions being arrived at after long

and mature reflection. Sherman never takes thought of
unexpected contingencies or failure. There is always a
remedy for any failure of a part of Thomas's plans, or
for the delinquencies of subordinates. Sherman never
hesitates to answer; Thomas is slow to reply. One is
quick and positive; the other is slow, but equally positive. Thomas thinks twice before speaking once; and
when he speaks, his sentences are arranged so compactly, and, as it were, so economically, that they convey his
idea at once. It is given as advice, but men receive it
as an order, and obey it implicitly.

The habits of the two men are radically different.
Sherman is an innovator on the customs not only of the
army, but every phase of social life, and is at least one
generation ahead of the American people, fast as it im-
agines itself. Thomas belongs to a past generation, and
his exceedingly regular habits belong to the "good old
time." He has been confirmed by long service in the
habits of camp, and appears never to be satisfied unless
living as is customary in camps. In September, 1862,
his division of Buell's army was encamped at Louisville,
Kentucky, his quarters being in the outskirts of the city.
While encamped here, Colonel Joe McKibbon, then a
member of General Halleck's staff, arrived from Washington City and delivered to Thomas an order to relieve
Buell, and assume command of the Army of the Ohio.
In order to put himself in communication with the commander-in-chief, Thomas was compelled to ride into the
city and take rooms at the hotel nearest the telegraph
office. He employed the day in communicating with
General Halleck, urging the retention of Buell, and in

declining the proposed promotion. Late at night he re-tired to his bed. But the change from a camp-cot to clean feathers was too much for the general. He found it impossible to sleep, and at a late hour in the night he was compelled to send Captain Jacob Brown, his provost-marshal, to his head-quarters for his camp-cot. The re-organization of the army, the murder of General Nelson by Jeff. C. Davis, and other events occurring about the same time, conspired to keep the general a guest or pris-oner at the hotel for a week. During all that time he slept as usual on his cot, banished the chamber-maids from his room, and depended for such duty as they usu-ally performed on the old colored body-servant who had attended him for many years.

System and method are absolutely necessary to Thom-as's existence, and nothing ruffles or excites him so much as innovations on his habits or changes in his customs. He discards an old coat with great reluctance; and dur-ing the earlier part of the war, when his promotions came to him faster than he could wear out his uniforms, it was almost impossible to find him donning the proper dress of his rank. He wore the uniform of a colonel for sev-eral months after he had been confirmed a brigadier gen-eral, and only donned the proper uniform when going into battle at Mill Spring. He was confirmed a major general in June, 1862, but did not mount the twin stars until after the battle of Stone River, fought on the last day of the same year, and then they found their way to his shoulders only by a trick to which his body-serv-ant had been incited by his aids. This methodical and systematic feature of his character found an admirable illustration in an incident to which I was a witness during the battle of Chickamauga. After the rout of the principal part of the corps of McCook and Crittenden, Thomas was left to fight the entire rebel army with a single corps of less than twenty thousand men. The enemy, desirous of capturing this force, moved in heavy columns on both its flanks. His artillery opened upon Thomas's troops from front and both flanks; but still they held their ground until Steedman, of Granger's corps, reached them with re-enforcements. I was sitting on my horse near General Thomas when General Steedman came up and saluted him.

"I am very glad to see you, general," said Thomas in welcoming him. General Steedman made some inquiries as to how the battle was going, when General Thomas, in a vexed manner, replied,

"The damned scoundrels are fighting without any system."

Steedman thereupon suggested that he should pay the enemy back in his own coin. Thomas followed his suggestion. As soon as Granger came up with the rest of his corps, he assumed the offensive; and while Bragg continued to move on his flanks, he pushed forward against the rebel centre, so scattering it by a vigorous blow that, fearful of having his army severed in two, the rebel abandoned his flank movement in order to restore his centre. This delayed the resumption of the battle until nearly sunset, and Thomas was enabled to hold his position until nightfall covered the retirement to Rossville Gap.

Thomas is not easily ruffled. It is difficult alike to

provoke his anger or enlist his enthusiasm. He is by no means blind to the gallantry of his men, and never fails to notice and appreciate their deeds, but they never win from him any other than the coldest words in the coldest, but, at the same time, kindest of commendatory tones. He grows really enthusiastic over nothing, though occasionally his anger may be aroused. When it is, his rage is terrible. During the campaign in Kentucky, in pursuit of Bragg in 1862, Thomas was second in command of the army under Buell. The new recruits committed many depredations upon the loyal Kentuckians. While the army was passing a small stream near Bardstown, called "Floyd's Fork of Salt River," Thomas was approached by a farmer whom he knew to be a good Union man, and who made complaint that one of the general's staff officers had carried off the only horse left on his farm. The general turned black with anger at such an accusation against one of his staff officers, and demanded to know who and where the offender was. The farmer pointed to a mounted infantry officer, who was attached to one of the regiments and not to the general's staff. The general rode up to him and demanded to know where he had obtained the horse which he rode. The officer replied that he had "impressed" him. The general knew the man had no authority to impress horses, and, choking with rage, he poured on the devoted head of the delinquent a torrent of invective. He drew his sword, and, putting the point under the shoulder-straps of the officer, ripped them off, and then compelled him to dismount and lead the animal to the place whence he had stolen him. He also required him to pay the farmer for his trouble and the loss of service of the animal.

When the battle of Mill Spring began it found Thomas in a bad humor, and on the first opportunity he had for "pitching into" any one he did not fail to take advantage of it. The victim was Colonel Mahlon D. Manson, a rough, excitable, but gallant old Indianian, who was acting brigadier in command of his own and two or three other regiments. Under the old organization of the volunteer army no adequate provision for aids for acting generals had been made, and Manson's only aid, his regimental adjutant, happened to be out of the way; so, when the battle opened, and he had posted his regiments to receive the attack, he hastily rode back to General Thomas to report in person the disposition he had made of his forces. It happened that in doing this Manson lost his hat, and he made his appearance before Thomas hatless, with disheveled hair, unwashed face, and incomplete toilet, and Thomas's pent-up rage vented itself on him. He had no sooner begun to state his position to Thomas than that officer interrupted him with,

"Damn you, sir, go back to your command and fight it."

Excited as Manson was, he caught the full meaning, and the perhaps unmeant insinuation of the general's words, and returned to his command much chagrined. Thomas's anger did not last long after finding this vent. He grew pleasanter before the day was over, was in spirits long before Zollicoffer's rout was complete, and when he came to write his report a week afterward, spoke very highly of Manson.

The self-control and coolness of Thomas under fire,

and amid the excitement and dangers of battle, is absolutely surprising, and, until I had seen at Chickamauga repeated instances of his imperturbation, I did not believe that human nature was capable of it. In relating one of the episodes of the battle, an account of which I published at the time, I alluded, I thought then, and think now, very happily to the general as the "Statue Thomas." During that terrible conflict the statue warmed into life but twice. At daylight on the second day, before the battle had been resumed, General Rosecrans rode along the line of battle, examining the position which the troops of McCook and Crittenden had taken as best they could, without other guide than the sound of cannon or other director than stern necessity. He rode up to Thomas's quarters near the left centre of the field and asked him several questions regarding the battle of the day before. Thomas alluded briefly to the events of the fight, and in speaking of his brilliant charge exclaimed rather warmly, "Whenever I touched their flanks they broke, general, they broke," repeating the last words with unusual zest and evident satisfaction. I was listening with great eagerness and looking squarely at the general, when he caught my eye, and, as if ashamed of his momentary enthusiasm, the blood mounted to his cheeks and he blushed like a woman. His eyes were bent immediately on the ground, and the rest of his remarks were confined to a few brief replies to the questions addressed to him.

The other instance to which I was a witness occurred during the afternoon of the second day's battle, and in the midst of a lull which had followed the retreat of

McCook and Crittenden and the falling back of Thomas's right division. The general was sitting in the rear of the line of battle of his right as re-formed, engaged in watching a heavy cloud of dust in the distance, and in such a direction that it might be the enemy, or it might be the reserve forces of Gordon Granger, which had been posted some distance in rear of the battle-field at Rossville, and which it was hoped would march to the aid of the army. The doubt under which he labored cast a visible cloud over the general's spirits, and excited his nerves to an unusual degree. He had no disposition to resume the fight, and, fearful of the result of the next attack of the rebels, was anxious to avoid a resumption of the battle. He consequently watched the development of the cloud of dust in the distance with painful anxiety. If it dissolved to reveal friends, then they were doubly welcome, for fresh friends insured the safe retirement of that fraction of the army which still held its ground. If it disclosed the enemy, then the day and army were lost, and it became the duty of those who formed this "last square" at Chickamauga to throw into the teeth of the victorious enemy a defiance as grandly contemptuous as that of Cambronne, and die. There was no escape if the troops advancing from the rear were, as it was feared, the cavalry of the enemy. General Tom Wood, hearing some one express himself to this effect, threw in a word of encouragement by saying that it was evident it was not cavalry, "for," said he, "don't you see the dust rising above them ascends in thick misty clouds, not in spiral columns, as it would if the force was cavalry," a remark which indicated the close observation of General Wood. The anxiety of General Thomas increased with every moment of delay in the development of the character of the advancing columns. At one time he said nervously to his staff, " Take my glass, some of you whose horse stands steady—tell me what you can see." I was standing near him at the moment looking through a field-glass, and remarked that I felt sure that I could see the United States flag.

"Do you think so? do you think so?" asked the general, nervously.

Shortly after, Captain G. M. L. Johnston, of General Negley's staff, reported to Thomas for duty, and the general requested him to venture toward the advancing force, and learn, if possible, to which army it belonged. Johnston was gone for some time, running the gauntlet of the rebel sharp-shooters, who were fast enveloping Thomas's left wing. During his absence the anxiety of Thomas increased until it grew painful to the observer, and the relaxation which followed the revelation of the fact that the coming force were friends was a positive relief to the by-standers. As Johnston returned with General Steedman the nerves of Thomas calmed down, and his excitement was hardly visible save in the petulant tone and manner in which he cursed Bragg for fighting without any system. During the fight which ensued he remained as passive and apparently as unconcerned as if he were in the safest place imaginable.

During the morning of the second day of the same battle I was again near General Thomas when the rebels made a vigorous attack on his breast-works. He and a single staff officer were sitting a little in the rear of the centre of the line, and just in range of the shells which the enemy was throwing with great vigor and rapidity. While thus exposed, a shell passed between the general and his aid, causing them to look at each other with a quiet smile. A moment afterward another shell took the same route. The general, instead of smiling this time, turned to his aid and said,

" Major, I think we had better retire a little," and fell back a few yards to a small wood.

On the night after this battle, and when the troops had retired to Rossville, General Thomas was asked by Colonel B. F. Scribner to take a cup of coffee at his campfire, and did so. Scribner had been slightly wounded in the head, and the clotted blood still stood upon his face, left there in order to prevent the wound from continuing to bleed. Thomas sat down by Scribner, drank his coffee, saw the wound of Scribner, talked of commonplace matters for half an hour, but never by word or act alluded in the slightest way to the fact that he had just fought one of the most important battles of the war, and saved the army from annihilation. No one could have known from Thomas's remarks that a battle had been raging, or that his host had been wounded.

One of the great faults of Thomas's character is due to this extreme solidity of his nervous system. Without rendering him exactly selfish or acrimonious, it has made him cold and undemonstrative in manner, and rather insensible to the emotions. He is generous without being enthusiastic, and kind without being at all demonstrative. He has been compared to Washington, but the comparison was made by General Rosecrans, who, by the way,

knew nothing whatever of human nature, and could not
read it even with the best spectacles of saddest experience; and the comparison holds good only thus far, that
Thomas, as Washington was, is portly of person and dignified of manner.   His undemonstrative manner has given
to many the idea that he was incapable of strong affections, firm friendships, or noble emotions; and the only
enemies whom he had were men with whom he had been
on terms of friendship, and who, falling under disfavor,
looked in vain to him for some demonstration of aid.
There are two or three instances, not proper to relate in
detail, which have given Thomas's fellow-officers the idea
that he was selfishly cold; but I do not think such to be
the case, for, though cold and undemonstrative, Thomas
has never revealed aught of the selfish or envious in his
character.   His blood ran as sluggishly as oil upon water, but it was from principle, if such a thing could be,
and I think it was in this case.   One of the subordinate
commanders of Thomas's army, who distinguished himself at Stone River and Chickamauga, was an Indiana
colonel named Ben F. Scribner, a brave officer, who, from
his action at the battle of Perryville, Kentucky, went by
the name of "gallant little Scrib"—a sobriquet bestowed
upon him by General Lovell H. Rousseau, his immediate
commander.   After the battle of Chickamauga, Scribner
was not treated fairly in the reorganization of the army
by Rosecrans, and complained to General Thomas, his
corps commander, of the injustice done him.   During the
conversation Colonel Scribner used the expression that
he could not but feel that a serious wrong had been done
him, when Thomas slowly and sadly said,

"Colonel, I have taken a great deal of pains to educate myself not to feel."

This remark gives a wonderful insight into Thomas's nature, and will explain much in his manner that is a mystery to thousands who have studied his character.

General Garfield used to relate a story which gave rather a comical turn to the general's undemonstrative style, and one which I do not remember to have ever seen in print. In fact, it has been a somewhat doubtful question with me as to whether I should be justified in relating it, and only do so with the warning, "*Honi soit qui mal y pense.*" When General Thomas relieved Rosecrans at Chattanooga in 1863, General Garfield remained with him for a time as chief of staff. One morning the two officers were riding around the town, examining the defenses which were then being built, when they heard some one hailing with the cry,

"Hello, mister! you! I want to speak with you."

On looking around, General Thomas discovered that he was the "mister" wanted, and that the person who had hailed him was one of those East Tennessee soldiers who were always easily distinguishable from the Northern soldiers by their peculiar rough, uncouth, and backwoods appearance. He stopped, and the man approached him and began,

"Mister, I want to get a furlough."

"On what grounds do you want a furlough, my man?" asked the general.

"I want to go home and see my wife," replied the East Tennesseean.

"How long since you saw your wife?" asked the general.

"Ever since I enlisted—nigh on to three months."

"Three months!" exclaimed the general, good-naturedly. "Why, my good man, I haven't seen my wife for three years."

The East Tennesseean stopped whittling the stick which he had in his hand, and stared for a moment incredulously at the general.

"Wall, you see," he said at length, with a sheepish smile, "me and my wife ain't that kind."

Shaking all over with laughter, the general put spurs to his horse and galloped away, leaving the astonished soldier unanswered.

I should have enjoyed hugely hearing Thomas laugh aloud. During the three years in which I saw him almost daily, and under all sorts of circumstances, I never saw him *smile* but once, and that was under circumstances so peculiarly ridiculous that it would have provoked laughter from Patience on a monument, or even the grief that she smiled at. A low comedian, named Alf. Burnett, from one of the Cincinnati theatres, essayed to become a war correspondent, and during the summer of 1863 made his appearance in the camp of General Rosecrans, quartering himself at Triune with Colonel James Brownlow, son of the famous Parson Brownlow, and at that time in command of an East Tennessee regiment. Burnett was very good as a mimic, and particularly excelled in his delivery of a burlesque sermon in which the sentence "He played upon a harp of a thousand strings, spirits of just men made perfect," frequently occurred as a refrain. Colonel Brownlow on one occasion invited Burnett to deliver this sermon before his regiment, and, as a joke upon the chaplain of the command, that worthy was requested to announce the occasion of its delivery, and when the time arrived to open the services with a hymn. Burnett began his burlesque sermon, and had gone through a considerable portion of it before the chaplain and the soldiers began to suspect how much they had been outraged. As soon as he perceived the nature of the performance, the chaplain approached Burnett, took him by the back of the neck, marched him to the camp limits, and with the injunction to "go and sin no more," kicked him out of the camp. The facts were at the same time represented to Rosecrans, who expelled Burnett from the department, but, at the solicitations of some friends, the mimic was allowed to return to make his explanations. After hearing Burnett's explanations, Rosecrans insisted on hearing the "Hard-shell Baptist sermon," and Burnett gave it in his best style. Rosecrans was delighted, declared it was inimitable, and told Burnett he should remain at his quarters, should deliver it nightly, and would have put him on his staff if Burnett had asked it. The sermon became Rosecrans's hobby; he thought and talked for a time of nothing else, and one night invited General Thomas to quarters to hear it. The general and his staff came, and the performance began with songs which did not interest, and continued with the sermon, which, much to Rosecrans's surprise, did not amuse "old Thom." But, after Burnett's farce had been finished, Rosecrans called upon Colonel Horace Porter, of the Ordnance Department, for a song, and Porter gave a comic Irish song in the best brogue, accompanying himself by imitating the playing upon Scotch bagpipes. Porter was one of the most dignified, quiet, se-- date, and elegant officers of the army at Rosecrans's head- quarters; and the ridiculousness of his attitude, the con- trast with his usual appearance and manner, was too much for General Thomas, and he " smiled" almost audi- bly several times during the song. I never afterward saw the fun stirred up in Thomas.

The contrast between Thomas and Sherman may be extended even to their personal appearance and habits; and in these, as in character, the difference is most mark- ed. Thomas's figure is very striking. Something of his height is lost to the eye by the heaviness of his figure. If he were as thin as Sherman, he would look the six feet two or three inches which have been ignorantly attribu- ted to him. He is really about five feet ten or eleven inches in height, but so much does his heaviness detract from the appearance of height that he does not appear so tall. Thick-set, robust, and healthy, he moves heavily and slowly, but by no means feebly or unsteadily. His beard and hair were sandy at the beginning of the late war, but they have since become silver sprinkled, and add to the great dignity of his appearance. His features are all large, with the exception of his nose—a long, thin Grecian feature which Napoleon would have admired. His lips are rather thick, rounded, and red. His chin and jaws, large and squarely cut, with his great, steady, though not bright eyes, indicate, more than any others of his features, his firmness and positiveness of character. His countenance is at all times severe and grave, but not necessarily stern. He seldom smiles; but the constant seriousness of his countenance is not repulsive. It may be said to be forbidding. It certainly forbids trifling. The simplest-minded man, seeking audience of him, will understand, on being received by the general, by a glance at his countenance, that he must be brief and to the point. His presence is no place for loungers. His visitors must have business to transact or retire, and they never require any other hint than the countenance of the general. He is a man in earnest, and it does not take long to discover it. He is perhaps as free from display and pretension as any man in the army. He never does any thing for "effect." His manner admits of no familiarity. There is dignity in every gesture, but not necessarily either grace or love. His style of living in camp is comfortable and even elegant. His mess consists of himself and two aids. His mess ware is principally silver of elaborate finish. I breakfasted once or twice with the general during the Chickamauga campaign. On the occasion of each visit daylight and breakfast were announced simultaneously by an elderly, dignified, and cleanly-attired colored servant, who brought me an excellent punch, with "Colonel Flynt's compliments," as an appetizer. The breakfast-table was spread under the fly of the tent, which served as a kitchen, and on it smoked fresh beef, ham, and strong black coffee. At each silver plate was a napkin of the purest white, artistically folded in the latest style of the first-class hotels, a silver water-goblet, a china cup, and the usual knives and silver forks. Better beef and better coffee could not have been found in the country in which the army was campaigning, while the hot rolls and potatoes, baked in the hot ashes of a neighboring fire, would have made many a French cook blush.

When beginning the campaign of Atlanta Sherman endeavored to effect an important innovation in the habits of his army by carrying out to the very letter his instructions to "move light," *i. e.*, without extra baggage. In order to impress upon his officers the necessity of setting a good example to the men, he published an order, in which he stated that the "general commanding intended making the campaign without tent or baggage." The hint was lost on most of the officers, and among others on Thomas, who moved in his usual heavy style, with a complete head-quarter train and the usual number of tents, adding indeed to the usual allowance a large wagon arranged with desks, which, when covered by a hospital-tent fly, made a very complete adjutant general's office. The campaign began, and Sherman made several days' march without his tent, sleeping any where that night overtook him, but before reaching Resaca he was very glad to take up his abode near Thomas's head-quarters, and make use of his tents and adjutant general's office.

No one has ever accused General Thomas of being a genius either militarily or otherwise. He neither plans campaigns with the aptitude and originality of Sherman, nor fights battles with the vigor and abandon of Sheridan. Thomas's success has been obtained by long service and patient industry, and he is an example of what may be accomplished by the unremitting toil of a practical man. He is possessed naturally of that good, clear sense which is often inappropriately called common sense, but which is of no common order at all. He has never been brilliantly educated, and is neither a brilliant thinker nor converser. He is doubtless well versed in West Point lore and the art of war. His education has been derived principally from a long and varied experience with the world, which has rendered him pre-eminently a practical man. His mind consequently takes naturally, as has been before stated, to method, and every thing he does is completed (in the full sense of the word) in a methodical manner. There is little that is original in his plans or his mode of executing them, but all are distinguished for their practicability and completeness. His calculations leave a wide range for contingencies, delays, and accidents, and are not easily disturbed by untoward incidents and unexpected developments. He never goes into a campaign or battle without knowing exactly how to get out of it safely, in case the necessity for retreating arises. He has on more than one occasion furnished the means of getting the armies of others out of danger. At Stone River, when Rosecrans was defeated and his council of war proposed to retreat, Thomas showed that the safety of the army depended upon remaining and assuming the defensive. At Chickamauga, when the same leader left his army in the midst of a terrible battle and at the beginning of a rout of the greater part of it, Thomas again came to the rescue, and covered the retreat in a manner which saved the day and the army.

With his troops Thomas is a most popular leader. He has the deep-seated and deep-rooted affection of his men, which is not the less sincere because it is undemonstrative. He is looked upon by the army with a sort of affectionate reverence, and he possesses in the highest degree the confidence of his men. To this more than to any other feeling, person, or circumstance, the nation owed the safety of its army at Chickamauga. This feeling of confidence in its leader did more to hold his corps together on that day—did more to keep up the *esprit du corps* of his command during the terrible attacks to which it was subjected, than did all the discipline which had otherwise been drilled into the men. The men of the two routed *corps* were just as good, just as brave, and just as tenacious fighters as were Thomas's men, but they had no faith at all in the wisdom of their leaders, McCook and Crittenden, who were not men of either inspiring presence or iron qualities. Men will not stand and fight under officers in whom they have not the most implicit faith. Such confidence is reposed in Thomas to the fullest degree, and is accompanied by an affectionate regard which adds to its strength.

Soldiers, as I have had occasion to remark elsewhere, have a very natural mode of expressing their affection by titles of endearment, indicative of the peculiarities of the subjects of their admiration. Thomas has been christened with dozens of "nicknames." When he was at West Point and in the regular army in Mexico, he was called "Old Reliable," from his recognized and proverbial fidelity to the service. During the Mill Spring and Stone River campaigns he won from his men the sobriquet of "Old Pap Safety." This was subsequently boiled down into "Pap Thomas," by which name he is called more frequently than by any other. His slow gait, and quiet, dignified style of riding, gained him the title of "Old Slow-trot." "Uncle George" and "George H." are often used by the men in facetious hours, and the titles always linger on the tongues of the soldiers like sweet morsels. And though these titles are used by the men with an air and in a tone indicating familiarity with their leader, none of them ever knew him, in his communication with them, to sacrifice his dignity in the slightest degree. They have no difficulty in reaching his ear. They always find a patient listener and a sound adviser, and a kindly mannered and pleasant director. He never laughs and jokes with soldiers or officers, but his mild voice and quiet manner win him more of the love of his men than any momentary familiarity could do. I have known him to halt in the march and spend ten or fifteen minutes in directing stragglers to their commands.

General Thomas is the purest man I met in the army. He was the Bayard of our army—"*sans peur, sans reproche,*" and I have endeavored in vain to find a flaw in his character. His character is free from every stain, and he stands forth in the army as above suspicion. He has gone through the war without apparently exciting the jealousy of a single officer. He has so regulated his advancement—so retarded, in fact, his promotion, that when, as the climax to two years' hard service, he fought a great battle and saved a great army, and was hailed and recognized by the whole country as a hero, not one jealous or defeated officer was found to utter dissent to this popular verdict.

There was at one time some ill feeling between Grant and Thomas, growing out of the anomalous position in which both were placed by Halleck when the army was besieging Corinth, but I believe that was cleared up. General Grant was made second in command under Hal-

leck, and his army was given to Thomas, who remained
in active command in the field.   Grant's position was really none at all; it was not recognized by regulations or
uses, and was felt by him to be an insult put upon him
(he imagined at one time) at the instigation of General
Thomas.   Such was not the fact, however, and General
Grant so became finally convinced.

The late rebellion was the school of many of our best
officers, and dearly did the country pay in its best blood
the tuition of some.   Bull Run was the price which the
country paid for having its erroneous idea of war violently corrected.   The failure of the first assault on Vicksburg and of the attack on Kenesaw Mountain were fearful prices paid to correct certain errors of judgment in
Sherman's mind.   We paid for M'Clellan's violation of
a well-known rule of war in placing the Chickahominy between his battalions.   Numerous similar instances
might be named, showing how the country has been
compelled to pay terrible penalties of blood for the ignorance of unworthy and incompetent leaders; but enough.
Thomas's training in the art of war has cost the country
not a single disaster or sacrifice.   On the contrary, he
has saved the country, on more than one occasion, the
fearful penalty it was about to pay for the ignorance of
other leaders.   He has been prominent in three grand
campaigns.   Two of them he has conducted on his own
plans and in person.   In the other he acted as second in
command.   The two which he planned and conducted
were complete successes; and the other, as far as he was
concerned, a magnificent triumph.   His first campaign
in the war for the Union was that against the fortified

camp of Zollicoffer at Mill Springs, Kentucky. His plan embraced an assault upon the rebel works; but before he could get into position to do this the enemy marched out of his works and attacked him in his camp, failing in an attempt to surprise him. The rebels failed also in the battle which ensued, and were terribly defeated, with heavy loss, and at the sacrifice of the organization of their army. Night alone, under cover of which it crossed the Cumberland River, prevented the capture of the entire rebel force. Fourteen pieces of artillery, fifteen hundred horses, with all the stores of the enemy and a large · number of prisoners, fell into our hands. This victory was complete, and doubly welcomed as the first positive success since the battle of Bull Run. The country hailed it as the first sign of the rejuvenation and reorganization of the army. The rebel "army of Western Kentucky" has never been heard of since that disastrous day; and George B. Crittenden, its commander, sank at once into disgrace and oblivion as a consequence of his defeat.

In the campaign and battle of Chickamauga Thomas was second in command to Rosecrans, but in all its important actions his is the principal figure. The story of Chickamauga has been often, and, in one or two instances, well told; but the whole truth about it must be reserved until time shall permit the historian to tell it without fear or favor. Thomas stands forth the undisputed hero of that day—the single spirit upon whom all depends. He is the central figure. There are no heroes beside him. The young and noble ones who died, as Lytle and Burnham, Van Pelt and Jones, and those not less noble spirits who distinguished themselves and lived to be rewarded, as Baird and Dick Johnston, old Steedman and young Johnston, who guided his columns to the assault, Wood and Harker—all these surrounding Thomas but add to his glory as the parhelion adds to the beauty of the sun. On the first day at Chickamauga Thomas did his share toward the destruction of a great rebel army, but it was in vain. The fruits of his victory were frittered away by the incompetency of others. There was no general advance when he advanced. On the second day it was too late; the enemy had succeeded in crossing his whole army over the Chickamauga, and the opportunity to destroy his forces in detail was gone forever. Circumstances then devolved upon Thomas the task of saving a great army, not destroying one. The duty was nobly performed, and the army nobly saved; and though those who were not present, and who judge of the battle from hearsay, may be mystified by the circumlocution and vagueness of official reports, those who staid at Chickamauga know very well that Thomas *alone* retrieved that disaster and saved Rosecrans's army.

A short time after I had published in Harper's Magazine the sketch of General Thomas, of which this is a revised edition, I received many letters from old friends complaining that I had not done him justice in using the expression "Thomas originates nothing," and many were the instances quoted showing his originality of mind and plans. None of the arguments or examples given were convincing, however, and I have left the expression unchanged. One of these complainants stated that General Thomas was the originator of the plan to go through Snake Creek Gap in order to get upon Joe Johnston's rear and flank; but I am inclined to think this an error. The writer narrated that a few days after starting on the Atlanta campaign in May, 1864, Sherman, having thoroughly reconnoitred Rocky Face Ridge, the defensive line of the enemy, decided that it was necessary to storm and carry the position. Sitting one day on the railroad bank in front of Buzzard Roost. Gap, he confided this opinion to General Thomas.

"It can't be done, general," Thomas answered; "the ridge can not be carried."

"But it must be," said the impetuous Sherman, with his usual petulance. General Thomas repeated his observation.

"But then we can't stay here," urged Sherman; "we must go ahead—we can't stop here. There is nothing left but to assault the ridge."

"Have you tried every other means, general? Can't we go around them?" asked Thomas, at the same time unfolding his map.

"Yes, yes, we have tried all other means."

"Why can't we go through Snake Creek Gap?" asked Thomas. The voices of the two, according to my informant, here became lowered; the two generals bent their heads over the map; and it is claimed by Thomas's admirer that the result of that conversation was the occupation of the mountain gorge of Snake Creek Gap. Although told with much detail and precision, I am not at all disposed to credit this story, and I am convinced that, though not without foundation, there is an error somewhere. Another admirer of General Thomas wrote me claiming for him the credit of having originated and planned "Sherman's march to the sea."   He states that, shortly after the occupation of Atlanta, and while Hood's army was still in Sherman's front, General Thomas proposed to General Sherman to take the 14th and 20th *corps*, and march through the state to Savannah or some point on the coast equally important. The plan was not immediately acted on; information was received of Hood's purpose to flank Atlanta and go northward, and General Thomas was sent to Nashville to organize the forces there in order to meet him. Hood did move north, and Sherman decided to leave him to the care or the mercy of Thomas, while he, with the 14th, 15th, 17th, and 20th corps, twice the force originally said to have been proposed by Thomas, and really three times the force actually necessary for the movement, made the march which Thomas had planned. I very much doubt the full truth of this statement, though I do not know that it is untrue in any particular. But whether or not he planned it matters little; Thomas at Nashville may be said to have executed it, and to him, and not to Sherman, belongs the credit of its success. I have always wondered how Sherman came to delegate the subordinate, Thomas, with the lesser half of the army, to fight the main battles and conduct the real campaign, while he, the superior officer, with the greater half of the force, made a detour in which no danger was encountered—no danger, in fact, apprehended—and which could have been better effected with half the force.

When the London Times characterized Sherman's march to the sea as the "Anabasis of Sherman," and declared that it was virtually a retreat, the London Times was exactly right, but the American people "could not see it." But the stupidity of the rebels made that retreat a success instead of a disaster to us. Had the Fabian policy of Joe Johnston prevailed—had Atlanta been surrendered without a struggle, and had the rebels been content to cover Macon with their infantry and employ their cavalry in destroying the single railroad which inadequately supplied Sherman's army, the retreat to Savannah and the sea would have been instead a retreat to Chattanooga. When Hood removed his army from Sherman's front, he presented that already doubting general with a second alternative, whereas he had but one before, and permitted him to choose of two routes by which to retreat. Sherman chose, for the sake of the morale of his men and of the people, to "retreat forward" to Savannah instead of "advancing backward" to Chattanooga, and went off at a tangent to the sea. His unexpected detour did not interfere with Hood's plans. The rebel had no more and no fewer enemies to fight than he would have had if Sherman had followed him. Sherman could not have concentrated his forces at Nashville in time to meet Hood, for portions of the last force which, under General Steedman, fell back from Chattanooga to re-enforce Nashville were cut off by the enemy and did not reach the field at all. With this view in his mind, apprehending no danger from Sherman, and believing he could defeat Thomas, Hood pushed on, with what result is known. He met Thomas at Nashville, and the consequence was his annihilation. The success of Thomas made Sherman's march a success, and hence the former deserves the full credit for the latter's achievement. How great this credit is can be seen by forming in the mind an idea of the consequences which would have attended a failure on Thomas's part. Had he been defeated Nashville would have fallen; Hood would have marched into Kentucky and appeared on the line of the Ohio, while Sherman, making his appearance a thousand leagues away on the South Atlantic coast, would have found himself written down a great failure instead of a great general.

The battles of Nashville were not greater in result than grand in execution, and are, to my mind, Thomas's finest examples of grand tactics. I can not here allude to them in detail. The operations were conducted in a manner characteristic of the man. The retreat and concentration at Nashville was a masterly performance, executed without confusion and completed without loss. The battle before the city was one of hard blows and simple manœuvres, fought after ample preparation and due deliberation. The columns were heavy and massed, and the lines strong and deep. The action was slow and measured. In the midst of the engagement there were numerous lulls—pauses employed in dreadful preparation, in re-arranging lines and massing columns. There were numerous deliberate assaults of strong positions, and in every minute detail of the general plan there was visible a combined effort of each part of the army to reach some vital point of the enemy's position, the key of the battle-field. When this was won the battle was ended. The victory was the result of cool, deliberate action. The troops were tools in the hands of their leader, and were made willing and trusty instruments through the absolute and unbounded confidence which they felt in him.

In the three campaigns of Mill Spring, Chickamauga, and Nashville, the career of General Thomas is chiefly embraced. In the minor events of his military career there is nothing to detract from the glory which attaches to him in these.

ULYSSES S. GRANT.

CHAPTER III.

GRANT AS A GENERAL.

THE clearest conception of the characters of Generals Sherman and Thomas is obtained by contrasting them. A correct estimate of General Grant may be had by forming in the imagination a character combining the peculiarities of both Sherman and Thomas; for in the person of the lieutenant general the very opposite qualities which distinguish the others meet and combine with singular grace and felicity. General Grant does not make so effective, or, so to speak, so dramatic a picture as Sherman, nor does he present so dignified, that is to say, so stately an appearance as Thomas; yet he combines in himself the originality and energy of the first, with the deliberation, coolness, and pertinacity of the latter. Without the constant fire and fury of Sherman, without the occasional sudden, fiery impulse of Thomas, Grant, always cool, calm, and dispassionate, is also always firm, always decided, and always progressive. Sherman is as mercurial as a Frenchman, and as demonstrative as an Italian; Thomas as phlegmatic as a Dutchman, and as tenacious as an Englishman; while Grant in every characteristic, in doggedness, pertinacity, positiveness, and taciturnity, is thoroughly American, and nothing else. Grant is a true sailor, in that he dreads both the storm of battle

and the calm of inactivity, and his appropriate motto is
"*In medio tutissimus ibis.*"   Thomas delights most in
calm—is always calm himself, even in the midst of rough-
est seas.   Sherman, on the contrary, delights in tempests,
and would now be nothing if there had been no storm.
Professor Mahan, who was the tutor of Grant and Sherman, has furnished a very handsome illustration of the
contrast between them by comparing the first-named to a
powerful low-pressure engine "which condenses its own
steam and consumes its own smoke, and which pushes
steadily forward and drives all obstacles before it," while
Sherman belongs to the high-pressure class of engines,
"which lets off both steam and smoke with a puff and a
cloud, and dashes at its work with resistless vigor."
Grant has Sherman's originality of mind, and, like him,
gave expression to several new and striking thoughts
upon the subject of the rebellion and its suppression, but
they were invariably clothed in the full, rounded, and
stately periods of Thomas rather than the sharp, curt,
and nervous language of Sherman.   He has planned
several campaigns with not less of originality than that
displayed by Sherman, but they have always been executed with the deliberation and persistence which is so
prominent a characteristic of Thomas.   Sherman has
given us several splendid illustrations of strategy and .
logistics, as witness his marches in Mississippi, Georgia,
and the Carolinas, but his battles will never be quoted
as brilliant examples of grand tactics.   Thomas has dis- '
played his abilities chiefly in the tactics of the battle-
field, and has given us at Mill Spring and Nashville two
splendid illustrations of the offensive, and at Chickamau-

ROBERT E. LEE.

ga a magnificent example of defensive battle; but his marches, which are always slow and labored, are never likely to become famous. Grant has excelled in both these important branches of the art of war, and has given us brilliant examples of each, proving himself a master in each branch of the art of war. He uses the strategy of Sherman to reach his chosen battle-field, and then employs the grand tactics of Thomas to win the victory. At the risk of becoming tedious in endeavoring to impress this idea on the mind of the reader, I can not here repress the desire to again call attention to the natural and singular manner in which the three great generals of the war alternately appear in contrast and comparison as the great strategist, the great tactician, and the great general of the age.

After the great success of Grant below Richmond, culminating in the surrender of Lee, the rebels, though they had persistently ignored any latent greatness in Grant, were delighted to frequently discover similarities between the victor and the vanquished, and numerous were the comparisons which were instituted commendatory of Lee, and patronizingly of Grant. The two, as men and as generals, should rather have been placed in contrast; for, save in the silent, observant thoughtfulness which distinguishes both, they have hardly a trait in common. It is impossible to compare the most positive man of the war with the least resolute of the rebellion; the strongest of the true with the weakest of the false cause; the grandest character with the most contemptible; a great and successful general on the offensive with a weak and unsuccessful general on the defensive. As a general, Grant

always assumed the offensive, and was uniformly successful.   The opposite is strictly true of Lee.   Lee's first
offensive campaign in Western Virginia against McClellan was a failure; his first defensive efforts against the
same leader a great success.   His second offensive movement against Pope failed, and his third offensive movement, culminating at Antietam, was a great disaster.   His
second and third defensive battles, Fredericksburg against
Burnside, and Chancellorsville against Hooker, were successful.   His fourth offensive campaign signally failed at
Gettysburg.   His next campaign was defensive.   It was
fought in a country naturally strong for defensive purposes, in opposition to the man to whom he is compared,
where he should be contrasted.   Though conducted with
energy and stubbornness, it was finally a great defeat, and
annihilated Lee's army as it should have done his pretensions to great generalship.   Lee saw fit only to be a
soldier and obey, not a leader to direct.   He had none
of the attributes of a revolutionist or of greatness; else,
when seeing and declaring that the cause of the rebel
leaders was hopeless, he would, as morally the strongest
man in the South, and practically the head of the rebellion as the head of the army, have declared that no more
blood should be uselessly shed, no more of war's desolation be visited upon the people.   But it does not seem
ever to have entered the head of this man that, perceiv-
ing the cause hopeless, and wielding the power which
temporarily sustained that cause, it was his duty to for-
bid its farther prosecution at the price of blood.   Had
Lee possessed the courage, decision, and positiveness of
Grant, he would himself have been peace commissioner

instead of Stephens and his colleagues, and he alone the contracting power. A truly great and honest soldier in Lee's position, and with the convictions of the hopeless-lessness of the rebel cause expressed by him in 1865, would have made peace, even if he had been compelled to put Jeff. Davis in irons to do so. As a man, compared with Grant, Lee has none of the characteristics natural to greatness; and when he joined the rebels for the sake of no great principle involving honor, but simply, as he declared in a letter to his sister, because he did not wish to raise his hand against relatives and children, although he believed them engaged, if not in a bad cause, at least in one for which there was no just occasion, he sank all individuality, and became a traitor out of mere indecision of character. If Lee is never hung as a traitor, he ought to be as a warning to all people who have not minds and opinions of their own. For this, the weakest act of a weak existence, there is no counterpart in Grant's life, but a thousand, or rather, I should say, one constant and unvarying contrast.

The resemblance between Generals Grant and Thomas in personal appearance and character is more marked than between the former and Sherman. The comparison between Grant and Sherman must indeed be confined to their military characteristics. The resemblance is most noted in the fertility of invention which distinguishes both in a higher degree than any two men hitherto developed by the war. Neither ever lacks for resources. Grant, with an inventive faculty truly wonderful, extricates himself from all difficulties with an originality not less admirable on account of the boldness with which his designs are accomplished. The originality of his designs, not less than the boldness with which he acts, adds to the certainty of success. If one resource fails he has another at hand. He creates opportunities, and, though he is no Cadmus, at whose will armed men spring from the ground, yet he may be said to originate the materials of action, and to supply by his energy and his spirit, his invention and tactics, many of the deficiencies existing in his physical force. He is not easily disheartened, but seems greatest in disaster or when surrounded by difficulties. He is not easily driven from the prosecution of a plan. He carefully examines its merits before he decides upon it, and fully tests its practicability before he abandons it for another. That to which he is compelled to resort by reason of the failure of one is not less matured than the first. It may be said with truth that he has never been forced to abandon any general plan upon which he had determined, though the campaign against Richmond was modified by circumstances and facts developed at the Wilderness and Spottsylvania. The purpose of the campaign overland was the destruction of an important line of railroad, and the desolation of a rich country, by and in which the enemy was enabled to exist at the very doors of Washington, and by thus forcing him to abandon his threatening and offensive attitude, enable Grant to place the army operating against Richmond in its only true strategical position south of the James River. It is now apparent to all that, had the attack of General W. F. Smith on Petersburg in June, 1864, proved successful—as there was every reason to suppose it would, and really no good reason why it did not—the capture of Richmond would have followed immediately. There exists a notable resemblance between this campaign of Grant's and that of Sherman against Atlanta. Both were prosecuted against large armies posted and fortified in a country naturally difficult to penetrate, and in which the enemy had all the advantages arising from defensible positions. Both were characterized by brilliant flank movements made in the very teeth of the enemy. And though Sherman's campaign embraced none of the desperate and lengthy battles in which Grant engaged, it is marked by several combats of unusual desperation, generally occurring on the march and fought for position.

Like Sherman, Grant is a fine mover and feeder of an army. The marches of each are made with great precision, and their logistical calculations are marked by great accuracy. If such were not the case, the dangerous flank movements of the one at the Wilderness and Spottsylvania Court-house, and of the other across the Allatoona Mountains and around Atlanta, might have resulted in very grave and serious disasters. Both generals have a full and genuine appreciation of the importance of economy of time in the collection, and of quantity in the distribution of supplies; and in view of the fact that both have at all times operated at a great distance, and at times entirely disconnected from their bases of supply, the regulation and completeness with which their vast armies have been fed is surprising, and calls forth the fullest admiration for the administrative ability which each has displayed. The energy which Grant possesses, in a degree fully equal to that of Sherman, differs matcrially, however, in character from that of that erratic warrior. There is nothing nervous about it, nor can it be said to be inspiring like that of Sherman, but it is no less effective. Sherman's energy supplies all that may be lacking in his subordinates, and retrieves their blunders and delays. Grant's energetic manner of working soon teaches subordinates that delinquencies are not allowable. The comparison might be extended farther and to other features, while some minor traits of opposite characteristics might be mentioned. Both are unselfish and unambitious, or it would perhaps be a better expression to say both are unselfishly ambitious, holding their own interests second to those of the country. Sherman acknowledges Grant to have been the first to appreciate and encourage him after his consignment to that tomb of military Capulets, Jefferson Barracks. Grant attributes much of his uniform success to the skill of his second in command. Neither ever wearies of sounding the praises or of admiring the qualifications of the other. Among the points of character in which they differ is temper, that of Grant being exceedingly good in the sense of moderate and even, while Sherman's is very bad in the sense of irritability and unevenness. There can be no doubt that both are good, generous, and unselfish men at heart.

The persistence with which Grant pursues an object or executes a plan, the tenacity with which he fights, his practicability, reservedness, and taciturnity, are the strongest points of resemblance between himself and Thomas. It is difficult to say which excels in these qualities. Grant's famous dispatch from Spottsylvania, "I propose to fight it out on this line if it takes all summer," was written with compressed lips—the reader naturally reads it with clenched teeth—and fairly and graphically illustrates the perseverance and stubbornness of the man. It is even more forcible than the memorable dispatch of Thomas, "We will hold Chattanooga till we starve;" and in better taste than that of Granger's, "I am in possession of Knoxville, and shall hold it till hell freezes over." Grant's criticism on the Army of the Potomac, which is doubtless as just an opinion of that army as has ever been uttered, illustrates this trait of his character still more forcibly and elegantly. A short time after he assumed personal supervision of Meade's army, General Oglesby asked him what he thought of its *personnel*.

"This is a very fine army," he replied, "and these men, I am told, have fought with great courage and bravery. I think, however, that the Army of the Potomac *has never fought its battles through*." It certainly fought them through at the Wilderness, Spottsylvania, and on the Appomattox, and fully confirmed Grant's faith in the superior endurance of the men.

It is also related of Grant that, when young, he was very fond of playing chess, and played with great skill, but found among his opponents one who was his superior, and who used to win the first games of a sitting with ease. But Grant was never content to remain beaten, and would insist on his opponent playing until he got the better of him in the end by "tiring him out," and winning at chess as at war by his superior endurance.

The following story of Grant may be apocryphal. If true, however, it is a fine commentary on that trait of his character under consideration.   If not true, it shows that the feature is such a prominent one that anecdotes have been originated to illustrate it.   The story runs that immediately after the battle of Shiloh, General Buell began criticising, in a friendly way, what he termed the bad policy displayed by Grant in fighting with the Tennessee River in his rear.

"Where, if beaten, could you have retreated, general?" asked Buell.

"I didn't mean to be beaten," was Grant's reply.

"But suppose you had been defeated, despite all your exertions?"

"Well, there were all the transports to carry the remains of the command across the river."

"But, general," urged Buell, " your whole number of transports could not contain over ten thousand men, and you had fifty thousand engaged."

"Well, if I had been beaten," said Grant, " transportation for ten thousand men would have been abundant for all that would have been left of us."

It is not to be lightly concluded that the act of Grant in encamping on the same side of the river and within thirty miles of the enemy was bad policy.   If he had encamped on the east side of the stream the rebels would have made the river, instead of the railroad at Corinth, their line of defense, and rendered its navigation very difficult for gun-boats and impossible for transports.   The stream could not have been made the base of operations as was intended.   It is doubtful if we lost more men in the battle of Shiloh than we should have lost in attempting to force the passage of the stream.   Grant's position was faulty because it was not fortified. His camp ought to have been intrenched. In the absence of works, he depended for protection on the flooded streams which in a measure surrounded his camp, but which failed to retard the rebel advance.

Grant's disposition to persevere has had a natural effect in creating in him a firm reliance upon himself. It is very seldom that he calls councils of war or asks advice in any shape. He fears no responsibility, and decides for himself. General Howard, himself a man of very marked characteristics, has noticed and alluded to this confidence, adding that it amounted almost to the superstitious fatality in which Napoleon was so firm a believer. This self-reliance is doubtless, however, merely the full confidence which has resulted from the habit of independent thought and action of a man of unusually strong, iron will, determination, and tenacity of purpose. Though his language often indicates this confidence in himself, it never degenerates into boasting.

During the battles of the Wilderness an aid brought the lieutenant general news of a serious disaster to the Second Corps, which was vigorously attacked by A. P. Hill. "I don't believe it," was the prompt answer of Grant, inspired by faith in his success. The aid was sent back for farther reports, and found that the reported disaster had been exaggerated.

Among the most admirable qualities of Grant's mind and character, and in which he is most like Thomas, is his practicability. Grant, like Thomas, is not a learned scholar, but has grown wise from worldly experience. His wisdom is that which results from a combination of common sense trained to logical reflection with practical observation. He deals with all questions in a plain, business-like manner, and with all absence of ostentation or display, and in a systematic style, which enables him to dispatch a great deal of business in a very short time. His practicability renders him remorseless in the execution of his plans. When he has decided it to be necessary, he pushes his massed columns upon the enemy, and orders the desolation and depopulation of a country with the same coolness, not to say indifference, with which he would announce a common event of little importance. His administration of the affairs of the Army of the Potomac, now universally acknowledged to have been of the highest ability, fully displayed this characteristic of practicability.

A fine illustration of his practicability is found in a story related of him when operating before Fort Donelson. On the night before the surrender, the preparations of a portion of the rebels to evacuate the fort led General McClernand to believe they were meditating an attack, and he communicated his suspicions to Grant, at the same time sending him a prisoner who had been captured but a short time before. On reading McClernand's dispatch, Grant ordered the prisoner's haversack to be searched. It was found that it was filled with rations. "If the rebels intend to hold the fort, they would not encumber their men with rations. They are preparing to leave," was the very sage and practical reasoning of the general; and he immediately ordered McClernand to assume the offensive. The result was that a commanding ridge near Dover, south of the fort, was carried, and only a

portion of the garrison escaped; the remainder capitu-
lated.

During the battles of the Wilderness a rebel shell
dropped within a few feet of Grant and Meade, making
a furrow in the ground and bursting some distance beyond. Grant, without a word, drew from his pocket a
small compass with which he calculated the course of the
shell. In five minutes afterward he had a piece or two
of artillery posted near by, and opening upon, soon silenced the rebel battery, whose location had been betrayed by the course of the projectile. As soon as this had
been done, he asked the elevation of the guns which had
done such good work. On being told, he soon established, by a calculation well known to every artillerist,
the important fact of the exact distance of the enemy's
line from his own.

Another illustration of his practicability is also an instance of his magnanimity—a feature of his character
equally prominent. The terms of surrender granted to
General Lee—the dismissal of the captured army on pa-
role, was a piece of strategy which was completely veiled
by the apparent magnanimity of the conqueror. It was
a splendid stroke of policy. The tender of such terms
placed it at once out of the power of General Lee to decline them. His army could not have been kept together
an hour after learning that they had been generously
offered and refused. Lee's reputation demanded his acceptance of them. The rebel troops thus dismissed had
to reach their homes by passing through Joe Johnston's
army. The tale of their utter discomfiture and capture,
and the generous treatment accorded them, Grant knew,

would be whispered in the ears of Johnston's men, to the utter demoralization and disbandment of that army.

At Donelson and Vicksburg Grant's terms had been unconditional surrender. Such a surrender was important for the moral effect to be produced at the North. The surrender of Lee was demanded, and the most generous of terms granted, in order to produce the desired moral effect at the South. To my mind, this action illustrates the greatness of Grant more forcibly than any one other act of his life.

General Grant fully appreciates, as does Thomas, the philosophy of silence. His staff have learned to imitate his taciturnity; and there is, consequently, an air of industry and business about his head-quarters which no one who visits them can fail to observe. He has, throughout his career, published no foolish proclamations and made no visionary promises. His victories have been followed by no high-sounding addresses to his armies; but he has confined his compliments to a plain recital of the deeds of his men and the results of their achievements. He has, moreover, gone through the war without having made a single speech. At Lexington, Kentucky, in January, 1864, Grant met with a spontaneous reception from the citizens on his arrival from East Tennessee. At the request of the populace he made his appearance in front of his hotel, and, on being told that on account of his short stature he could not be seen by those on the outskirts of the crowd, he good-naturedly mounted a chair and bowed two or three times to the people. A speech was called for, but he contented himself with requesting Leslie Coombs, who was present, to state to the people that he "had never made a speech in his life, knew nothing about the business, and had no disposition to learn."

I have elsewhere, in endeavoring to show how Grant is a combination of the strategist, Sherman, and the tactician, Thomas, used the expression that he employed the strategy of one to reach his chosen battle-field, and the tactics of the other to win the victory. Grant's own definition of strategy will perhaps make this idea plainer. Shortly after the battles of Chattanooga, he was sitting in his head-quarters at Nashville, with his feet comfortably stretched before the fire, while he enjoyed himself with puffing and chewing his cigar with that completeness of repose which strangers to his habits have called a dullness of facial expression. Quarter-master General Meigs sat near him, while General W. F. Smith, who had but a short time before made himself quite a reputation with Grant by the skillful operations in Lookout Valley in October, 1863, paced the floor apparently absorbed in thought. Meigs, noticing this, broke the silence, which had lasted for several minutes, by asking,

"What are you thinking about, 'Baldy?'"

On receiving no reply from the absorbed officer, he turned to Grant and remarked, with a laugh,

"'Baldy' is studying strategy."

Grant removed his cigar from his lips and said, with a serious air, "I don't believe in strategy in the popular understanding of the term. I use it to get up just as close to the enemy as practicable with as little loss as possible."

"And what then?" asked Meigs.

"Then? 'Up, guards, and at 'em!'" replied the general, with more than usual spirit; then again lapsing into his accustomed taciturnity.

Grant has "crept" upon the enemy in this war on several occasions to some purpose, and with an effect which proves that his strategy is of a superior order. His strategic march to the rear of Vicksburg is already accepted as an illustration of the art of war, and not many years will elapse before it will be quoted as such in the military academies of the country. The combinations against Richmond are full of fine strategic marches and manœuvres. The flank movement around Spottsylvania Court-house, and the march upon Petersburg, accomplished in the face of the enemy, are not less brilliant than that of Vicksburg; while the defeat, pursuit, and capture of Lee are by far the most brilliant operations known to the history of modern warfare. General Grant's marches closely resemble in their general outlines those of Sherman. They are executed with all the energy and certainly as much of the skill as those of Sherman, but on a larger scale, with larger forces, and in the face of greater natural obstacles. In none of Sherman's operations has he made the passage of such streams as the Mississippi or James Rivers. The mountains of Georgia furnish no more difficult passes than those of Virginia. The marches of Sherman in Georgia and South Carolina are wonderful and brilliant, but they were made in the face of an enemy totally inadequate to cope with him. Those of Grant in Mississippi, Tennessee, and Virginia, are not the less wonderful because made in the face of a strong, watchful enemy, who, in Virginia at least, had an admirably mobilized army, and because accompanied by weeks of hard contested encounters.

The numerous battles of Grant are the most important and the most successful of the war. From his first victory at Fort Donelson, through Shiloh, Corinth, and Iuka, Vicksburg, and Chattanooga, to the battles before Richmond, and the surrender of Lee, he has been almost uniformly successful, and his victories have been more complete, and productive of more substantial fruits than those of any other commander. As his strategy is that of Sherman on a larger scale, so his grand tactics are those of Thomas on more extensive fields. The movements and the manœuvres of the two men are the same. The movements are always deliberate and heavy; the manœuvres are always executed by massed columns formed in deep lines. Grant, like Thomas, appears to decide in his own mind the key-point of the enemy's position, and to direct his assaults to the ultimate possession of that point. He devotes every energy, and, when it is necessary, every life, to the attainment of this success, knowing that this ends the conflict. When it is gained, as at Chattanooga and during the engagements of April 2d before Petersburg, the battle is won. If he fails to reach this key of the field, as in the first assault at Vicksburg and at the Wilderness, he is beaten. If he wins the point and the victory, he immediately pursues the retreating foe, as at Chattanooga and Petersburg. But if he fails, he does not abandon the field. His mind is too rich in resources for retreat. Ceasing to be Thomas, he becomes Sherman again, and has recourse to strategy, whereby he forces the enemy to a field where his grand tactics will stand

a better chance of success. A critical examination of
Grant's campaigns will reveal these features fully developed. He fully comprehends the specialty of Sherman,
strategy, as well as that of Thomas, grand tactics, and is
master of both. He has displayed in his campaigns, all
of which have been of mixed operations, all the persistence and pertinacity of Thomas combined with the originality of design and resources of mind of Sherman. But
in none of his campaigns have these peculiarities been
better or more brilliantly illustrated than in the campaign and battles of Chattanooga, and the not less wonderful campaign around Richmond. The first is an example of his tactics, the latter of his strategy.

The operations of Hooker and W. F. Smith in Lookout
Valley, which were a part of the Chattanooga campaign,
and which resulted in raising the siege of that strong-hold
by opening river communication with the base of supplies, was not less original in conception or bold and brilliant in execution than the famous march around Vicksburg. Bragg was compelled to abandon all hope of
starving out the garrison or capturing Chattanooga, and
he determined to attempt the seizure of Knoxville with
a portion of his army under Longstreet while he kept up
a show of besieging Chattanooga with the remainder. It
was this movement which gave Grant the opportunity
for the display of his tactical abilities. Burnside, in advising Grant of Longstreet's approach to attack him, reported that he (Burnside) held a line on the Tennessee
River, from London to Kingston, possessing unusual natural advantages, and expressed the opinion that he could
easily defeat Longstreet in any attempt he might make

to cross the stream. Grant immediately ordered Burnside to make no defense of the line which he held, but to fall back to Knoxville and stand a siege, promising to relieve him in a few days. The result of this was that Longstreet was deluded into crossing the Tennessee, and thus placed himself far beyond supporting distance of Bragg. Grant's strategy had thus far resulted in dividing the rebel army into two. He immediately went to work to defeat the parts in detail.

Bragg, learning of the approach of Sherman to Grant's aid, attempted, on November 23, 1863, to evacuate his strong position before Chattanooga, and retire for safety beyond the mountains. Grant, unwilling to let him off so cheaply, made a movement to detain him, and by commencing his proposed operations a day sooner than originally intended, he forced the rebel leader to remain in his rifle-pits and accept battle. Grant in nowise changed his plan as determined upon six days before the operations began, except that he commenced them eighteen hours sooner than intended. On the afternoon of November 23d he did that which he had previously intended to do on the morning of the 24th. It was the movement of Granger's *corps* into a position from whence, at the proper time, it was to assault the rebel centre. In this position the *corps* was compelled to lie idle, and in waiting for the auspicious moment, for eighteen hours longer than it was originally intended it should. This assault, which was made on the 25th, and was the closing scene of the battles, has been erroneously called one of those "blind, uncertain strikings which won the Alma and Magenta," when in reality Grant had determined upon it six days before it was executed, and spent two entire days in watching from the very front of the line for the moment at which to attempt it. The entire three days' engagement is remarkable for the consistency with which the plan was followed out. General Halleck pronounced the battle to be the " most remarkable in history," and Meigs called it the "best directed battle of the war." Never have operations in war better illustrated the vast advantages of the offensive.

The several battles of Chattanooga were fought on purely offensive principles, and I have often thought since that the secret of Grant's success may be discovered in the fact that he has always taken the offensive. I have heard men call him "the lucky Grant," and the newspapers speak of his good fortune; but it is not luck —it is not good fortune. It is "*Le genie de la guerre.*" He does not depend upon circumstances or good fortune, but controls both. One such illustration from Grant, as witnessed at Chattanooga, shows more forcibly and graphically the vast advantages of offensive warfare than can all the maxims of Napoleon or Jomini. From the moment that Bragg at Chattanooga was compelled to abandon his attempts at an orderly retreat and evacuation of his position, his movements were forced upon him, and his army was really controlled and commanded by Grant. Every movement made by the enemy may be said to have been ordered by Grant. Bragg, in command of the rebel army, was merely his mouth-piece. The plan of the battle contemplated the breaking of the enemy's centre; but this was so strongly posted on a mountain ridge almost inaccessible, that, in order to render success possible, it was necessary to force him to weaken his forces holding the centre. This was accomplished after two days' labor by the attacks upon either flank of the rebel line by Hooker and Sherman, and was no sooner made than perceived by Grant, who instantly ordered the assault of the centre, which resulted in the victory, and the capture of several thousand prisoners and sixty pieces of artillery. To complete the success of the operations, Burnside about the same time defeated Longstreet at Knoxville (Fort Saunders), and Sherman approaching to the relief of the besieged, the rebels abandoned the siege and retreated to Virginia, rejoining Lee soon after at Fredericksburg.

In conception, execution, and result, the closing operations of the war—the campaign to the rear of Richmond—must be considered as by far the most remarkable and brilliant movements of the rebellion. There is every evidence necessary to show that the campaign, as deliberately planned, was energetically carried out. The battles of April 1st and 2d, south of Petersburg, were absolutely necessary to the solution of the strategic problem. The object was to gain a position on the right flank of Lee, in order to force him not only to evacuate Petersburg, but to compel him to evacuate it in such a way that he would have to retreat by roads on the north side of the Appomattox River. By the success of this battle Lee was thus forced north of the river, and Grant gained a route to Burkesville Junction—the only point to which Lee could retreat—which was parallel with that of the rebels, and which, while separated from them a great part of the distance by a river, was also much shorter and without any natural obstructions such as lay in Lee's way. Lee had to retreat by the longer route, which was practically made still longer by the necessity of recrossing the Appomattox River. The consequence was that Grant reached Burkesville Junction by the time Lee reached Amelia Court-house, and not only interposed himself as an impassable barrier to the junction of Johnston and Lee, but also continually presented a force between Lee and Lynchburg. By keeping this force thus "heading Lee off," while at the same time he continually attacked him in flank and rear, Grant forced him, on the seventh day of the pursuit, to surrender his whole force. From the moment of occupying Burkesville, Grant held Lee in a position from which, if defeated in battle, he had no line of retreat. He was forced to make a stand in a position in which, had he given battle, he would have been forced to an unconditional surrender or equally disastrous dispersion.

An idea of the character of General Grant must, of course, be formed from the developments of the war. His life at West Point, and his subsequent career in Mexico and in civil life, displayed no particularly prominent trait of character other than an adaptation to the practical in life. At West Point he is remembered as a quiet, studious, and taciturn youth, only remarkable for the decision which has since been so prominent a characteristic of the man. He was neither a book-worm nor an idler, and graduated neither first nor last, but in that medium rank in his class which has given to the country several of its most thoroughly practical and successful men. In Mexico he was distinguished only for the bravery which he displayed at Chapultepec.

In his manners, dress, and style of living, Grant displays more republican simplicity than any other general officer of the army. In manner he is very unassuming and approachable, and his conversation is noticeable from its unpretending, plain, and straightforward style. There is nothing declamatory nor pedantic in his tone or language. His rhetoric is more remarkable for the compact structure than the elegance and the finish of his sentences. He talks practically, and writes as he talks; and his language, written and oral, is distinguished by strong common sense. He seldom indulges in figurative language; but when he does, his comparisons betray his habits of close observation. He dresses in a careless but by no means slovenly manner. Though his uniform conforms to army regulations in cut and trimmings, it is often, like that of Sherman, worn threadbare. He never wears any article which attracts attention by its oddity, except, indeed, the three stars which indicate his rank. His wardrobe, when campaigning, is generally very scant, while his head-quarter train is often the smallest in the army. For several months of the war he lived in a log hut of unpretending dimensions on the James River, sleeping on a common camp-cot, and eating at a table common to all his staff, plainly furnished with good roast beef, pork and beans, "hard-tack," and coffee. It is related of the general that when the march to the rear of Vicksburg began, he announced to his army the necessity of "moving light"—i.e., without extra baggage. He set an example by sending to the rear all his baggage except a green brier-root pipe, a tooth-brush, and a horn pocket-comb. The story of his appearance in the Senate Chamber in February, 1865, is still fresh in the minds of the public. He had no sooner left the hall, after paying his respects to the senators, than one of the Democratic members rose and asked the consideration of the Senate upon what he termed the evident and gross mistake which had been made in appointing Grant a lieutenant general, and declared it to be his opinion that "there was not a second lieutenant of the Home Guard of his state who did not 'cut a bigger swell' than this man who had just left their presence !"

The general is not lacking in self-esteem. He very naturally desires to be popular, likes to be well spoken of, but succeeds better than Sherman in concealing what vanity he possesses. He often excites admiration by the modesty of actions which in others would be considered exceedingly immodest; as, witness the quiet manner in which he accepted a present of a hundred thousand dollars from the citizens of New York.

Those who are disposed, like himself, to be fatalists, may imagine in the significance of Grant's surname, and the manner in which he obtained his baptismal name, encouraging omens of his success and that of the cause in which he is engaged. The surname Grant (derived from the French word *grande*, great, or valorous) is that of a Scottish clan, whose motto, as given in Burke's "Encyclopædia of Heraldry," appears to have been adopted by General Grant. It is as follows: "*Stand fast, stand firm, stand sure.*" The slogan of the clan was "Stand fast, Craigellachie." I believe there is no doubt that General Grant is of Scotch descent, and from the Grants and Duffs of Aberdeenshire. One of his aids, and a distant relation, Colonel Duff, was born at Duff House, "in the shadow," of which Mr. James Gordon Bennett, who was the first to appreciate and proclaim Grant's ability, records that he also was born. The general's proper christian name received at baptism was Hiram Ulysses; but on entering West Point he received, by the mistake of the person who nominated him, the name of Ulysses Simpson, which, abbreviated, gives the same initials as those used to indicate the government of which he is the servant. "United States Grant" is an appellation much more common than Ulysses S. Grant; while the patriotic friends of the general have given this title several facetious variations, such as "Uncle Sam," "Unconditional Surrender," and "United we Stand Grant."

The confidence of the fatalist is not necessary to courage. There is a courage superior to the mere indifference to danger, and this quality Grant possesses to the fullest degree. Sherman calls him one of the bravest men he ever saw. His coolness and his clear-headedness under danger and amid excitement is remarkable, and is superior to that of Thomas, who, next to Grant, is the coolest and most clearly administrative man under fire now in the army. During the battles of Chattanooga Grant and Thomas established their head-quarters on "Orchard Knoll," immediately in the rear of the centre of the field, and from which they could have a full and close view of the column which was to make the assault on the rebel centre. From the moment the signal for the attack was sounded, the scene was of the most exciting character; but during that important half hour in which the victory trembled in the balance, Grant and Thomas remained passive, cool, and observant. They were standing together when the assaulting column had reached half way to the summit of Missionary Ridge, when a portion of it was momentarily brought to a halt, and when the stream of wounded retiring down the hill made the line look ragged and weak. At this moment Thomas turned to Grant and said, with a slight hesitation, which betrayed the emotions which raged within him,

"General, I—I'm afraid they won't get up."

Grant, continuing to look steadily at the column, hesitated half a minute before answering; then taking the cigar he was smoking between his fingers, he said, as he brushed away the ashes,

"Oh, give 'em time, general," and then as coolly returned his cigar to his mouth.

Fifteen minutes later I met him on the summit of the hill, riding along with head uncovered, receiving the plaudits of the men who had won, but who had not yet secured the victory. The rebel centre had been broken, but the right wing, which had just repulsed Sherman, was yet intact, and, turning about face, attacked the troops which had carried the centre of their line. Our line was much broken, and the troops excited to such a degree at the victory they had gained that they had become almost uncontrollable, and on the appearance of General Grant, who, following in the wake of the advancing columns, had appeared in their midst on the summit as the white-plumed helmet of Henry IV. had appeared at Ivry, the men gathered around him shouting and hurraing, grasping his hand and embracing his legs. But, while coolly receiving these demonstrations of affection and delight,

Grant was not blind to the danger, and was using the necessary efforts to get his troops in readiness for the expected attack, which, but for his precaution, I am satisfied would have badly damaged us. He conveyed his fears intuitively, as it were, to his staff, and each one exerted himself to get General Turchin's brigade into position as ordered by Grant. Mingling in the very thickest of what now became the hottest fire of the day, they urged forward the troops, and personally gave directions for their disposal. Turchin, finding some men moving a piece of artillery to the rear in his way, raved and swore in broken English until he had got his men up to the works, and Lieutenant Turner as heartily cursed the fellows who were retiring the gun, and while doing so got seriously wounded. General Meigs, quarter-master general, busied himself in preparing friction primers for the captured guns which General Grant was ordering into position, but got so excited over the great victory gained that he gave the task up in despair to Captain Ross, of General Grant's staff. General Turchin pushed forward his troops, and no sooner had they appeared in line of battle in the fort, than suddenly the battle ceased and was over. As if with one accord, the rebels ceased to struggle. They broke in utter and total confusion, and rushed down the hill. Volley after volley followed them as they fled, but they did not halt. On they rushed, struggling and striving, reckless of all now save safety.

During the siege of Vicksburg Grant personally superintended the mounting of a number of Columbiads on a part of his line. While the men were cutting the embrasures in the works he stood upon the epaulement, and, though the rebels made a mark of him for their bullets, very composedly whittled a rail until the guns were placed to suit him.

Whittling and smoking are among Grant's favorite occupations. He is a true Yankee in these respects. It is recorded of him that, during the battles of the Wilderness, he was engaged in whittling the bark of a tree under which his head-quarters were established; and on all occasions, great and small, he smokes. He is a more inveterate smoker than either Sherman or Rosecrans, but he smokes in a different style and for a different effect. Both Sherman and Rosecrans take to tobacco as a stimulant to their nervous organizations. Grant smokes with the listless, absorbed, and satisfied air of an opium-smoker, his mind and body being soothed into repose rather than excited by the effect of the weed. Neither Sherman nor Rosecrans are neat smokers, the velvet breast-facing of their coats and their shirt-bosoms being generally soiled. Grant, on the contrary, is very neat, and smokes only the best of cigars. He smokes almost without cessation, and is never at ease when employed at any thing which forbids smoking as an accompaniment. During the famous interview with Pemberton before Vicksburg he smoked with his usual composure. "We pardon General Grant for smoking a cigar as he entered the smouldering ruins of the town of Vicksburg," said a rebel paper after the surrender. "A little stage effect," it added, "is admirable in great captains." But Grant never smokes dramatically. His cigar is a necessary part of himself, and is neither assumed nor abandoned for state occasions. He has been known to forgetfully smoke at reviews, and has frequently been brought to a halt and notified by sentinels or guards over commissary stores, "No smoking allowed here, sir." On entering the Senate Chamber to be presented to the Senate, he had to be requested to leave his cigar outside.

Sherman's errratic disposition caused him to be suspected of lunacy. Grant's imperturbation and his dullness of expression, added to exaggerated tales of his excessive use of strong tobacco as an opiate, was the origin of the story which prevailed at one time to the effect that he drank to excess. In early life he may have indulged in occasional sprees, but he does not drink now at all. Swearing is not a habit with him, and his phlegmatic temperament is seldom so ruffled as to cause him to indulge in an oath. He seldom jokes, and rarely laughs. His great "weakness" is Alexandrian, and consists in his love for fine horses. When quite a boy he was remarkable for tact in managing horses, "breaking" them with astonishing ease. When he was only fifteen years old persons came to him from a great distance to have him teach their horses to pace. This is not a great and exclusive quality of the man, however, as it is well known that thousands of negroes on Southern plantations were noted for the same knack or tact. It was doubtless the result of the innate love of the boy for horses, a love now as strong in the man and the general. He is said to be the best rider in the army.

Grant's undemonstrative manner has nothing of the repulsive about it. He has won and retained many warm friends. The friendship between him and Sherman has become historical, and is often quoted as in agreeable

F

contrast to the numerous bitter and disgraceful jealousies which have too often been made public, but which exist in the army to an extent not suspected by those who have no intimate acquaintance with its secret history. There is much of romance in the story of Grant and Sherman's friendship. It began in 1862, and has ever since continued to grow in strength. When the armies of Halleck were lying—literally so, indeed—before Corinth, Grant was, to all appearance, shelved in disgrace. He was second in command, but to be second in command then was to be the "fifth wheel to the coach." Grant was much chagrined at his position, and felt in tenfold degree each petty indignity which Halleck heaped upon him. One day General Sherman, who commanded one of the divisions of the wing under the command of General George H. Thomas, went to General Grant's quarters, bolted with his usual abruptness into his tent —they didn't stand on ceremony in the field—and found the general actually weeping with vexation. Sherman asked the cause, and, for the first time, Grant recounted the indignities which he had endured, the troubles he had encountered, and the false position in which he had been placed before the country.

"The truth is, Sherman," he said, "I am not wanted. The country has no use for me, and I am about to resign and go home."

"No you are not," returned Sherman, impatiently; "you are going to do nothing of the sort. The country does need you, and you must stay here, bear these petty insults, and do your duty."

He gave Grant no time for argument, compelled him,

in a measure, to stay, cheered him up and kept him in the field until the appointment of Halleck, as commander-in-chief, left the command in the West vacant, and Grant again came into power.

Years afterward, at the close of the war, Sherman, returning from his march through the Carolinas, having just received the surrender of Joe Johnston, found himself placed in a false light before the country by this same man Halleck. When he reached Washington City he was boiling over with rage at the indignity which Halleck had placed upon him by telegraphing that he had directed his troops to move without reference to Sherman's truce or orders, and his naturally bad temper became threateningly violent and uncontrollable. He denounced Halleck in unmeasured terms, and, had the latter been in Washington, a personal collision might have occurred. But, before the two could meet, Grant saw Sherman, and the scene enacted in the tent before Corinth three years before was re-enacted, save that the parts were changed. Grant appeared as the peacemaker, and as positively, though in a very different manner, advised Sherman to ignore Halleck and frown him down. Sherman was wise enough to take the advice, and the "great marplot" will make his chief appearance in history as one whom these men could afford to ignore.

Grant has always been generous to his subordinates. His careful consideration of the interests of his staff and general officers is proverbial, while his generous treatment of inefficient officers, whom he has been compelled to relieve, is well known. In the first action in which he commanded, the battle of Belmont, his troops at first gained an advantage over the rebels. They began to plunder the rebel camp in spite of all that the general could do to stop them. At last Grant, who knew that Confederate re-enforcements were coming up, got some of his friends to set fire to the camp, so as to stop the plundering. Then he got his troops together as well as he could, and retreated; but, in the mean time, the Confederate re-enforcements came up, attacked, and defeated him. There were five colonels under Grant who had not by any means supported him efficiently in his attempts to stop the plundering and collect his troops. Grant expected to be deprived of his command on account of the defeat, and one of the colonels, fearful of the same fate, called to see him about the prospect. He gave him no satisfaction, but, on the colonel's departure, turned to a friend and said, "Colonel —— is afraid I will report his bad conduct."

"Why do you not?" asked his friend; "he and others are to blame for not carrying out your orders."

"Why," said the generous Grant, "these officers had never been under fire before; they did not know how serious an affair it was; they have had a lesson which they will not forget. I will answer for it they will never make the same mistake again. I can see by the way they behaved in the subsequent action that they are of the right stuff, and it is better that I should lose my command, if that must be, than the country should lose the services of five such officers when good men are scarce." Grant did not lose his command, and three out of the five officers afterward greatly distinguished themselves.

The impression prevails to some extent among persons unacquainted with Grant in the field, the only place where he shows to great advantage, that he owes all his success to Sherman, Thomas, Sheridan, and his other chief subordinates. The fact is, the indebtedness is on the part of the subordinates. Grant owes his reputation to them just as ever schoolmaster owes his to the ability displayed by his scholars; but the indebtedness of the pupil to the tutor who educates his mind and directs his talent is not by any means repaid by this reflected credit. Sherman was a complete failure; he was looked upon, indeed, as a lunatic, until Grant saw what he was capable of, and directed his great abilities into the proper channel. Sheridan met with an uninterrupted series of defeats until Grant singled him out for his cavalry commander, and then the " belligerent cadet" met with an uninterrupted series of victories. Wilson stands similarly indebted; and Meade's greatest successes were obtained under Grant's direction.

It is not only with such men as Sherman, Sheridan, Logan, Howard, and others, with whom he bears the most intimate relations, but with his whole army, that Grant is a well-beloved leader. He has gained the universal admiration of his men by no clap-trap display or familiarity at the expense of discipline, but by a constant and watchful care for their interest. It is a boast in the Army of the Tennessee, which Grant commanded in person for nearly three years, that the men never wanted for food; Grant's commissary stores were always well filled. He was always careful to protect his men from the imposition of sutlers and army speculators, generally by fixing the prices of all articles sold in his department; and he cut red tape for the benefit of the private soldier with a remorseless hand.

When sitting for their photographs Grant and Sherman have dispensed with their cigars, and the consequence is an imperfect picture. None of the many artists who have painted them in oil have had the independence to supply the deficiency of the photographs, and add the cigar, which is a necessary accompaniment of the men, and which must be an important feature of every pen-picture which will be made of them. The addition of the cigar would doubtless detract from the dignity of the picture, but it should be remembered that artists paint as well for posterity as for the present generation. History will preserve in its picture of Grant his peculiarities, and, among others, the fact that he was an inveterate smoker. Why should not the artists preserve such a peculiarity as this, as well as the outlines of his figure and expression of his face? Is it any more important for posterity to know that his eyes were blue than that he smoked incessantly?

Grant is not so tall as Sherman nor so heavy as Thomas. His short stature would have made it difficult for him to enlist in the British army. He is but an inch above the minimum standard of officers of our army, but, being straight and somewhat spare, he has the appearance of being above medium height. Sheridan and Logan are the only major generals in our army who are shorter in figure than Grant. His forehead is high and square. His hair was originally a dark brown, but at forty-three, his present age, it is fast becoming sprinkled with iron-gray. His eyes are sharp and expressive, though small, peering out from under his overarching brow with great brilliancy. His nose is aquiline. His mouth is small,

and he has a habit of closely compressing his lips.   His
chin and cheeks are covered with a heavy beard, which
he never shaves, but keeps closely cropped or trimmed.

Though the war in which he has won his reputation is
now ended, the future has still much to do in establishing the position which Grant has to hold in history.   To-
day he enjoys the confidence of his countrymen to a degree unknown to military leaders during the war.   If
ultimately successful in the end—if he directs his course
through the mazes of the political campaign which has
followed hard upon the close of the war as well as he has
his military career, posterity will delight, and will find
little difficulty, in tracing out a comparison between his
character and that of the country's first great leader.
This it is hardly proper for the present age to do; and
such a comparison, if made in detail, would doubtless
shock the modesty of General Grant more than it would
the nation's sense of propriety; but if consistent in character and success to the end, the historian of the future
will not be content to draw simply the comparison which
I have imperfectly outlined, but will liken him to one
who in every respect was greater than the Sherman or
Thomas to whom, combined as in one man, I have compared him.   But, whether successful to the end or not,
if he remains, as at present, aloof from politics and far
above partisanism, General Grant, like Washington, will
live forever in the memories of his countrymen as a
good and honest man.

CHAPTER IV.

SHERIDAN AS A CAVALRYMAN.

VERY few wars of as short duration as was that of the late Southern rebellion produced as many as three great and original military leaders of the calibre of Sherman, Thomas, and Grant. The ancients could boast of but one Alexander, one Cæsar, one Hannibal to an era; modern times of but one Frederick, one Suwarrow, one Napoleon to an age. It took half a century of constant and almost universal revolution to produce Napoleon and his prodigies. Only this country, of all the universe, can to-day boast of possessing a general universally conceded to be a great military genius, and it has more than one. The rebellion, which at its outset boasted of commanding nearly all the military talent of the country, produced in the end only one really great soldier—Joseph E. Johnston; all the rest were mediocre—hardly respectable, indeed, if Stonewall Jackson, who was a fair, though unequal counterpart to Sherman, be excepted. The loyal cause, which was thought to be weak in its leadership, produced in the end all the really able statesmen of the revolution, and, with the two exceptions nôted, all the great military leaders. These latter are not confined to the three whom I have already sketched. Many of Grant's subordinates developed a genius for war of no

PHILIP HENRY SHERIDAN.

ordinary quality, and won on hard-fought fields fame and reward as successful leaders. No general was ever seconded by such numbers of able lieutenants, not even Napoleon ; and nearly all of Grant's chief subordinates won splendid reputations for skill, energy, and daring, the three attributes of greatness accompanying and necessary to success. When one looks at the developments of the war in this respect, he may well accept without question Grant's declaration, lately made in his usual modest style, that the country could readily have found another than himself to bring about the end of the war successfully.

Philip Henry Sheridan, who is one of the most noted and noteworthy of these subordinates of Grant, must always be looked upon as one of the miracles of war, not so much from the result as the manner of his achievements. If he were neither a great strategist, like Sherman, nor a great tactician, like Thomas, nor both, like Grant, he would still be a successful leader. I have endeavored to show in the preceding chapters that the lieutenant general is, as a military leader, complete in himself, possessing all the attributes of generalship ; while Sherman, embodying nervous intellectual force, and Thomas, representing physical power, are constituted by nature, as well as by the choice of Grant, to be his chief subordinate commanders. Sheridan, in character, is like neither of the others, but is an original genius, and a leader not unworthy to rank with Sherman and Thomas, or to hold position as the third subordinate commander of General Grant. He may be said to be an Inspiration rather than a General, accomplishing his work as much, not to say more, by the inspiriting force of his courage and example as by the rules of war. He supplies to the army the passion and fire which is smothered in Grant and Thomas, and imperfectly developed in Sherman. He renders an army invincible more by the impartation to it of his own courage and fire than by any system of organization, and appears to accomplish by this imparted enthusiasm all that results under the leadership of the others from discipline. When the future historian sums up Sheridan's character, with all the facts yet hidden, as they must be for some years to come, laid profusely before him, he will hardly rank Sheridan with those who have carefully and wisely planned. He belongs rather to that class of our officers who have, by skillful and bold execution, won the distinctive classification of "fighting generals." He can not be said to have developed any strategic genius, and his tactics have been of a strange and rather eccentric character, but it can not be denied that, in every battle in which he has been prominently engaged, he has given brilliant examples of his courage, vigor, and skill as a quick, dashing, and stubborn fighter. He is pre-eminently a "fighting general." He claims to be nothing else, and can afford to rest his claim on his deeds during the rebellion. His entire career in private and public has shown him to be impetuous, passionate, bold, and stubborn. He was born a belligerent. His natural element is amid the smoke, his natural position in the front line of battle. He fights vigorously and roughly, and when the tide of battle flows and ebbs most doubtingly he holds on most grimly. In private life his great energy is a little curt, and his fiery temper a little too quick, but his abruptness and belligerency are too honest and natural to excite condemnation; while his manner, when not excited or opposed, is distinguished by great courtesy, modesty, and pleasantry. In battle the wildest and most impetuous of warriors, in peace he is the "mildest mannered man" that ever scuttled canal-boats on the James or crossed sabres with a rebel. He is as impetuous as Sherman and as persistent as Thomas. He is cool and collected in the minor matters over which Sherman grows nervous, and fiery and bold in great dangers in which Sherman grows coolest and calmest. Sherman's energy is that of the brain, inspired; Sheridan's that of the blood, inflamed. In history Sheridan will stand forth as a type—a representative leader, even more boldly, if not more prominently, than Sherman, or Thomas, or even Grant. His was a specialty—he was great in a peculiar line of duty; history and romance will unite to make him the type of the "modern cavalier," and he will enjoy, in some degree, the semi-mythical existence which all representative men hold in history.

Sheridan is descended from the same class of the north of Ireland emigrants which produced Andrew Jackson and Andrew Johnson, save that the parents of the latter were Protestants, while those of Sheridan were Catholics. Having settled, on their arrival in this country, in a more populous, thriving, educated, and free district, Ohio, they were enabled to offer their son better educational advantages than were the parents of Jackson and Johnson, who had settled in the less civilized district of North Carolina, and hence young Sheridan became possessed of a good common-school education in his native place, Perry County, Ohio, where he was born in 1831.

Any number of statements have been made as to Sheridan's birthplace. Some writers have declared it to be Boston, while still others have said it was Somerset, Ohio. He was born, according to his own statement, near the town of Somerset, in Perry County, Ohio, on the 6th of September in the year named. The necessities of his family early forced him to manual labor, while his own inclination led him to study. He was a quick though somewhat careless student, while his great animal spirits made him early a rather wild and belligerent youth, fond of a boyish frolic and a trick, always lively and always generous, sometimes thoughtless in wounding the feelings of others, but quick to generously heal when in fault. When quite young, Sheridan was variously employed in his native county in doing odd "chores," among others that of driving a water-cart about the streets of Somerset, Ohio, and in sprinkling the dusty thoroughfares of that old-fashioned town. When about twelve years of age he entered the employment of a Mr. John Talbot, in Somerset, Ohio. Talbot was an old gentleman who kept a country store in which was sold every thing useful and ornamental, embracing dry goods and groceries, confectionery and hardware, from. rat-traps to plows, and from woolen socks to ready-made overcoats, and Sheridan found himself in a position to learn a little of every thing —every thing, at least, in the country grocery line. Mr. Talbot was a man who delighted in being thought, if not by others, at least by himself, a patron of youth, and he patronized young Sheridan, and was, as he afterward declared, "a friend to him when a friend was every thing." When Sheridan grew older and famous, Talbot still continued to patronize him, and once said, alluding to his former protégé, that, on taking him into his service, he "perceived that he was smart and active, and took some pains to instruct him not only in selling goods, etc., for that," he adds, with great candor, "was our duty and interest," but when a leisure moment offered he taught him to improve his "slight knowledge of writing, arithmetic, pronunciation," etc. Young Sheridan did not remain long with Mr. Talbot, but gave up his service for that of a gentleman named Henry Dittoe, in the same trade and in the same town as that of Mr. Talbot. While still here he attracted the attention of the Hon. Thomas Ritchey, then member of Congress from the Congressional district in which Perry County was located, and, owing to the influence of an elder brother and the favorable impression he made upon Mr. Ritchey, Sheridan obtained, very unexpectedly to him, the appointment of cadet to the West Point Military Academy. This was immediately after the close of the Mexican War, when it was a very difficult matter to obtain appointments for others than the sons and orphans of officers who had fallen in the war.

He therefore got into West Point pretty much as Mr. Lincoln used to say General Rosecrans won battles, "by the skin of his teeth." The fact is, he got out of the Academy with the honors of graduation in pretty much the same way. The characteristics which had distinguished him as a boy in his native town soon made him noted at West Point as the "best-natured and most belligerent cadet" in the Academy. In fact, his belligerent disposition retarded his advancement in youth and as a cadet as much as it has since advanced him. He fought so much at West Point, was so unruly, and "so full of deviltry," that, despite his fine scholarly attainments, the future great cavalryman graduated so low down in his class that he could only be commissioned in the lowest arm of the service instead of the highest, in which he has since so distinguished himself. As it was, he was a year longer in his course than nine tenths of his classmates. He entered in 1848, and should have graduated in 1852, but went over until the next year. I have been told that, at this late day, he required only "five points" more to his number of "black marks" to exclude him from the honors of graduation; and if he had not, toward the close of the session, by skillful management and unusual control over his quick temper, won the good opinion of one or two of his tutors, the future major general would have been forced to leave the Academy as he had entered it, instead of having the brevet of second lieutenant of infantry in his pocket. One of his instructors, who had admired his generous character, employed the argument that belligerency was not a fault in a soldier, and this is said to have done much in securing him the needed approval of the West Point staff of instructors and the honors of graduation. The argument was too powerful to be resisted by educated soldiers, and Sheridan was consequently sent forth fully authorized to be as great a belligerent in time of war as he desired.

Sheridan's class at West Point produced very few remarkable men. The three ablest of his classmates, McPherson, Sill, and Terrill, perished during the rebellion. McPherson, who graduated at the head of the class, was a brilliant student, an admirable engineer, but never a great leader. The student predominated in his organization, and he lacked in decision and nerve. He rose very high in rank in the regular army, but it was owing less to his available talents and practicability than to the care of Grant and Sherman, with whom he was a great favorite. Terrill made a fine soldier as an artillerist, and won well-deserved renown and promotion by his admirable handling of his battery at Shiloh. He was very ambitious of advancement. I was present at his death at Perryville.. His brigade was pushed by General McCook, the corps commander, into a forest, in which the enemy surprised and defeated his troops, who were raw recruits, scattering them in every direction. Terrill's horse was shot under him, and, being thus dismounted, and left without a command, he turned—the ruling passion strong in death—to the artillery, and assumed command of a couple of batteries fighting in General Rousseau's line. Thus returned to the arm of the service for which education and inclination adapted him, he did magnificent service. While thus engaged, and while in the act of sighting a gun of Bush's Indiana battery, he was mortally wounded, and died a few hours afterward, with a message to his wife unfinished on his lips. Joshua W. Sill, who was, perhaps, the superior man of the class of 1853, fell in a similar manner at Stone River. The enemy had thrown himself upon Sheridan with great energy, and succeeded in forcing him to retire. Sill was one of Sheridan's brigade commanders, and in aiding the general to rally the retiring troops, and in leading them to a charge, he was shot and instantly killed as the enemy were temporarily repulsed. Sill was a practical man, of great resources, energy, and courage, small of stature, and compactly built. He was beloved and admired in the army for his great courtesy, kindness, and good sense. . There were also in Sheridan's class others who became generals in the volunteer service during the late rebellion. William Sooy Smith commanded infantry during the greater part of the war, but conducted the cavalry expedition from Memphis in 1863, intended to co-operate with Sherman in Mississippi, but miserably failed. R. O. Tyler and B. F. Chamberlain were well known for services in the Potomac Army. General John M. Schofield attained to some prominence during the war, although he had more to do with combating the prejudice which existed against him in the War Office and the army than in fighting the rebels. William R. Boggs, who graduated fourth in Sheridan's class, failed as a rebel brigadier, and at the close of the war turned his attention, like Lee, to teaching young ideas how to shoot. John R. Chamblis, H. H. Walker, and John S. Bowen, who were also rebels, were failures. Hood was the only success among the seceding members of the class. He owed his rapid promotion from colonel to lieutenant general in the rebel army to something of the same qualities which won his promotion for Sheridan. Hood was not less bold and impetuous than Sheridan, but he lacked Sheridan's sound sense and quick judgment, and doubtless would not have made the rapid progress he did but for the aid and friendship of Jeff. Davis. Sheridan and Hood met in battle but once during the rebellion. It was at Chickamauga, and that encounter cost Hood his leg, although Sheridan was defeated. Hood commanded a division of Longstreet's corps, Sheridan one of McCook's divisions.

Eight years of almost profound peace followed Sheridan's graduation, and little opportunity offered for advancement. In May and June, 1855, Sheridan, then promoted to be a lieutenant, was in command of Fort Wood, New York Harbor, but in the July following he was ordered to San Francisco in charge of a body of recruits. On arriving there he was detailed to command an escort of cavalry intended for the protection and assistance of Lieutenant Williamson and the party engaged in the survey of the proposed branch of the Pacific Railroad from San Francisco to Columbia River, Oregon. Sheridan succeeded shortly after in getting himself detached from this command and ordered to join a battalion of dragoons under Major Raine, of the Fourth Infantry, then on an expedition against the Yakima Indians, and expecting active service and severe warfare. In this expedition he distinguished himself by gallantry at the "Battle of the Cascades" of the Columbia River (April 28, 1856). Although his action on the occasion is not described, it is not difficult to imagine it as of the same character as the later deeds of daring which have distinguished him. He was rewarded for his gallantry by being placed in command of the Indian Reservation of the Coast Range. Here he was engaged for a year in keeping the Conquillo Indians on Yakima Bay in proper subjection, and in building the military post and fort at Yamhill.

From this distant post he was recalled in 1861 to find himself promoted, by the resignation of large numbers of the Southern officers of the army, to a captaincy in what

was then Sherman's regiment, the Thirteenth Infantry.
He was ordered to join his regiment at Jefferson Barracks, and thus became attached to the Trans-Mississippi,
or Army of the Southwest, in which he saw his first service in the present war. Although this army had gone
through a campaign under Lyon, the preparations for
another under Fremont, and was then under command
of Halleck, it was so far from being organized that Sheridan could find no active duty, and was placed upon a
military commission to inquire into certain alleged irregularities of the Fremont administration of Missouri
affairs. About that time General Curtis, who had assumed command of the troops in the field, was ready to
begin an active campaign, and Sheridan was appointed
acting chief quarter-master, with which the duties of commissary were at that time blended. He was out of place
and felt it, and his success as a quarter-master was very
indifferent indeed. He used to laugh and say many
months after that providing "hard-tack and sow-belly,"
as the soldiers called the crackers and pork which formed the chief ingredients of their rations, was not exactly
in his line; and he was very fond of relating, in connection with the remark, his first experience in restricting
the contraband traffic in salt with the rebels. As chief
quarter - master, it was his duty to take such steps as
would not only provide for his own troops, but deprive
the rebels of contraband supplies. Hearing that Price,
then at Springfield, was suffering for salt, he employed
every means to stop the export of that article beyond
our lines; and, congratulating himself on his success,
used often to say, with a chuckle, that "the rebels were

actually starving for salt." When the advance of the army took place, and Price was hastily driven out of Springfield, the only article left behind was, much to Sheridan's disgust, an immense quantity of salt which had been smuggled through our lines. He ever afterward professed himself disgusted with his quarter-mastership, and fortunately soon after got himself under arrest and sent to the rear.

Officers generally look upon arrests as misfortunes. Sheridan's arrest was the turning-point in his fortunes, since it placed him, after a brief delay, on the staff of a rising major general and in the line of promotion. The circumstances of his arrest are not without interest, as showing one or two of his characteristics. Like many regular officers of the army as organized in 1861, Sheridan was in favor of carrying on the war by striking hard blows at the organized armies of the rebels, and generously providing for the people, who, while remaining at home, under United States protection, as non-combatants, still surreptitiously furnished men and material to the rebels. It is difficult to conceive the "Ravager of the Shenandoah Valley" entertaining any of these false notions of sympathy, yet such were Sheridan's feelings at the time, so strict a stickler was he for military discipline. He has overcome this too delicate and nice consideration for the interests of rebel aiders and abettors, and, like the country, has been educated by war in the belief that treason is to be fought with fire. Feeling thus during the Pea Ridge campaign, Sheridan was particularly disgusted with the ravages committed by a regiment of Kansas Jay-hawkers in General Blunt's division, and used often to denounce them in unmeasured terms. He was so much embittered against the regiment and opposed to their style of warfare, that when General Blunt ordered him to impress a large amount of provender from the citizens for the use of the army, he replied in any thing but decorous terms, declining to execute the order, and intimating in conclusion that he was not a Jay-hawker. General Blunt, of course, relieved him and preferred charges against him. Sheridan was ordered to report to Halleck. The letter was forwarded as evidence against him, and fell into Halleck's hands. That officer, having a just appreciation of a good joke, laughed heartily over the letter; and, sharing Sheridan's prejudices against "jay-hawking" and "bummers" generally, he caused the charges to be withdrawn, and in May, 1862, ordered Sheridan to duty on his own staff as acting chief quarter-master.

It is a singular fact that Sheridan was a protégé and favorite of both Halleck and Grant, who had not a thought, feeling, or interest in common. To have equally pleased Halleck, the theoretical, and Grant, the practical soldier—Halleck, the wily and polite lawyer, and Grant, the simple-minded, straightforward soldier—Halleck, who attempted to rise by arts, and Grant, who trusted solely to action for promotion, required very great qualities in a mind as young as Sheridan's. The secret of his success in pleasing both doubtless lies in the fact that he attempted to please neither. Sheridan has been one of the most honest of our generals. There was nothing tricky about him; his comrades all felt that he used no underhand influence to rise. Yet to the friendship inspired in these two very opposite natures by his honest and straightforward conduct Sheridan is doubtless somewhat indebted for his rapid advancement from a captaincy to a major generalcy in three years. When one reflects upon the rapidity of his promotion, the days of France under the empire appear to have come to us, and Bulwer's preposterous promotion of his hero in the play becomes highly probable. "Promotion is quick in the French army," said old Damas. Verily not more so than in the national army of the United States during the rebellion.

General Halleck was at the time of this occurrence before Corinth, and thither Sheridan repaired, to find himself suddenly and unexpectedly transferred from the regular to the volunteer service as colonel of the Second Michigan Cavalry, in place of Gordon Granger, who had been promoted. Halleck had, with an appreciation which he subsequently frequently displayed in organizing the United States armies, noticed Sheridan's qualities, and placed him in the branch of the service for which he was best qualified: But even Halleck did not fully appreciate the admirable qualities of his young protégé, and failed, when intrusted shortly after with the absolute organization of the armies, to advance him to the position for which the quicker appreciation of Grant afterward singled him out, after observing his conduct in one battle only.

His promotion to colonel aroused the ambition of Sheridan, who had before modestly hoped to eventually become a major. He now had opportunities to distinguish himself, and immediately went to work to improve the opportunity, determined to win rank and fame before the close of the war, which, having now changed its character, also gave promise of being long and adventurous, and full of occasions for one in his arm of the service.

His regiment was brigaded with that of Colonel W. L. Elliott, who, as the ranking officer, became brigade commander, and under his leadership Sheridan made his first campaign as a cavalryman. It was the famous raid around Corinth and upon Beauregard's communications at Boonesville, which was noted at the time as one of the first and most successful adventures of our then rapidly improving cavalry, and won for its leader a reputation for dash that the loyal press, with very questionable taste, continually compared to the daring of Stuart and Morgan in their bloodless raids against weak outposts and unguarded rear-lines. This irregular warfare of the rebel cavalry had not, up to that time, partaken of the bloody character which has since been given the cavalry encounters of the war, and Elliott and Sheridan were among the first to expose the fallibility and weakness of the boasted rebel cavalry when vigorously opposed. Elliott never accomplished any thing afterward, and it is half suspected that Sheridan did the work on the occasion which made Elliott famous.

It was but a short time after this affair that a second opportunity to distinguish himself was offered Sheridan on the same field, and, taking advantage of it, he fought his first cavalry battle.

This engagement, although of a minor character, served to illustrate his characteristics as a quick, dashing, stubborn fighter, as more brilliantly developed in Sheridan at more important engagements. The rebels were commanded by General James H. Chalmers, who attacked Sheridan's single regiment with a brigade of cavalry, evidently expecting little resistance. Sheridan was not required, by the importance of the post he commanded nor the position of the army whose front he covered, to hold his ground, and could have with propriety declined battle, and fallen back on the infantry line; but it was not in the heart of the "belligerent cadet" to decline an invitation to battle from any gentleman. He drew up his regiment in line, and received the attack in handsome style. Chalmers's first repulse taught him that he should have to proceed with his attack more systematically, and he brought up his line for a more regular and general assault. While he was thus engaged, Sheridan, with perhaps more enterprise than sound discretion, in view of the insignificance of the stake for which he contended, sent a detachment on a detour to the rear of the rebel position. These, by strenuous exertions, succeeded in effecting this purpose, and made an attack from that direction, while Sheridan, attacking from the front, succeeded in surprising the rebels and driving them from the field in confusion. Chalmers, his opponent in this engagement, subsequently won, under Bragg and Forrest, a character for belligerency similar to that now enjoyed by Sheridan, but he was not as uniformly successful, and his belligerency got him into difficulty. Bragg arrested him for his failure to carry the works at Munfordsville, Kentucky, in September, 1862, when Chalmers had assaulted them without orders. He subsequently got into like difficulties with Forrest, but his readiness to fight and general good qualities brought him safely out of his troubles. In the engagement at Boonesville his readiness to fight was evinced to Sheridan's satisfaction, while Sheridan's superior endurance and enterprise were made apparent to the rebel at the same time.

It was this success which made Sheridan a brigadier general. It has always been an unfortunate feature of our army organization that there is no provision for the promotion of the deserving in the branch of the service in which they have won distinction, and for which they have evinced high qualifications. A colonel of cavalry shows himself eminently deserving of promotion by his services in that branch, and he is promoted to be brigadier general of *infantry*, and not only taken from the line of the service for which he is best fitted, but, though promoted in rank, is sent to command an inferior arm of the service. By this fault of organization not only does the army lose the service of the person thus promoted out of his sphere, but often the promotion becomes the ruin of the recipient, who may be totally unfitted for this new line of duty. There are numerous examples of this. Among several of these failures, which have resulted from this cause, two of the most notable were of persons in Sheridan's own class. I have elsewhere already noticed how Terrill, who, as a captain of artillery, gained a great reputation for his successful handling of his battery at Shiloh, and who was promoted to be a brigadier general of infantry, to utterly fail and throw away his young life in his chagrin and desperation. McPherson's success outside of the engineer corps was no greater. He graduated at the head of his class, distinguished himself as an engineer, was promoted rapidly from captain to corps commander, only to find himself totally unfitted for such duty, and in time to waste, by his inadaptation to infantry and his lack of decision, the rich fruits of Sherman's successful strategic march through Snake Creek Gap upon Resaca.

Sheridan's fate was not exactly the reverse of this, for, when taken from the cavalry, for which he was eminently fitted, and made brigadier general of infantry, his success at first was not encouraging; but under the various tests which these charges have proved to be, he was more uniformly successful than any officer I remember placed in the same position. I know, indeed, of no general officer who was subjected to so many tests as Sheridan. He was alternately commanding cavalry and infantry, then both together, constantly changing from one line of operations to another, and thus being subjected to the study of new lines and new topography, besides being forced to meet and overcome the prejudices against new commanders local to every army. In fact, Sheridan may be said to have begun his career anew three several times, and his ultimate success in spite of these obstacles shows the superiority of his mettle.

Immediately on his promotion Sheridan was placed in command in Kentucky of a division of raw troops, for the organization of which he was not so well fitted as for fighting them. The command was under General Nelson. Shortly afterward Nelson was killed, and the reorganization of his army, and its incorporation with that of General Buell, placed Sheridan in command of a division of partly disciplined veteran troops. A short time subsequently the army was again reorganized by Rosecrans, and Sheridan was given a division and assigned to the corps of General A. McD. McCook. Sheridan's division suffered defeat at Stone River and Chickamauga. But amid those disasters and defeats the fighting qualities of the "little cadet" found illustrations as brilliant, but not so familiar as those of his greater victories at Cedar Creek, Five Forks.

Stone River was a battle in which the endurance of the soldiers rather than the generalship of their leaders gave us possession of a field in which the enemy retained, until his abandonment of the field, the tactical and strategic advantage. Each corps, and even each division, "fought on its own hook;" there was no generalship, no plan, no purpose on our part. The official reports tell very elaborately of a grand plan, and how, despite the reverses of the first day, it was carried out to brilliant and successful completion, but that plan was arranged after the battle was finished. There was no such plan before the battle, for, like all of Rosecrans's battles, Stone River was fought without any definite plan. Bragg was the tactician of Stone River. He assumed and held the offensive during the whole engagement, and our forces were kept continually on the defensive. It is a singular fact, that so ignorant was Rosecrans of the position of the enemy, so absolutely without a plan was he, that on the very morning of McCook's disastrous defeat he ordered General Crittenden to occupy the town which the enemy were covering in strong force, declaring that they had evacuated it. General T. J. Wood protested against the blind obedience which General Crittenden would have given to this command, and, pending the reference of the remonstrance to Rosecrans, McCook was attacked and whipped. The soldiers fought the battle on our part, not the general commanding the army; and it was Thomas, Rousseau, Sheridan, Negley, Wood, and Palmer, as leaders, who saved the day, and retrieved the disaster precipitated by McCook's incompetency, and Rosecrans's incapacity, from extreme nervousness, to direct a large column of troops. Sheridan's division was posted on the left of McCook's corps, which, being struck in flank and rear, was very quickly and unexpectedly doubled up and thrown back upon Sheridan's division, which was thus forced, while fighting a division in its front, to turn and form a defensive *crotchet* to the whole army, thus being compelled to expose one or the other of its flanks. It was forced back by superior numbers until its line of battle described three sides of a square, and these being broken after a terrible resistance, it was forced to retreat through a dense forest of cedars, in which artillery could not be moved, to the line formed by the reserves under General Rousseau. While the rest of the corps had been rapidly driven, Sheridan's division fought for hours desperately, losing all the brigade commanders, seventy other officers, and nearly one third of the men killed and wounded. The other divisions of McCook's corps, under Jeff. C. Davis and R. W. Johnson, were never rallied until they reached Nashville, while Sheridan's fell back upon the line of reserves and fought for two days afterward. This result was entirely owing to the personal exertions, daring, and skill of Sheridan; and his conflict formed such a brilliant episode of that badly - managed battle, and his abilities shone so prominently in contrast with the delinquencies of others, that he was at once made a major general.

In the dark cedars at Stone River he kept his men together, when almost surrounded or entirely cut off, only by being at all times along the front line of battle with them; by well-directed encouragement to the deserving, and the blackest reproaches to the delinquents; by alternate appeals and curses, and a constant display of a daring which was inspiring, and in the presence of which no man dared betray himself a coward.

"The history of the combat of those dark cedars will never be known," wrote the only historian who has as yet truly written of Stone River, Mr. W. S. Furay, of the Cincinnati Gazette, a young man of very extraordinary abilities, and the most conscientious of all the war correspondents whom I met in the army. "No man," he adds, "could see even the whole of his own regiment, and no one will ever be able to tell who they were that fought bravest, or they who proved recreant to their trust. It was left to Sheridan to stay the successful onset of the foe. Never did a man labor more faithfully than he to perform his task, and never was leader seconded by more gallant soldiers. His division formed a kind of pivot, upon which the broken right wing turned in its flight, and its perilous condition can easily be imagined when the flight of Davis's division left it without any protection from the triumphant enemy who now swarmed upon its front and right flank; but it fought until one fourth of its number lay bleeding and lying upon the field, and till both remaining brigade commanders,

Colonel Roberts and Shaeffer, had met with the same fate as General Sill."

When Sheridan had extricated his command from the forest and got in line with the reserves, he rode up to Rosecrans, and, pointing to the remnant of his division, said,

"Here is all that is left of us, general. Our cartridge-boxes contain nothing, and our guns are empty."

The Tullahoma campaign, which followed that of Stone River, offered few opportunities for the display of any other quality of the soldier in Sheridan than that of energy. The pursuit of Bragg, which formed the main feature of that campaign, required rapid marching, but no fighting. After the expulsion of the rebels from Tullahoma and Winchester the general pursuit was abandoned, as the enemy had reached the mountains, and only Sheridan's division and Stanley's cavalry received orders to pursue the enemy across the mountains to the Tennessee. Sheridan moved with great alacrity, hoping to reach the bridge over the Tennessee at Bridgeport in time to save it from destruction. He moved so rapidly that he reached the river before Stanley's cavalry, which had been ordered by an indirect route through Huntsville. He succeeded in saving the greater part of the bridge. He used to tell with great glee that on reaching Bridgeport he found numbers of the rear-guard of Bragg's army sitting on the burned end of the bridge, and asking his advance on the opposite bank of the river if "they were part of Stanley's cavalry." The infantry had moved so rapidly in pursuit that the enemy had all the while mistaken them for cavalry.

Sheridan has since displayed the same energy in moving, with better effect. The surrender of Lee was, without doubt, the effect of the admirable and vigorous execution by Sheridan of Grant's plan of operations from Five Forks to Burkesville Junction. It will be remembered that Sheridan, by rapid movements, placed his forces at Jettersville before Lee had reached Amelia Court-house, and thus cut off all retreat to Danville. His dispatches relating to those operations partake of the vigor of the actual movements, and handsomely illustrate his energy.

"I wish you were here yourself," he wrote to Grant—a compliment that the little lieutenant general may be proud to point to. "If things are pressed," he added, "I think Lee will surrender."

"Press things," was Grant's order. It needed no other. Sheridan pushed forward rapidly, struck right and left, punishing the enemy wherever found, and at last forcing Lee to surrender. Grant returned the compliment with interest in writing his final report of the closing operations of the war. He describes, in his peculiarly forcible language, that, on the eve of the battle of Winchester and the beginning of Sheridan's valley campaign, he went to Sheridan's quarters to examine his plans, forces, material, etc., and found that he had only a single instruction to give his lieutenant—"Go in!"

"Press things" and "go in" are instructions as laconic as they are indefinite. They betray Grant's practicability and plainness, and honor Sheridan. It is, perhaps, better to be the one addressed in such terms than even the author of them. Sheridan is not less plain and forcible in his language than Grant, as witness his various reports, the quotations above, and his opinion of Texas. "If I owned," he once said, "Texas and hell, I would sell Texas and live in the other place."

The battle of Chickamauga, as far as McCook and Sheridan were concerned, was only a repetition of Stone River. McCook's corps, consisting then of Davis's, Sheridan's, and Negley's divisions, was again defeated. General Negley, very unfortunately for that gallant officer and gentleman, was taken from his division in the heat of battle and ordered to the command of a number of batteries, and the division suffered badly, while the other division, under General Jefferson C. Davis, was scattered in every direction. Sheridan, who had formed the extreme right, had a desperate though ineffectual fight, but, after being separated from the rest of the army, eventually cut his own way out, brought in his division about half organized, and took his place in the line at Rossville, to which Thomas fell back at night. On this occasion, as at Stone River, Sheridan was a subordinate. The disaster to his division was general to his corps, and resulted from the incapacity of others, and not his own bad management. He was powerless to avert, he could only partly retrieve the disaster. On both occasions he did so with a skillful hand, by the most strenuous exertions, and at great personal risk.

Chattanooga was the battle in which Sheridan caught the eye of Grant, who there selected him without hesitation for the important position which he subsequently filled. Sheridan's division formed the right of the centre column, which, in the engagement at Chattanooga on November 25, 1863, assaulted and carried Mission Ridge, and, breaking the rebel centre, assured the victory. His men were kept in position waiting for the signal to assault for over thirty-six hours, and they and their leader had grown very nervous, half fearing the battle would be won too soon by Sherman and Hooker, and the chance for glory stolen from them, when at last the wished-for signal came, and away to the charge sprang the assaulting columns. General T. J. Wood commanded one column, and he and Sheridan strove with a lofty ambition, in which there was nothing that a saint could condemn, to reach the summit first. Sheridan gloried in the deed. He could not contain himself, and yet he rode along the front line, half leading, half directing his men, as clear-headed as if the cross-fire of the twenty rebel batteries that opened upon his men were directed against charmed lives, and he knew them to be futile as against him. During the charge he took a canteen of whisky from his aid, Captain Avery, and, filling a cup which he carried, raised it with a gesture toward Bragg's head-quarters, which were plainly visible on the mountain crest, saying, in imitation of the soldiers, "How are *you*, Mr. Bragg?" Before he could drink the liquor, a rifle-ball carried away cup and beverage. Sheridan exclaimed, "That's damned ungenerous!" There was no time for more, and he spurred forward, and soon again formed part of his front line. His horse was killed under him, and he led the remainder of the assault on foot, reaching the summit with the first, and, as horses were not plentiful on the ridge, he sprang upon one of the fifty captured guns, swinging his sword over his head, and shouting for joy with his men, while, at the same moment, he poured invective after invective on the heads of the rebels whom he was unable to pursue. Before the battle was ended, Grant, having left his head-quarters in Orchard Knob, rode along the summit of the ridge, and before the fire of the enemy had ceased he had marked Sheridan for future use. Chattanooga was the flood-tide of his fortunes, and, without knowing it at the time, he that day launched his bark anew. Henceforth his abilities were not to be lost by his being made subordinate to men of inferior calibre. He was henceforth to win great successes, not retrieve, in some degree, the great disasters of others.

Sheridan did not know for months after of his good fortune on that day. On the contrary, his friends soon after had reason to' imagine that he was again under a cloud. It was but a few months after this memorable battle that Gordon Granger and Sheridan were relieved of their commands. It was generally known that Granger had offended Grant by his delay in moving with Sherman to Burnside's aid at Knoxville, and it was supposed that both he and Sheridan were laid on the shelf. I met the latter as he passed through Nashville, and he told me that he did not then exactly know his destination, except that it was Washington City. The announcement was soon made, however, that he had been placed in command of all of Grant's cavalry on the Potomac, and those who knew Sheridan learned to appreciate more highly the clearness with which Grant read the characters of his subordinates. Returning Sheridan to the cavalry service was not by any means the least important of Grant's services to the country.

It was not intended, in the scope of this chapter, to give a detailed statement of the events of Sheridan's life. The purpose was rather to make the public more familiar with his character than his history. The prominent points of his later career are as well known to all as myself. I have often had cause to regret that I have no personal recollections of Sheridan's remarkable campaign in the Shenandoah Valley. I should have been particularly glad to have had an opportunity to witness and to analyze the wonderful effect of Sheridan's presence on his men during the rout at Cedar Run. It can not be accounted for on any theory, however philosophical, framed by a person who was not an eye-witness, while it might be comprehended in the light of a minute and graphic description of the manner of the general on that occasion. His success in restoring order, and then confidence, was doubtless due to his decisive manner, while the subsequent restoration of *morale* was owing to the promptness with which the offensive was resumed. The control which Sheridan then held over his men is certainly very remarkable, in view of the short time during which he had commanded them, and the condition in which he found them on this day. Absent at the beginning of the battle of Cedar Creek, it will be remembered that he pushed forward to the front to find his troops retreating rapidly, and, although not pursued, much demoralized. Demoralized does not necessarily, as I have found by experience on more than one doubtful field, imply defeat. Sheridan appears to have felt so; for, on being told by a colonel whom he met that the " army was whipped," the indomitable Sheridan exclaimed, " You

are, but the army isn't." His presence seemed to inspire
the men with a new purpose. He possesses a secret similar to that of Cadmus. Though not making soldiers
spring ready-armed from the earth as Cadmus did; he
creates an enthusiasm which gives additional power and
strength to those he has. On the occasion alluded to, so
powerful was this inspiring presence that, in an incredible short space of time, he had his routed men reformed
in line, and ready to receive the onslaught of the enemy.
But the enemy, intent on rifling the captured camps, had
not pursued in force, and Sheridan found waiting was in
vain. The confidence of the troops had been restored by
the presence of their leader, the facility with which he
re-established the broken lines, and the cheering language
and encouraging tone of his conversation and orders. He
fully re-established the morale of the men when, finding
the enemy failed to pursue, he ordered an advance. The
fact that he did advance on the same day of the rout
serves to show, among Sheridan's other great qualities as
a leader, his decision and daring. There are few generals, in our own or any other service, who would have
conceived the idea, or for a moment entertained the purpose of immediately resuming the offensive. Two years
before, pursuit after a victory, not to mention pursuit after a defeat, was held to be impossible. The fact that
Sheridan was able on this occasion to resume the offensive with complete success shows how absolute was the
confidence of the men in this comparative stranger, who
had plead, entreated, cursed, and browbeat the flying
army into order again. The magnificent ride from Winchester to the field, which at the time was made in all

the accounts the salient feature of the battle, grows commonplace when compared to "Little Phil's" ride among the routed masses of his corps.   He may be said to have been every where at once, for his presence was felt in every battalion.   His orders, so brilliantly illustrated and varied by his peculiar and numerous oaths, found their natural echoes in the cheers of the men, in whose hearts his presence restored confidence.   The rapidity with which he rallied his broken lines and brought order out of chaos is incredible even to those who have seen the "belligerent cadet" in the midst of battles; and to one who has never witnessed the singular effect which the reception of orders to attack have on men, it will still remain incredible how he so far restored the confidence and morale of his troops as to enable him on that occasion to snatch victory from defeat.

There was some occasion for the display of the same personal daring, and the exercise of the same influence by example, on the part of Sheridan, at the battle of Five Forks.   His *presence* on every part of that contested field, it is now generally conceded, had as much to do as generalship with the final result of that battle, where every thing depended on the persistence of the attack on the weak point which Sheridan had discovered.   It is doubtful if success would have followed the efforts of a general who had been content to *direct* the battle.   Sheridan *led*. He was in the front line, under the heaviest fire, at all times, waving his sword, encouraging his men, exhorting them to incredible deeds, and, as usual with him, swearing alternately at the enemy and his own skulkers.   He is represented by those present as the "impersonation of every thing soldierly." He rode up and down the lines, under fire, continually waving his sword, commanding in person, exhorting them to seize the opportunity within their grasp, and sweep their enemies to destruction. It is related of him, and the story is characteristic enough to be true, that, at the conclusion of the first day's unsuccessful battle at Five Forks, while striding up and down in front of his field head-quarters, apparently absorbed in deep and calm thought, he suddenly startled his staff by breaking out in a series of horrible oaths, in which he swore he would carry the rebel lines next day, or "sink innumerable fathoms into hell."

Despite several remonstrances which I have received from him and his friends, I must say that Sheridan occasionally indulges in oaths, but one can easily find it in his heart to forgive them. They are merely the emphasis to his language. Oaths are said to be fools' arguments. Sheridan throws them at one in a discussion not from a want of more forcible arguments, but from a lack of patience to await the slow process of logical conclusions. For this same reason he heartily despises a council of war, and never forms part of one if he can possibly avoid it. He executes, not originates plans; or, as Rosecrans once expressed it in his nervous manner, "He fights—he fights!" Whatever is given Sheridan to do is accomplished thoroughly. He does not stop to criticise the practicability of an order in its detail, and at the same time does not hesitate to vary his movements when he finds those laid down for him are not practicable. He does not abandon the task because the mode which has been ordered is rendered impossible by any unexpected event. If the result is accomplished Sheridan does not care whose means were employed, or on whom the credit is reflected. He grasps the result and congratulates himself, the strategist of the occasion and the men, with equal gratification and every evidence of delight. His generous care for the reputation of his subordinates, his freedom from all petty jealousy, his honesty of purpose, and the nobleness of his ambition to serve the country and not himself, his geniality and general good-humor, and the brevity of his black storms of anger, make him, like Grant, not only a well-beloved leader, but one that the country can safely trust to guard its honor and preserve its existence. It is easy for one who knows either of the two—Grant and Sheridan—to believe it possible that, during all the period in which they held such supreme power in our armies, not a single thought of how they might achieve greatness, power, and position, at the expense of country, has ever suggested itself to their minds. There are few other characters known in profane history of whom the same thing can be truly said.

Sheridan goes into the heat of battle not from necessity merely. The first smell of powder arouses him, and he rushes to the front of the field. It is related of him that when the engagement of Winchester began, he stood off a little to the rear, as Grant would have done, and endeavored to calmly survey the field and direct the battle. But it was not in his nature to remain passive for a great while. When the fight warmed up and became general, he could stand it no longer, and, drawing his sword, he exclaimed, "By God, I can't stand this!" and rode into the heat of the engagement.

The belligerent in Sheridan's organization is often aroused without the stimulus of the smell of gunpowder. In 1863, while Sheridan was encamped at Bridgeport, Alabama, he invited General George H. Thomas, then encamped at Deckerd, Tennessee, to examine the works erected at Bridgeport and the preparations going on for rebuilding the bridge. I was then at Deckerd, and being invited to accompany the party to Bridgeport, did so. At one of the way-stations the train halted for an unusually long time, and Sheridan, on asking the conductor, a great, burly six-footer, the reason, met with a somewhat gruff reply. Sheridan contented himself with reproving his manner, and ordered him to proceed with the train. The conductor did not reply, and failed to obey. After waiting for a time, Sheridan sent for the conductor, and demanded to know why he had not obeyed. The fellow answered, in a gruff manner, that he received his orders only from the military superintendent of the road. Without giving him time to finish the insulting reply, Sheridan struck him two or three rapid blows, kicked him from the cars and into the hands of a guard, and then ordered the train forward, acting as conductor on the down and return trip. After starting the train he returned to his seat near General Thomas, and, without referring to the subject, resumed his conversation with that imperturbable dignitary.

On another occasion Sheridan detected an army newsvender in some imposition on the soldiers, and, without waiting for an explanation, he seized him by the back of the neck and thumped his head against the car, although he had to stand on tiptoe to do it.

Sheridan's appearance, like that of Grant, is apt to disappoint one who had not seen him previous to his having become famous. He has none of the qualities which are popularly attributed by the imagination to heroes. "Little Phil" is a title of endearment given him by his soldiers in the West, and is descriptive of his personal appearance. He is shorter than Grant, but somewhat stouter built, and, being several years younger and of a different temperament, is more active and wiry. The smallness of his stature is soon forgotten when he is seen mounted. He seems then to develop physically as he does mentally after a short acquaintance. Unlike many of our heroes, Sheridan does not dwindle as one approaches him. Distance lends neither his character nor personal appearance any enchantment. He talks more frequently and more fluently than Grant does, and his quick and slightly nervous gestures partake somewhat of the manner of Sherman. His body is stout but wiry, and set on short, heavy, but active legs. His broad shoulders, short, stiff hair, and the features of his face, betray the Milesian descent, but no brogue can be traced in his voice. His eyes are gray, and, being small, are sharp and piercing, and full of fire. When maddened with excitement or passion these glare fearfully. His age is thirty - four, but long service in the field has bronzed him into the appearance of forty, yet he is one of the most elegant of young bachelors, and answers fully to the description of the first Scipio, "*Et juvenis, et cœlebs, et victor.*"

JOSEPH HOOKER.

CHAPTER V.

FIGHTING JOE HOOKER.

THE name and fame of General Joe Hooker are, as they ought to be, dear to every American, for he is eminently a national man. Born in Massachusetts, he has resided in every section of the country, and is cosmopolitan in habits and ideas. Nature never made him for one part of the land. He has fought over every part of the country from Maryland to Mexico, from the Potomac to beyond the Rio Grande, and from a private citizen of the most westerly district of California, he rose to command as brigadier general of the regular army in the most easterly department of the reunited country. Every Californian, if not every American, *is* proud of Joe Hooker, for he is a representative man of that peculiar race of pioneers drawn from every state of the Union and nationality of the globe.

Hooker is naturally a fighting man, a belligerent by nature as much as Philip Sheridan, and he insists on forcing every dispute to the arbitrament of arms. Actual blows satisfy him best, and, from the very nature of his mental organization, "war to the knife" is an admitted motto with him. A curious accident gave Hooker the title of "Fighting Joe;" but few of the multitude who read of him under that appellation, and none of those who, in the heat of political and partisan discussion, which during the war seemed to partake of the extreme bitterness created by the conflict, endeavored to ridicule both person and expression, suspected how accurately the title described the character of the man. A man born with this disposition would naturally seek the army. Hooker entered West Point and studied his way through with a zeal and industry which must have placed him higher than twenty-eight in a class of fifty graduates had he not, like Sheridan, suffered for his belligerency in the estimation of the staid and steady professors of that institute. He was not a student, nor was he an idler, nor yet a plodding, industrious, dull scholar, who learned with great difficulty, and retained only what he was taught. On the contrary, he was quick to learn, original in applying what he learned, and critical of the ideas and facts taught him. At West Point he as frequently criticised the rules of war laid down by the authorities of the past age as in the field as a general he was free in criticising his contemporaries. He got through the course creditably in 1837, and managed, being still young, and the belligerency of his nature not fully developed, to exist in the quiet position of adjutant of West Point. Afterward he also managed to endure the monotony of the adjutant general's department for five years, until the war with Mexico broke out, when he sought adventure, promotion, and fame in the active service. The Mexican War was the great opportunity of many young lives, the practical schooling of nearly all who distinguished themselves during the late war for the Union. To Hooker, young, ambitious, and belligerent, the opportunity was highly welcomed. The declaration of war was hailed by him with an intense joy that would have horrified his Puritan fathers if they could have been cognizant of it.

Hooker's career in Mexico was not remembered when the rebellion began, or he would have earlier stood high in the confidence of the government, for it was among the most brilliant of the many successes attained by the many very able young men engaged in that war. To have risen under the old and very faulty organization of the army in a short war, in which there were few casualties, from a lieutenant to be brevetted lieutenant colonel of the regular army, was no small achievement. Hooker was successively brevetted captain, major, and lieutenant colonel "for gallant and meritorious conduct" in the several conflicts at Monterey, in the affair at the National Bridge, and in the assault of Chapultepec. He was detailed, if I remember rightly, early in the campaign as adjutant general on the staff of General Gideon Pillow, and, though Gabriel Rains and Ripley were associated with him on duty, it was generally understood and felt that the young chief of staff furnished all the brains and most of the energy and industry to be found at the headquarters of the division. Pillow, Rains, and Ripley became somewhat notorious during the late rebellion as officers of the rebel army. During the war with Mexico sectional feeling ran high on the subject of supporting the administration in the prosecution of an offensive war, and very often young Hooker was compelled to hear tirades uttered by these Southern officers against his native state, which gave only a lukewarm support to the war of invasion which that against Mexico was deemed, but he never allowed them to pass unreproved or unresented. A less positive character than Hooker might have been influenced in his state allegiance by such surroundings in a camp composed almost exclusively of Southern soldiers, and at a head-quarters where prevailed the most intensely bitter sectionalism which then disgraced the army. The discussions which grew out of the objections which the young chief of staff took to the peculiar views of the embryo rebels only served to confirm him in his adherence to and love of the government; and none of the old army officers entered into the war for the Union with more alacrity or with a clearer conception of the desperate purposes and characters of the traitors than did Joe Hooker.

The peace which ensued in 1847 found Hooker with the natural belligerency of his quick temper fully developed, his ambition fired, and his restless activity of mind and body increased. He had no disposition to return to the monotony of the adjutant general's office, or to that quiet of garrison duty, that a captain of artillery, which he had become, would have to endure. The unadventurous career which a professional life in a settled country among civilized people promised was also without charms to his restless mind. He remained in the army only as long as the prospect of service in Mexico and on the Pacific Coast had any promise of activity; but soon finding that the peace which followed the Mexican War was likely to be profound and undisturbed, he resigned his commission, and plunged into the excitement of pioneer life in the newly-discovered gold regions of California. He purchased a ranche across the bay from the city of San Francisco, and for a short time became interested in the, to him, novel duties of a farmer. It is natural to suppose that this monotonous existence soon became painfully dull to a person of Hooker's restless disposition. The ranche was neglected for other objects affording more excitement and adventure; but by the year 1860 this existence had lost many of its charms, and Hooker again found the "horrors of peace" upon him. Peace, it must be known, has its horrors for some men, just as the calm has its terrors for the seaman. The consequence was that Hooker fell into some of the bad habits which follow idleness. He was a "fish out of water," with nothing of an agreeable character to do, and he restlessly ran into some excesses, which I have heard his California friends allude to as the process of "going to the dogs." His business-character suffered, but not his social standing. His ranche was neglected and went to ruin. His health became somewhat impaired, when, fortunately for him, the rebellion broke out. He hastened to Washington to offer his services to the President.

He succeeded after much difficulty in obtaining a commission, and gladly launched again into active service. He became a changed man. He had abandoned his bad habits with the ease and readiness of a man of resolute and determined mind, and now, engaged in that profession which had every charm for him, he began in earnest the prosecution of the true aim of his life. He believed in fate and destiny; believed that strong minds and brave hearts control their own fortunes; and, with firm confidence in himself, announced to his friends, who congratulated him on his appointment, that one day he

H

would be at the head of the army, of which he was then only a brigade commander.

If Hooker's military career be examined critically, it will be found that his success as a leader has been due to the impetuosity, boldness, and energy with which he fights. His presence on a battle-field may be said to be calculated to supply all deficiencies in the discipline of the troops. His presence and demeanor inspired his troops with the qualities of courage and daring which distinguished himself, and restored morale to broken columns with the same success as that which ever marked the presence of Philip Sheridan. As commander of the Army of the Potomac, General Hooker never met with brilliant success. He assumed command at a time when the bitter jealousies which disgraced that army most impaired its energies and retarded its action. He had little of the love or admiration, and, consequently, little of the genuine support of his subordinate commanders; while he was, by reason of his promotion, farther removed from immediate direction of his troops, and the inspiration of his presence was lost on those who had learned to believe in him.

Success with Hooker depended upon his immediate presence with his troops, and to remove him from close intimacy with them was to impair his effectiveness. No one will attempt to deny that Hooker held such an inspiring control over his men, and that his presence among his troops in battle had much to do with their effectiveness. He was what has been called "a powerful presence." He was destined for a leader, not a director of troops, and hence his great success has been as the leader of fractional corps of great armies. His battles on the Peninsula; his vigorous pursuit of the rebels from York-town; his conduct throughout the "battle-week on the Chickahominy," and his engagement at Malvern Hill, were the deeds which are familiarly known throughout the country. His success as the commander of a *corps* in the West has become not less familiar to the public; and his achievements at Lookout Mountain, Resaca, and before Atlanta, will be the basis for the establishment of his true character as a military man. I do not mean by this to say that Hooker can not command with success a great army. I have no personal knowledge of his career as a commanding general, but from his mental organization it is evident that he is greater as a leader than as a director of men. My personal recollections of Hooker's battles are confined to a few, the most remarkable of which was the battle of Lookout Mountain. The "battle above the clouds," as the assault of Lookout Mountain was called, was one of the most remarkable operations of the war. The mountain which was carried is fourteen hundred feet above the Tennessee River, and was held by a force of at least six thousand rebels strongly fortified. It is not a regular slope from the summit of Lookout to the foot, but the first twenty-five or thirty feet of the descent is perpendicular rocks, or what is generally understood to be meant by "palisades." These are very high and grand, and there are but two routes by which they can be overcome. One of these is a gap twenty miles south of the point on the Tennessee River where the assault was made. The other is by a road to Summertown, which winds up the east side of the mountain, ascending the palisades by a steep acclivity and narrow road. General Hooker's plan of operation was to get possession of the road. To do so was to gain possession of the mountain. He must be a regular mountaineer who can unopposed make the ascent of the Lookout without halting several times to rest; and the story of the assault seems incredible to one standing on the summit, where the rebels were posted, and looking at the rough ascent over which Hooker charged. Only a general in whom the disposition to fight was largely developed could have conceived such a project, and only troops inspired by the presence of one whom they knew to be a brave and daring leader could have executed the ambitious plan. It was planned in all its details, and executed in all its completeness by Hooker. The original intention of General Grant, who was commander-in-chief, was to attack Lookout with a force only sufficiently large to keep busy the rebel force occupying it while the main attack was made elsewhere. The destruction of a pontoon bridge, which connected Hooker's camp with that of the main army, forced Grant to leave him a much larger corps than he had at first intended, and he then gave Hooker permission to assault the mountain with all his force. The order was received about noon on the 25th of November, 1863, but before nightfall General Hooker had planned and had executed an attack which was as brilliant as daring. Two months' observation of the mountain from his camp in the valley had given him a full knowledge of all its outlines, its roads, etc., and it is easy to believe that the plan which Hooker decided upon had had for some time a place in his mind.

It was as unique in conception as it proved successful in execution.

A small force under General Osterhaus was ordered to make a feint upon the enemy's rifle-pits at the point (or "nose," as Rosecrans calls it) of the mountain, while with Geary, and Ireland, and Crufts, and Whitaker, General Hooker moved up the valley west of the mountain until a mile in rear of the enemy's position; the troops then ascended the side of the range until the head of the column reached the palisades which crown the mountain, and formed in line of battle at right angles with them; they then marched forward as Osterhaus made a sharp attack as a feint, and, by taking the rebel works in flank and rear, secured about thirteen hundred prisoners. The enemy fled around the "nose" of the mountain, closely pursued, to a position on the opposite side, where Hooker again attacked. After one or two desperate efforts the rebel works were carried, but it was at such a late hour (midnight) that it was impossible to dislodge them from the Summertown road, a route by which they evacuated during the night. Hooker made a great reputation by his unique plan, and the vigor with which he executed it. The battle on the other parts of the line were suspended for that day, and Hooker on the mountain became the "observed of all observers." The troops in the valley watched him and his Titans with equal admiration and astonishment; astonishment at the success attained, and admiration of the daring displayed. When our troops turned the point of the mountain, taking the rebels in rear, capturing many and pursuing the rest rapidly, the troops in the Valley of Chattanooga cheered them repeatedly. As the lines of Hooker would advance after nightfall, those in Chattanooga and the valley could see the fires built by the reserves springing up and locating the advancing columns. As each line became developed by these fires, those on the mountain could plainly hear the loud cheers of their comrades below. One of the expressions used by a private who was watching the fires from Orchard Knob grew at once into the dignity of a camp proverb. On seeing the line of camp-fires advanced beyond the last line of rifle-pits of the enemy, a soldier in General Wood's command sprang up from his reclining position on Orchard Knob and exclaimed,

"Look at old Hooker: don't he fight for 'keeps?'"

"Fighting for keeps" is army slang, and signifies fighting in deadly earnest.

Those who remained in Chattanooga described this combat as the most magnificent one of the grand panorama of war which the various battles of Chattanooga proved to be. General Meigs has graphically described it at a moment when it was just dark enough to see the flash of the muskets, and still light enough to distinguish the general outline of the contending masses. The mountain was lit up by the fires of the men in the second line, and the flash of the musketry and artillery. An unearthly noise rose from the mountain, as if the old monster was groaning with the punishment the pigmy combatants inflicted upon him as well as upon each other, and during it all the great guns on the summit continued, as in rage, to bellow defiance at the smaller guns in our forts on the other side of the river, which, with lighter tone and more rapidly, as if mocking the imbecility of its giant enemy, continued to fire till the day roared itself into darkness.

General M. C. Meigs has given the combat its name of the "battle above the clouds." It is true that Hooker fought above the clouds, but more than this, he manufactured the clouds that he might fight above them. During the night before the engagement a slight, misty rain had fallen, and when the sun rose, cold and dull, next morning, a fog hung over the river and enveloped the mountain, serving as a convenient mask to Hooker's movements. As the day advanced, however, the fog began to lift, and was fast disappearing, when the battle on the west side of the mountain began to rage heavily. Then the smoke of Hooker's musketry and artillery began to mingle with the mist and clouds; they grew heavy again, and settled down close upon the mountain, so that at one time the clouds thus formed hid the contending forces from the view of those in the valley, and Hooker literally fought the battle above clouds of his own making.

The "inspiring presence" with which Hooker is endowed, and to which I have alluded, has had many illustrations. McClellan, with whom Hooker was no favorite, acknowledged that the loss of Hooker's presence by wounds, during the battle of Antietam, cost him many valuable fruits of that conflict. While such an acknowledgment is disgraceful to McClellan, who could thus admit that the absence of one corps commander out of five could lose him a battle, it is highly complimentary to Hooker, who appears, by the way, to have been the only officer at Antietam who was fighting for any definite object, any vital or key-point of the field.

The well-known effect of Sheridan's presence at Cedar Creek was not more remarkable in restoring the morale of his army than was that of Hooker at Peach-tree Creek, Georgia, in retrieving the disaster which was there threatened. The Army of the Cumberland was surprised at that point on the 20th of July, while on the march, and, being vigorously attacked, was in great danger of being routed. It was a well-known fact that the presence of Hooker every where along the line of the threatened and almost defeated army kept the men in line, at the work, and finally saved the day. Were it within the purpose of this sketch to do so, no better illustration of the fighting general could be given than a detailed account of this battle, in which Hooker was the central—only figure. The country is as much indebted to him personally for the victory as to Sheridan for Cedar Creek, Rousseau for Perryville, or Thomas for Chickamauga.

Hooker is "his own worst enemy"—not in a common and vulgar acceptance of that term, now universally applied to those who indulge their appetite at the expense of the brain. His weakness is not of the vulgar order, but has been the disease of great minds immemorial. His great crime against weak humanity lies in the fact that he was born a critic. Iago was not more positively critical than Hooker, though the latter is not necessarily "nothing if not critical," as was Othello's evil genius. Hooker can not resist the temptation to criticise; and, being unable to appreciate that questionable code of morality in which policy dictates that the truth is not always to be spoken, he has made himself life-long enemies. He can attribute with perfect justice every fail-

ure of his life to that one " weakness of the noble mind."
It accelerated his retirement from the service in 1853 ;
it originated the difficulties which nearly prevented his
re-entry into the service in 1861 ; it retarded his promotion, lay at the root of all his difficulties as commander
of the Army of the Potomac, made enemies of his subordinates, and defeated his every plan, and at last forced
him to resign command of the army. It nearly defeated
his every effort to regain a command. It cost him many
difficulties in the event, and finally forced him to retire
from active command under Sherman just as the war
was being wound up with the grand *crescendo* movement
of Grant. He was bitterly assailed by the press, and per-
secuted by fellow-officers for his various criticisms, and
even accused of insubordination by men who did not
know that from time immemorial the orders of generals
have been freely criticised by subordinates, who did not
fail to obey them, however. Diogenes was not the only
critic of Alexander the Great. Napoleon would have
suffered even more than McClellan from criticism if he
had been as poor a soldier, for McClellan had but one
honest critic, Hooker, and all of Napoleon's marshals frequently criticised his movements. Criticism forced the
arbitrary Czar of Russia to abandon the chief command
of his army in the face of Napoleon's invasion of 1812,
and turn over the command to a general who was not
one of his favorites. Hooker was, indeed, the only genuine military critic which the war produced. Sherman
occasionally indulged in critiques, but his temper interfered with his judgment, and made his criticism as absurd
as vain. Fremont was merely a critic without being a

general, and found fault for the love of fault-finding. General Meigs, who also tried his hand at criticism, was simply good-natured, not critical. Cluserét and Gurowski were simply Bohemians, and Assistant Secretary of War Dana won reputation only as "Secretary Stanton's spy."

The candor of Hooker's criticisms make them highly palatable. One naturally admires the decision which marks them, and, though some may consider his reasonings incorrect and his deductions unjust, they must enjoy the perfect independence with which they are uttered. His criticism on the battle of Bull Run first brought him to the consideration of Mr. Lincoln, who read characters at a glance. His famous criticism on McClellan, in which he did not hesitate (he never hesitates either to censure or to fight) to attribute the failure of the Peninsular campaign to "the want of generalship on the part of our commander," gave him more publicity than his early battles. The late President used to remark that he had never had occasion to change the favorable opinion which he formed of Hooker on hearing his criticism on the battle of Bull Run. The criticism on McClellan indicates the character of the critic as that of a quick, resolute, decided man, ready to take all responsibilities. The character has been fully established by Hooker since he uttered that remarkably free criticism. Hooker's opinion of McClellan has been attributed to envy of the latter's position, but I think that he formed his conclusions of the man long before the war of the rebellion. A circumstance which happened during the Mexican War gave him his idea of McClellan, and is so admirable an illustration of McClellan's character that I am tempted to relate it here. Attached to Pillow's head-quarters, where Hooker was chief of staff, was a young American, since celebrated as an artist. He had long been resident in Mexico; was imprisoned on the approach of our forces to the city, but managed to escape and reach our army. Here he volunteered to act as interpreter to General Pillow, and accompanied the army in this capacity through the rest of the campaign. One day, while encamped in the city after its capture, Captain Hooker requested the artist to make a drawing of a very superior piece of artillery captured during the assault. It happened that this gun was in the camp of a company of sappers and miners, and thither he repaired to make the sketch. On going to the company head-quarters, he found Gustavus Smith, the captain, and Callender, the first lieutenant of the command, absent, while Second Lieutenant George B. McClellan, the officer on duty, was making the rounds of the camp. The artist at once repaired to the gun which he wished to sketch, and was engaged in doing so, when McClellan, with an armed guard at his heels, stepped up, with the martial air of one " dressed in a little brief authority," and demanded to know who the intruder was, and by what authority he was there engaged in sketching. The artist, smiling at the manner of the young man, very quietly handed him Captain Hooker's authority for the work he was doing. On reading it McClellan dismissed the guard, and opened a conversation with the intruder, asking him various questions, and at last eliciting the fact that he had been for several years past a resident of the city of Mexico. Instantly McClellan's interest was excited, and he propounded innumerable questions to the artist on—not the history, wealth, resources, defenses, etc., of the city, as one would naturally suppose a young soldier might consistently do, but upon the condition, character, wealth, standing, etc., of the best families of the first society of the city! He asked particularly after the most fashionable, and aristocratic, and wealthy houses, and more particularly still about the leading dames of the fashionable circles. He finally concluded by complaining to his informant that he found it difficult to get introduced to the first families, and had been much disappointed in not getting admitted into the best Mexican society. The story was too good to keep, and Hooker, Pillow, and all the staff afterward enjoyed the artist's frequent relation of the story of the young man who "fought to get into the best Mexican society." I have often thought that the young Napoleon conducted his Potomac campaigns as if his purpose was to place himself on such a footing that, on arriving at Richmond, he would be readily admitted into "the best Southern society." Advising a man of McClellan's character, as Hooker once did, to disobey orders and move on Richmond, with the encouraging comment that he "might as well die for an old sheep as a lamb," was like throwing pearls to swine.

The criticism on McClellan and his want of generalship was mistaken by a great many for vanity instead of candor, and the press of the country heartily ridiculed Hooker's vanity. He was called an *exalte*, an enthusiast. He has certainly a good opinion of himself, as all great men, not only warriors, but philosophers, have invariably had of themselves. Many not less famous men have been vain of lesser qualities than Hooker boasts, and their own good opinions of themselves have been adopted by posterity. Hooker is proud of his mental abilities. Cæsar was proud of his personal appearance, and devoted more hours to the plucking of gray hairs from his head than he did to sleep. Vanity and valor often go hand in hand. Murat was equally brave and vain, and made his famous charges bedizened in gold lace, and resplendent with fanciful furs and ermine trimmings. Heroes are seldom sloven. Cromwell and Sherman, in their slovenliness, are paradoxes in nature as they are marvels in history.

Hooker's retirement from the army was accelerated, and his subsequent return to the service was retarded, as has been stated, by this habit of freely criticising the operations of the army. The history of his troubles is as follows: Immediately after the close of the war with Mexico, Hooker was called upon to testify before a court of investigation, which had the settlement of the difficulties between Generals Pillow and Worth growing out of the assaults on Chapultepec. In the course of his examination he very freely criticised some of the movements of General Scott, the commander-in-chief, and with that confidence in his own judgment which is a marked characteristic of Hooker, and which, strange to say, betrays nothing egotistical in it, told how he would have accomplished the same ends attained by Scott at less loss, by other movements. Scott, with good reason, was mortally offended; and when Hooker's resignation reached his hands in the routine channel of business, it was not delayed for lack of approval, but was forwarded with a recommendation that it be accepted. When Hooker wished, at the beginning of the rebellion, to return to the army,

General Scott stood in the way; and being supreme in authority, under the President, he permitted Hooker to beg for admission for some months, keeping him dancing attendance unavailingly at the doors of the war office.

Hooker lingered for several months at Washington endeavoring to get a command, only leaving the city to witness the Bull Run battle; but at last wearied out, and seeing no hope of attaining his ends, he determined to return to California.   Before leaving, however, he called upon the President, whom he had never met, to pay his parting respects, and was introduced by General Cadwallader as " Captain Hooker."   The President received him in his usual kind style, but was about to dismiss him, as time required that he should dismiss many, with a few civil phrases, when he was surprised by Hooker's determined tones into listening to his history.

"Mr. President," he began, "my friend makes a mistake.   I am not 'Captain Hooker,' but was once Lieutenant Colonel Hooker, of the regular army.   I was lately a farmer in California, but since the rebellion broke out I have been here trying to get into the service, but I find I am not wanted.   I am about to return home, but before going I was anxious to pay my respects to you, and to express my wishes for your personal welfare and success in quelling this rebellion.   And I want to say one word more," he added, abruptly, seeing the President was about to speak; "I was at Bull Run the other day, Mr. President, and it is no vanity in me to say I am a damned sight better general than you had on that field."   The President seized and shook Hooker's hand, and begged him to sit down; began a social chat, which, of course, led to a story, and thus on to a more intimate acquaintance. The President, who was Hooker's firmest friend afterward, used to take great pleasure in telling the circumstance, and the effect of the speech upon him. The boast was made in the tone, not of a braggart, but of a firm, confident man, who looked him straight in the eye, and who, the President said afterward, appeared at that moment as if fully competent to make good his words. He was satisfied that he would at least try, and, impressed with the resolute air not less than with the high recommendations of "Mr. Hooker," requested him to defer his return to California. Hooker remained in Washington, and among the numerous changes which shortly followed the battle of Bull Run and the retirement of General Scott was the transformation of "Mr. Hooker" into "Brigadier General Hooker."

Hooker sometimes indulged in sharp criticisms even in his official reports. During the battle in Lookout Valley he sent a portion of his left wing, under General Shurtz, to the assistance of General Geary; but the former became mixed as to his topography, and did not reach the battle-field until too late to aid Geary, who accomplished his task successfully. He reported, in extenuation of his failure, that he found a wide swamp in his path, and had been compelled to go around it. Hooker, in his official report, after stating General Shurtz's excuse, adds very quietly that he had thoroughly examined the country between General Shurtz's camp and the battle-field, and that no such swamp as described existed.

Another criticism on some of his subordinates during the battle of Lookout Mountain reacted on Hooker in consequence of being too delicately put by him, and too broadly by Grant in an indorsement.   During the assault of that mountain, General Walter Whitaker commanded the second line of the attacking column under Geary, and the formation being that of *échelon* on the right, Whitaker was some distance in the rear.   When Geary's front line reached and took the rebel position, a large number of prisoners and several cannon were captured, and turned over by the front line to Whitaker. Whitaker sent the prisoners to the rear, secured them and the guns; and in his official report represented them as his captures.   Geary, in his report, mentioned, as he had a perfect right to do, the captures as his, and thus the reports showed double the list of actual captures.   Hooker, in a quiet, sarcastic vein, whose irony is hardly visible to those not acquainted with the circumstances, alluded to this double report, and gave the full number of captured guns and men with an ironical exclamation point at the end of the sentence.   Grant turned the joke on Hooker by indorsing his report, with the statement that the amount of captured material enumerated exceeded the actual captures by the whole army!

When Burnside was in command of the Army of the Potomac he executed an order, which was afterward suppressed by the President, dismissing several officers of his army from the service for various reasons.   Among the number was General Hooker, dismissed, as might naturally be supposed, for having criticised the action of his commanding general at Fredericksburg.   The order, which was known as "General Order No. 8," was not carried into effect, and only saw the light through the treachery of a clerk in the adjutant general's office of the army. Instead of the order being carried out, Burnside soon after resigned, and Hooker assumed command of his army.

Hooker left the Army of the Cumberland in consequence of having freely criticised Sherman's movements on the advance on Atlanta. The failure of Sherman to promptly follow up his success in seizing Snake Creek Gap, and to retrieve the blunder of McPherson on retiring from before Resaca in May, 1864, was particularly provoking not only to Hooker, but to every other commander who saw Joe Johnston slip through Sherman's fingers in consequence of that delay, and Hooker very freely alluded to it as a blunder. The natural consequence of this, and subsequent instances of candid criticism on Hooker's part, was the creation of some considerable prejudice against him in Sherman's mind. Sherman was of too bilious a temperament ever to sacrifice an opportunity to vent his spleen, and when he found an occasion he took care to resent the insult of which Hooker had been guilty in criticising him, forgetting that Curtius and Alexander, Jomini and Napoleon had ever existed. The opportunity came. When McPherson, the commander of the Army of the Tennessee, was killed in front of Atlanta, Hooker was left the senior major general in command of a corps in Sherman's department, and he naturally expected to be placed in command, the more so as the President so desired. But Sherman appointed General O. O. Howard to the command, subject, of course, to the approval of the commander-in-chief. Mr. Lincoln telegraphed Sherman, requesting him to appoint General Hooker; and on Sherman's reiteration of his desire to have General Howard appointed, the President urged Hooker's appointment in stronger terms. General Sherman was determined that Hooker should not be appointed, and with an impertinence characteristic of Sherman, replied, that "his resignation was at the service of the President." Had Mr. Lincoln been a thorough military man instead of a good-natured and indulgent President, he would have at least punished Sherman for such an unwarrantable reply, but he only smiled at it and liked Sherman, as every body else did, all the better for what looked like independence rather than impertinence. The consequence was that Howard was appointed. A thousand worse appointments might have been made, and I don't know but what the methodical Howard better suited the command than Hooker would have done. Hooker took umbrage at the appointment of Howard—the insult was too glaring and offensive to be overlooked—and at his own request he was relieved of command under Sherman by the President, and given the command of the Department of the North.

It is not to be supposed, from what I have said about Hooker's disposition to criticise, that he is of a vindictive nature. His disgust is not irrevocable. He is always ready to forgive a blunder when retrieved by a success. He is particularly constant in his friendships. There are several instances of his friendship for men, which are remembered without being remarkable except for their constancy, and as illustrating the kindness of his heart. He was particularly devoted years ago to the interest of an humble friend whom he met in Mexico under rather singular circumstances. During the battle of Churubusco he was sent by Pillow with an order to one of the brigade commanders. Being compelled to cross a ditched field—very common in Mexico—he went on foot, with only his sabre at his side. While crossing the field he was suddenly attacked, not by Mexican Lancers, but by a Mexican bull, who dashed unexpectedly at him. He immediately turned and gave battle in the true *matador* style, thrusting with his sabre whenever an opportunity offered, and springing out of the way, with all the activity of a bull-fighting Spaniard. He was fast getting weary of the sport, however, when he saw at a distance a private of the Mounted Rifles, and called on him to shoot the beast. After much trouble he at last attracted the attention of the soldier, who quickly obeyed orders, crossed the ditch and shot the bull, much to the relief of Hooker. The soldier immediately afterward disappeared, and Hooker found it impossible to discover him, though search was made through camp for the preserver of his life, as Hooker persisted in considering him. He did not give up the search, and at last discovered the man years after in Washington. He was in want. Hooker, having some influence, obtained him a position in one of the departments at Washington, where he still remains, a firm friend of Joe Hooker, and boasting of enjoying the friendship of the "commander of the best army on the planet."

Like most nervous men, Hooker is untiringly energetic. He goes at every thing, as he does at the enemy, with a dash. He talks at you with vigor, piles argument on argument in rapid succession—argument which requires not less vigorous thought to follow and answer—couples facts

with invectives, and winds up with a grand charge of resistless eloquence which has much the same effect as the
grand charge of a reserve force in battle.   He works with
the same rapidity—the same nervous, resistless energy,
and does not know what fatigue is.   He has energy
equal to Sherman, and in his organization and habits is
somewhat like Sherman, though more elegant.   Hooker
is the very impersonation of manly grace, dignity, deli-
cacy—a thorough-bred gentleman.   Hooker has energy
equal to Grant, but he has not Grant's patience, stoicism,
or imperturbability.   He is not content, like Grant, to
wait for results.   His strength lies in his momentum ;
Grant's in his weight.   It was perhaps because Hooker
so nearly resembles him, and because Howard had such
opposite characteristics, that Sherman preferred the latter
as commander of the Army of the Tennessee.   Howard
and Hooker have certain qualities in common, but yet are
as different in organization as Sherman and Howard.
Howard is, like Hooker, a finished gentleman, princely
in manners.   No one meeting them can fail to notice that
both are equally graceful, equally handsome, equally dignified, considerate, manly, and courteous.   But Howard,
unlike Hooker, is exceedingly methodical, is always calm,
self-possessed, and of a lymphatic rather than a bilious
temperament.   Hooker is ever sanguine.   It is not to
be supposed that, because he is a quick worker, he easily
flags in his hasty labor.   His energy never gives out, and
he is as persistent as Thomas, more so than Sherman, and
vies with Grant in this respect.

The title of "Fighting Joe" is very offensive to General Hooker, but I have chosen to use it as the heading for

this article because it accurately as well as briefly describes the character of the man.   It was given him by
an accident, but it was a happy one; and when history
comes to sum up the characteristics of our heroes, she will
apply it as indicative of Hooker's character.   The circumstances under which it was given are as follows: The
agent of the New York Associated Press is often compelled, during exciting times, to furnish his telegraphic
accounts by piecemeals, in order to enable the papers to
lay the facts before the public as fast as received, and
hence, in order to number the pages correctly, he has to
originate what are called " running heads," or titles, each
being repeated with every page.   When the account of
the battle of Malvern Hill was being received by the Associated Press agent at New York, there was such great
excitement in that city that it even extended to the telegraph operators and copyists, who were generally considered proof against such fevers of excitement.   In the
midst of the sensation which that battle created, one of
the copyists, in his admiration of the gallantry and daring
of General Hooker as detailed in the report, improvised
as a " running head" the title " Fighting Joe Hooker,"
which was repeated page after page.   Two or three of
the papers adopted it, in lieu of a better, as the head-line
for the printed accounts, and heralded the battle of Malvern Hill under that title.   The name "stuck," and has
been fixed on Hooker irretrievably.   Instead of accept-
ing the title as a decree of fate, he can not bear to hear it.
" It always sounds to me," he once said, when allusion
had been made to it, " as if it meant ' Fighting Fool.'   It
has really done me much injury in making the public be-

lieve I am a furious, headstrong fool, bent on making furious dashes at the enemy. I never have fought without good purpose, and with fair chances of success. When I have decided to fight, I have done so with all the vigor and strength I could command.

A very general idea at one time prevailed that General Hooker was a hard drinker, very often indulging to great excess, but this has of late been corrected. As far as my rather close observation goes, the impression was unfounded. It had its origin with that pestiferous class of humorists who devote their energies to the renewal of old jokes for the sake of modern application. Many of the false impressions which were afloat regarding Mr. Lincoln found their origin in the habit which the Joe Millers of the age had of crediting their stories, both witty and vulgar, to Mr. Lincoln instead of to the Irish nation as formerly. It is from these same fellows that Hooker has suffered, and three fourths of those who declared him to be a drunkard had no better foundation for the assertion than a story told as coming from Mr. Lincoln, in which Hooker was recommended to avoid Bourbon County in his passage through Kentucky. Hooker's style of living in camp was elegant, more from the attention of the staff officers who messed with him than from his own desire, taste, or exertions. He was always indifferent to personal comfort, though very particular as to personal appearance.

His complexion may have been the origin of the stories about his drunkenness, but every one familiar with him knows that his roseate hue is natural to him. His complexion is red and white most beautifully blended, and he looks as rosy as the most healthy woman alive. His skin never tans nor bleaches, but peals off from exposure, leaving the same rosy complexion always visible. The Spanish women in the city of Mexico, with whom he was a great favorite, described his complexion by an adjective, a mongrel Spanish word which I have now forgotten, but which I remember signified "the only man as beautiful as a woman."

El capitan hermoso, "the handsome captain," was a phrase as common with the Mexican ladies of the Mexican capital as "Fighting Joe" is now with the American public. *El buen mozo* was another phrase among them; while more intimate admirers called him *El guero*, "the light-haired." The light brown hair is now much tinged with gray, and, until lately, *El buen mozo*, the comely youth, despite the ravages of time, was a splendidly preserved young gentleman of fifty. But the tall, erect, muscular figure of *El capitan hermoso* has been bent and weakened, but not by age. His animal spirits are just as great as when he marched through Mexico, but his physical endurance is gone, perhaps, forever. His full, clear eye is just as bright to-day as it was when he was simply captain and chief of staff to General Pillow, but he can not spring as nimbly into the saddle at the sound of opening battle. On the 20th of November, 1865, while assisting at the reception of General Grant at the Fifth Avenue Hotel, New York, he was suddenly stricken with paralysis, and was carried to his residence in a helpless state. He lost the use of his right side, leg, and arm, and will, it is feared, become a confirmed invalid. His physicians declare that the paralytic stroke was the result of

a blow received by Hooker at the battle of Chancellorsville nearly three years before. The general became
very much reduced by this disease; his frame became
bent and emaciated, and something of the symmetry of
his features was lost. Very little hope of his ultimate
recovery is entertained by any other person than himself; but nothing can convince the sanguine general that
his health will not return to him in time.

LOVELL H. ROUSSEAU.

CHAPTER VI.

REMINISCENCES OF ROUSSEAU.

ALL failures find their special apologies, and some curious ones were originated by the admirers of McClellan to account for the singular ineffective policy of that officer. That policy is now generally known as the "McNapoleonic," in contradistinction to the Fabian policy, from which it differed only in that Fabian attained valuable results, while McClellan did not. Every thing was to have been effected by the young Napoleon, according to his admirers, by pure, unalloyed strategy, and the rebellion and its armies were to be crushed without bloodshed. This great strategist, according to these authorities, was without parallel; all the rest of the generals, like Thomas, Grant, Hooker, etc., were, according to the McClellan theory, *only* "fighting generals." Their battles were mere massacres; Grant was a butcher; they quote his Wilderness campaign even to this day to prove it, and declare that he lost a hundred thousand men in his battles north of the James, but never reflect that McClellan lost ninety thousand without doing any fighting, and while retreating instead of advancing to that same river. Sheridan, to their mind, is a mere raider, without an idea of strategy, and Thomas, Hooker, Hancock, and all the rest, were "*only* fighting generals."

Belonging to this "despised" class of fighting generals, of which Hooker and Sheridan, as I have endeavored to show, despite this McClellan theory, are brilliant graduates, are Major Generals John A. Logan, of Illinois, and Lovell H. Rousseau, of Kentucky. Each of these four is endowed mentally, and constituted by nature, to be a leader of men. Hooker and Sheridan have been confirmed generals by education. Rousseau and Logan owe every thing to nature, and are leaders, not generals, intuitively. The first two have been educated at West Point into being good directors of armed battalions, but it goes "against the grain" with either to confine himself solely to the direction of a battle, and hence they are often seen in battle obeying the dictates of nature, and leading charges which they should direct. Rousseau and Logan never enjoyed the advantages of West Point, and, as nature is unchecked in them by education, he who hunts for them on the battle-field must look along the front line, and not with the reserves. Neither Logan nor Rousseau would be content—it can not really be said that they are competent—to direct a battle on a grand scale: it would simply be an impossible task on the part of either, for they are neither educated nor constituted naturally to be commanders, in the technical sense of the term. They are neither strategists nor even tacticians. Both are bold, daring, enthusiastic in spirit; one has a commanding presence, and the other an inspiring eye, and the natural and most effective position of each is at the head of forlorn hopes, or leading desperate charges to successful issues.

The same contrast in person between "Fighting Joe

Hooker," tall, towering, and always graceful, and "Little Phil Sheridan," short, quick, and rough, can be traced between Rousseau, a huge, magnificent, ponderous, and handsome figure, and "Black Jack Logan," a somewhat short but graceful figure, in whose forehead is set the finest pair of eyes ever possessed by a man. The *personnel* of these four warriors differs very much. Hooker and Rousseau are very different types of the tall and elegant "human form divine," and Logan and Sheridan illustrate the graceful and the graceless in little men; but the great hearts of each beat alike, and on the battlefield the daring and boldness of each are equally conspicuous and effective.

Of all these heroes, however, Rousseau is most naturally a leader. His whole career, civil and military, illustrates him as such; and only in a country of the extent of ours, with such varied and complex interests existing within each other, could any man attain the success with which he has been rewarded, without at the same time gaining such fame as would have made his name as familiar in every home as household words, and invested him with a national reputation. It is a fact illustrative of the vast extent of the late war, and of the existence of the various sectional interests which were second to the great, absorbing feeling of devotion to the whole Union, that there are thousands of people in the East who do not know aught of the geographical position of Western battle-fields, or the history of the military career of the more distinguished officers of the Western armies. The case is also reversed, and such distinguished men as Meade, Hancock, and Sickles, and hundreds less renowned, are hardly known at the West.   The people of the East, naturally absorbed in the interests which are nearest and dearest to them, are intimately acquainted with the history and achievements of the chosen leaders of their sons and brothers of the Potomac armies, but know little in detail of the leaders of the Western armies. To the people of the East, Rosecrans is a myth of whom they remember only that he met disaster at Chickamauga; and of Thomas they know little more than that he was the hero of that same defeat.   They know little of McPherson, McClernand, Dodge, Blair, Oglesby, Osterhaus, and others, save that they " were with Grant" at Vicksburg and elsewhere.   Indeed, the whole army of the West enjoy in the East a mythical existence, and Logan and Rousseau live in our memories as undefinedly, though as firmly, as many of the characters of romance.   Nine out of every ten who are asked to tell who and what they are will be puzzled for a reply, and will state much that is pure romance, and nothing illustrative of their characters.   And yet no two men have been more prominent or more popular in the armies with which they were connected than these two rising men of the West.

General Rousseau, of whom it is proposed to speak in this chapter, is not a strategist nor a tactician according to the rules of West Point, in whose sciences he is uneducated save by the practical experience of the past four years of war.   He makes no pretensions to a knowledge of engineering, or strategy, or grand tactics, is not even versed in the details of logistics; but of all those who have won reputation as hard, pertinacious, and dashing fighters, none more deserve their fame than he.   His battles have been brilliant, if short; desperate and bloody contests, in which more has resulted from courage and the enthusiasm imparted to the men than from strategy and tactics. If examination is made into Rousseau's career, it will be found that he has ever been in the front line of battle, not only at Buena Vista, in our miniature contest with Mexico, at Shiloh, Perryville, and Stone River, but in every aspect, and under all circumstances of his career, always ahead, and leading his people in politics as in war. A self-educated and self-made man, of strong intellectual and reasoning powers, quick to resolve and prompt to act, he appears at all times in that noble attitude of one who has led instead of following public sentiment. In youth he was left the junior member of an orphaned family, of which his habit of decision made him the head and chief dependence. Emigrating in 1841 to Indiana, he made himself, by his talents, the leader of a party which had never attained success before his advent, and never won it after his retirement. His personal popularity retained him a seat in the Senate of Indiana for six years. In the middle of the term for which he was elected in 1848, he returned to Kentucky, and began the practice of law at Louisville. The Democrats of the Indiana Senate insisted he should resign, because a non-resident, but his constituents would not allow him to retire; and Rousseau threatened in retaliation to return to reside in Indiana and again run for the Senate. The Democrats were afraid of this very thing, and opposition to Rousseau's retention of his seat for the rest of the term was silenced. The Democrats contented themselves with trying to throw ridicule on him by calling him "the member from Louisville."

Returning to Kentucky in 1849, Rousseau was one of the few of her sons who were prepared to second or adopt the views then agitated by Henry Clay in regard to emancipating slaves. In 1855, when "Know-Nothingism" had swallowed up his .old party—the Whig—and held temporarily a great majority in his city, county, and state, Rousseau became the leader of the small minority which rejected the false doctrines of the "American" party. His bitter denunciation of its practices, its tendencies to mob violence, and his persistent opposition to its encroachments on individual rights, nearly cost him his life at the hands of a mob who attacked him while defending a German in the act of depositing his vote. He was shot through the abdomen, and confined for two months to his bed, but had the satisfaction to know, when well again, that the party he had fought almost single-handed had no longer an organized existence. He was also instrumental, in 1855, in saving two of the Catholic churches of Louisville from destruction at the hands of a mob of Know-Nothings, and gained in popularity with both parties, when the passion and excitement of the time had passed away, by these exhibitions of his great courage and sense of right and justice.

It was not merely, however, through the political excitement of the day that Rousseau won his popularity and established his character. For many years past—for at least two generations before the war—the courts of Kentucky have been noted for the many important and exciting criminal trials which have come up in them, and no bar presented finer opportunities for a young criminal lawyer. From the time of Rousseau's return to Kentucky in 1849 to the period when he went into the army in 1861, no important criminal case was tried in the Kentucky courts in which he did not figure on one side or the other. In 1843, the old system of pleading in the common law courts of England, as it existed before it had been clipped and modified by legislation, was in vogue at the Indiana bar, and on his advent in that state Rousseau soon found that no lawyer could practice respectably there without special pleading. A lawyer who was not a special pleader would in those days frequently find his case and himself thrown out of court, without exactly understanding how it was done. He therefore studied special pleading as a system in itself, taking the old English authors on the subject, and, after a few years' hard study and practice, soon made himself one of the best special pleaders in the West. When he returned to Kentucky, this system, not so thoroughly in use there, gave him several triumphs, which at once established his character and gave him plenty of practice. As a jury lawyer Rousseau has had no rival in his district since 1855; and the late Attorney General of the United States, James Speed, acknowledges himself indebted to Rousseau for several of his worst defeats before juries. Knowing the particular and peculiar legal talents of Rousseau, the attorney general employed him to aid in the prosecution of Jeff Davis for treason, and to assist Hon. John H. Clifford and William M. Evarts in the important duty of endeavoring to define treason.

There occurred in Louisville in 1857 a trial of a very remarkable character, which illustrates in a very interesting manner Rousseau's legal ability and his decision and daring. A family of five or six persons, named Joyce, were murdered, and their bodies burned in their house near the city. Suspicion fell upon some negroes on the adjoining plantation, and they were seized by the neighbors and threatened with hanging if they did not confess. One or two of them were hung up for a few moments and then let down nearly exhausted, but still persisted in declaring their innocence. Another, however, tied to a stake, and the fagots fired around him, agreed to confess, and, to avoid death by burning, confessed that himself and the others arrested with him had committed the murder. The negroes—four of them, all belonging to one man— were thrown into jail to await their trial. Their master was satisfied that they were innocent, and determined to engage the best available counsel for them. This was easier to propose than to do, for so great was the excitement among the people that, extending to the lawyers, no other counsel besides Rousseau could be retained, and he was compelled to undertake the defense unaided. He had always been very popular in the district in which the murder had been committed, and many of his old friends from the neighborhood visited him, and urged him not to sacrifice his popularity with them by defending such abased and brutal criminals as these negroes. In vain Rousseau urged that the greater the guilt the greater the necessity for a lawyer. His friends could listen to no reason, and saw no justification in defending negroes who deserved to be hung according to their own confession. When Rousseau intimated that he did not believe the confession, and alluded to the manner in which it had been extorted, they would go away in disgust, and many cursed him for "a damned abolitionist."

When the trial came on, the people of the district in which the murder had been committed crowded the court-house night and day. The sole surviving member of the family, a young man also named Joyce, occupied a seat within the railing of the court-room, while the crowd of his friends were kept outside of the bar. The feeling of animosity in the crowd against the negroes was only kept from breaking out into fury by the certainty of their conviction and punishment by law; but fears were justly entertained that some development of the trial might so excite the by-standers as to cause the instantaneous hanging of the negroes. This fear was fully justified, and an attempt to hang them was only frustrated by the prompt action and daring of Rousseau. The sole evidence for the prosecution was that of the negro who had confessed, and he was put upon the stand, after the usual preliminaries, to give his statement in open court. The negro went on, in a hesitating manner, to give, with many contradictions, the story of how the murder had been committed, and the house fired in several places. He stated that, after the house was almost encircled in flames, the youngest child of the murdered family, a little girl of two years, who had been overlooked in the hurry of the massacre, aroused by the light, sat up in bed and asked, calling to her mother, to know "if she was cooking breakfast." At this part of the evidence there was a deathlike stillness through the court-room. The crowd, horrified, seemed afraid to draw a breath for a moment, and the negro witness himself appeared to fully comprehend the danger of the situation and hesitated. At last one old gentleman—I think he was one of the jury—shading his eye with his hands as if to shut out the scene, uttered, in a pitiful tone through his clenched teeth, the sound which I can only express by "tut! tut! tut! tut!" The half hissing sound could be heard all over the court-room, and as it was heard a cold shudder ran through the crowd, followed a moment after by crimson flushes of passion on bronzed cheeks. In the midst of the silent excitement—for it was an excitement so profound as almost robbed men of the power of speech—young Joyce sprang to his feet and exclaimed,

"I want all my friends who think these negroes are guilty to help me hang them."

He was answered by a wild shout and by the click of hundreds of pistols. As he had spoken, young Joyce drew a huge knife from a sheath fastened to his body, and, encouraged by the answering cry of his friends, sprang toward the negroes. As he did so, however, Rousseau, who stood between him and the prisoners, caught him by the throat with one hand, and with the other clasped the wrist of the arm which held the uplifted knife. It was but the work of a moment for a powerful man like Rousseau to thrust Joyce back again in his seat and pinion him there while he turned and confronted the crowd, who had made a rush for the negroes, but who were being beaten back by the sheriff and one or two policemen. As soon as they saw the position of young Joyce, still held in his chair by the powerful arm of Rousseau, the crowd made a rush in that direction. Rousseau was again prompt and decisive.

"Mr. Joyce," he said, "tell your friends that while they hang the negroes I'll attend to you."

Joyce waved his friends back with the only hand left free, and quiet again succeeded. It is hardly probable that even this promptness would have saved Rousseau had he not been personally popular with the crowd. As the crowd shrank back he released Joyce and turned abruptly to the judge, who had ordered the sheriff to summon a force of the police to protect the prisoners, and said,

"Don't do any thing of the sort. Don't do any thing of the sort, your honor. We can protect the prisoners and ourselves. There are enough true men here to protect them from the fury of this young man."

"Where are your friends?" cried the still furious crowd.

"You are!" exclaimed Rousseau, turning abruptly to them—I might say on them. And then, without a single second's hesitation, he began a brief speech, in which he passionately urged and entreated them to aid him in preventing Joyce, whom he characterized as "this unfortunate young man," from committing a deed which would forever be a curse to him as long as he had a memory of it, and which would forever disgrace them as a law-abiding community. While he was yet speaking the crowd calmed down, and when he had finished painting the enormity of the offense and the remorse of the young man if he had been permitted to commit so great a crime, they cheered him, and through the room went frequent and repeated whispers, "He's right;" "he's right;" "Rousseau's always right!"

The trial thenceforth procceded in quiet until the an-

nouncement of the verdict of "not guilty," when another
terrible scene ensued; but provision having been made
for such an occurrence, the negroes were carried off to
jail for protection. The people were satisfied that the
negroes were guilty, and the verdict (obtained by Rousseau by showing the inconsistencies of the confession and
the circumstances, the threats and the terror, under which
it was extorted) only increased their passion. The jail
was surrounded, and the night after the acquittal the negroes were taken out by the mob and hung on the trees
in the City Hall grounds. During the riot the mayor
of the city, Mr. Pilcher, while endeavoring to quiet the
crowd, was struck by a missile in the head, and died
soon after from the effects of the injury received.

This and several other trials eventually resulted in increasing Rousseau's popularity. Two or three of his most
important cases embraced the defense of men accused and
undoubtedly guilty of aiding negroes to escape from slavery. It is hardly comprehensible that less than a decade
ago this offense was considered the most criminal act a man
could commit in Kentucky, or that men were sentenced
to fifteen years' hard labor for such offenses, or that con-
victs are still working out their term for these offenses
in Southern penitentiaries. To engage in the defense of
such criminals a few years ago, even in the latitude of
Louisville, was to be set down as an "abolitionist," and
but few of the Kentucky lawyers of the decade just before the war cared to bear such a character. Rousseau,
without courting the reputation, did not fear it; and his
manly bearing in all such cases, and in the political excitement of the time, so advanced him in popular estimation

that in 1860 he was elected to the State Senate of Kentucky without opposition and as the candidate of both parties, whose only rivalry with regard to him was as to which should first secure his acceptance of the nomination. It was while holding this position as state senator that Rousseau began his bold opposition to Kentucky neutrality, which brought him so prominently before the country, and opened to him that career in which he has won so much honor and such a high rank.

The true story of Kentucky neutrality is one of the most romantic episodes of the war. The visionary schemers who planned the Southern Confederacy were guilty of dozens of chimerical and fallacious schemes, whose shallowness is now so apparent that one wonders how the Southern people were ever deceived by them. The rebel leaders declared—and declared it so often that they actually believed it themselves—that the Northern people would not fight. They boasted, and boasted so frequently that they began after a time to believe, that one Southern man could really whip five Yankees. They deceived themselves for so many years with the doctrine of States Rights that leaders and people began to believe that a fraction of the body corporate could exist without the aid of the rest, and offered to this modern and enlightened age a national illustration of Æsop's fable of the stomach's folly. When the schemes of the rebel leaders were culminating, and they found that the people of the Border States were not disposed, like those of the Cotton States, to be hurried, regardless of consequences, into a war in which they had nothing to gain and every thing to lose, they instituted, with a shrewdness worthy the fame of a Philadelphia lawyer, the no less visionary schemes that there could be law without power, and that a portion of the body, and that portion the heart, could suspend its operations while the rest was being violently agitated. In Tennessee, where the first-named scheme was successful, the rebels deceived the Union men into advocating the doctrine of "no coercion." In Kentucky, where their complete success in carrying out the second design was frustrated only by the sagacity of Rousseau, the rebels deceived the Unionists into advocating the doctrine of "neutrality." Twice the people of Tennessee voted against co-operation with the rebel states; and when the rebels again dared to test the question at the polls, they embodied in the contest the principle that "the general government could not coerce a sovereign state," and into the support of this doctrine the anti-secessionists foolishly acquiesced. The first act of the President in calling for troops to enforce the laws was construed into coercion, and the state seceded. Three times the State of Kentucky voted by large majorities against secession, but the rebels did not despair, and, having failed to get the people to secede, or to declare against the right of coercion, they endeavored, with but partial success, to commit the authorities and the Unionists to what was called "a strict neutrality."

The rebels in Kentucky were under the leadership of a Cassius-like character named Simon Bolivar Buckner. He had been in the secrets and the interests of the disunion leaders for years before the first overt act of secession was committed, and for three or four years previous to 1861 had been engaged in schemes for carrying the state out of the Union, and for furnishing troops to the rebel army that was to be. The principal of these schemes was 'the organization of the very irregular militia of the state into a strong body, known as the " State Guard." Buckner, by every means in his reach—and his associates in treason, who were also in power, gave him great assistance—fostered this scheme. He created a martial spirit among the young men of Kentucky, and by the aid of Tilghman, Hunt, Hanson, and others, who eventually became rebel generals, extended this spirit to every part of the state. He was a man eminently fitted for such a task, and by his duplicity and skill undermined the faith in and love for the Union existing among the young men who formed the State Guard. Years before the majority of them suspected that secession would ever be attempted, they had grown to look upon the institutions, doctrines, and even the flag of the Union with indifference, if not contempt. The flag of Kentucky became the flag of the guard, and Buckner even attempted to expel that of the government from the organization. The various uniforms of the different militia organizations of different districts were discarded, under Buckner's orders, for a uniform of gray, which eventually proved to be that of the rebel army. The various arms of the different companies were discarded for weapons of a uniform calibre. The organization, which had originally embraced only companies, was extended to divisions and regiments, and brigades were formed and drilled in encampments as such. In fact, nearly a year before South Carolina seceded, the State Guard of Kentucky, with Simon Bolivar Buckner as Inspector General commanding, was simply a body of recruits for the embryo rebel army. It is slightly foreign to the subject, but I may as well add here the fact I have never heard stated before, that, at the same time, and undoubtedly for the same purpose, the martial spirit of the youth of all the Southern States was being encouraged. Militia organization of the various states were being thoroughly remodeled and systematized, the best of arms obtained, uniforms of the same kind purchased, and, to all appearances, the rebel army, as it afterward existed, was being recruited in 1858–9 and '60.

This organization, under Buckner, existed when neutrality was instituted, and the new doctrines gave it and the traitors who led it additional strength, while it served to cloak their designs. Great numbers of the leading Unionists of the state joined with the rebel leaders in support of this doctrine, ridiculous and inconsistent as it now appears to have been. A large majority of the people who had voted against secession also became committed to the visionary doctrine, until it came to be the accepted policy of the state; so that, when Lovell Rousseau, in the Senate, in May, 1861, denounced neutrality as a mask of the secessionists on the one hand, and a disgraceful yielding of the Unionists on the other, he found few who agreed with him, and less who seconded him in his avowed purpose of abolishing neutrality, and placing the state, at all times, in her proper position as a true member of the Union, amid the disasters of war as well as in the prosperity of peace.

The public were not prepared to follow him, and he was forced to accept neutrality as a compromise between union and secession, between right and wrong, but doing so under public protest in the Senate of the state, and declaring on every occasion which offered that it was a debasing position, which he intended to abandon as soon as he could induce the state to follow him. He found little support in this honorable war upon neutrality until the secessionists, under Buckner, went a step farther, and proposed, after hostilities had fairly begun, to make the neutrality of Kentucky an "armed neutrality," urging that the state troops be armed to resist encroachments from either rebel or Union troops. In this proposition Rousseau saw an opportunity for forcing a direct issue with the rebels, and he was quick to take advantage of it. He saw in it actual aid to the rebellion. Against this scheme, which proposed the appropriation of three millions of dollars to arm the "Kentucky State Guard," he at once began a crusade as earnest as it was untiring. He denounced the State Guard and its leaders as secessionists and traitors, stormed at them in Senate-halls and on the stump, and not only defeated the bill, but succeeded very happily in dividing the State Guard into two rival organizations, known as the "Home Guards" (Unionists) and "State Guardsmen" (rebels). He called it at the time "separating the sheep from the goats." It was a most fortunate achievement; for it not only saved thousands of young men belonging to the State Guard from being unwittingly drawn into the rebel army, but precipitated the designs of the rebels, and hastened the defection which was inevitable. This was accomplished under personal difficulties, opposition, and dangers, which only made the labor more delightful to a person of Rousseau's temperament. He delights in opposition; is in his element only when in the minority, and strongly opposed; and his belligerent disposition led him to gladly accept not only the numerous stump and street discussions and disputes, but even street quarrels and fights with the secessionists. The rebel sympathizers seldom dared attack him openly, his bold front, at all times maintained, making them prefer to exercise their strategy and trickery against him rather than come to open warfare. Upon him, as the head and front of the offending party, they poured all their abuse and vituperation, but dared to do little more.

This split in the State Guard soon proved a serious affair, and the " defection," as the traitors called the retirement of the Union men, became quite general. Every incident increased the feeling; every day saw the differences of opinions and the breach grow wider. On one occasion Buckner was reviewing the regiment of the Guard which was stationed at Lexington, Ky. The feeling between the partisans composing the regiment had become quite demonstrative, and on this occasion Captain Saunders D. Bruce, a Union officer of the regiment (subsequently colonel of the Twentieth Kentucky Infantry, now a resident of New York, and editor of the "Field, Turf, and Farm" newspaper), made his appearance in the line with two small United States flags as guidons for his company. Buckner, noticing them, approached Captain Bruce, ordered him to the front, in full view of the regiment, explained to him that Kentucky was neutral in the " unfortunate struggle" then going on, and directed him to replace the guidons by flags of the state. Bruce, without replying, turned to his company, and, as if about to obey, gave the orders, "Attention, company;" "Shoulder arms;" "Right face;" "Forward march," and away went the "Lexington Chasseurs" out of the line, and for that matter out of the State Guard. No attempt was made to stop the company, or to call Bruce to account for his "insubordination."

No sooner had the work of dividing the State Guard been thus accomplished, than Rousseau hastened to Washington to obtain permission from the President to raise troops in the state for the United States service. While on the way to Washington, he had an interview with General McClellan, then commanding the Western Department, at Cincinnati, and found him opposed to his scheme. McClellan sent to Washington his aid, Colonel Key (subsequently dismissed the service for disloyal utterances), to represent Rousseau's scheme as rash and ill-advised. At the same time, others were sent to Washington by the "mild-mannered" Unionists to urge the President not to grant Rousseau permission to raise troops, arguing that it would at once precipitate the invasion of the state by the rebels. Rousseau consequently found great difficulty in obtaining the required authority, but went at the question boldly.

He was introduced to the President and the cabinet by Secretary Chase, who was his energetic friend in the matter, and who subsequently aided him materially in getting around the President's objections to the project. Before he had finished shaking hands with the stalwart Kentuckian and soldier, the President good-humoredly said, "Rousseau, I want you to tell me where you got that joke about Senator Johnson, of your state."

The "joke" alluded to was one of the neatest of Mr. Lincoln's numerous dry humors, and was as follows: A state senator from Paducah, Ky., John M. Johnson by name, who had made himself notorious as a secessionist, wrote to Mr. Lincoln in May, 1861, a very solemn and emphatic protest, in the name of the sovereign State of Kentucky, against the occupation and fortification of Cairo, on the Illinois side of the Ohio River. Mr. Lincoln replied in a letter written in his own peculiar vein, apologizing for the movement, promising it should not be done again, and declaring that if he had half suspected that Cairo, Illinois, was in Dr. Johnson's Kentucky senatorial district, he would have thought twice before sending troops there. Rousseau had heard the story, and had repeated it in a speech in the Senate, and an explanation of how it had gained publicity was what the President requested. Rousseau explained.

"The joke was too good to keep, sir, and so Johnson told it himself."

The interview, thus auspiciously began, proved a failure. Cameron and Chase were the only ones in the cabinet who favored the enlistment of troops in Kentucky; and on their declaring this opinion, the President advised them not to be too hasty, remarking,

"You know we have seen another man from Kentucky to-day."

"I don't ask you to say who that man was, Mr. President," said Rousseau, suspecting it to have been Colonel Key, and anxious to forestall him, as he had declared his intention to oppose the scheme; "but Colonel Key is not a Kentuckian, and does not know or comprehend our people. If you want troops in my state, I can and will raise them; and I think it is your duty to our people in Kentucky to begin the work of enlistment there, for if the rebels raise troops and we do not, why, naturally, many young men will be led away from duty by their sympathies for kindred and associates; while if you begin the work of enlistment, the loyal youth will have something to guide and direct them in the right course."

In this way Rousseau represented to the President what he had done in the way of defeating the schemes of the rebels to arm themselves at the expense of Kentucky, and in dividing the state militia into two classes. He had inspired the loyal Home Guards with an *esprit du corps*, which would save the greater part of them from any connection with the secessionists; but he represented also that there were thousands of young men in the state who had not decided to follow either the rebel or loyal banner, and that, knowing this, the rebels were recruiting in every part of the state. Thousands of the young and thoughtless would be, and hundreds were being, drawn into the rebel army by this means, and he argued that the government ought to recruit in this neutral state as an encouragement to the young men to join the loyal army.

But the President took time to consider, and Rousseau withdrew. The next day Mr. Chase drew up in regular form the authority Rousseau desired, and Cameron signed it and gave him a commission as colonel, the rank dating from June 15th, 1861. Both Chase and Cameron promised to endeavor to obtain the President's sanction of the act, that Rousseau might feel perfectly free to go to work. Rousseau was granted another interview with the President, who, after some farther conversation on the subject, indorsed Rousseau's original application to be permitted to raise troops as follows:

"When Judge Pirtle, James Guthrie, George D. Prentice, Harney, the Speeds, and the Ballards shall think it proper to raise troops for the United States service in Kentucky, Lovell H. Rousseau is authorized to do so."

This he handed to Rousseau and asked, "Will that do?"

Rousseau read it carefully, and then replied, somewhat disappointed,

"No, Mr. President, that won't do."

"Why not, why not, Rousseau? These men are good Union men."

"Yes, sir, good men and loyal, Mr. Lincoln, but nearly all of them differ with me on this subject, are committed to the abominable doctrine of neutrality, and it would be too late when the majority of them conclude that it would be proper to raise troops. Then I fear the state will have seceded. I had hoped, sir, that what the War Department has done in my case would be acceptable to you."

"What has Cameron done?" asked the President.

"He has, by the advice of Mr. Chase, authorized me to raise two regiments in Kentucky."

"Oh!" said Mr. Lincoln, after reading the documents, "if the War Department has acted in the matter, I have nothing to say in opposition."

Rousseau, fearful that too much might be said, at once arose, shook the President's hand, and vanished.

On his return to Kentucky, Rousseau, in deference to the President's wishes, as implied in the indorsement of his paper, consulted James Speed, and through him called a meeting of the gentlemen named, and also of others in the city of Louisville and interior counties of the state. Much to the surprise of Mr. Speed, only himself, his brother Joshua, Bland and John P. Ballard, Samuel Lusk, Morgan Vance, and John H. Ward, a minority of the meeting, hardly respectable in numbers, were in favor of the project. Pirtle, Guthrie, Prentice, Harney, Bramlette, Boyle, and others, opposed it strongly, and in the end adopted resolutions to the effect that the time had not come; that it was then impolitic, unwise, and improper to enlist troops for the United States service in Kentucky; but adding that when the time did arrive, they all wished Rousseau, in whom they expressed every confidence, to head the movement. Rousseau had made up his mind that such would be the result of their deliberations (from which he had retired before the final action), and had decided upon his course; so that when Joshua Speed next day handed him the resolutions, Rousseau was neither surprised nor chagrined, but very much disgusted. A few minutes after leaving Mr. Speed on this occasion, he met Bramlette, subsequently governor of the state, and that gentleman began to defend the majority of the meeting of the night before for their action in the matter, when Rousseau interrupted him by asking if any thing had been said in opposition to the enlistment of troops by him in other states. Bramlette replied in the negative, when the two parted, and Rousseau immediately began the enlistment of Kentuckians, but established his camp and swore in his recruits in Indiana. Being compelled to do this was very humiliating to Rousseau, but it did not dishearten him, and he went at his work energetically. There were greater

K

obstacles in his way at that time than the mere opposition of men as to time and place.   When he began the work of enlistment, the government had no credit in Kentucky, and the expenses of enlisting and feeding his two thousand recruits were defrayed by himself and a gentleman living in Indiana named Samuel Patterson, whose name, for the sake of his devoted loyalty, deserves to go down to history.   Despite these obstacles, despite the fact that every paper in the state ridiculed the project and laughed at the projector, nevertheless Rousseau's recruits — the rebels called them "Rousseau's ragamuffins"—increased in numbers and grew in discipline until they became formidable, and eventually saved the city from rebel occupation.

From the time that loyal recruiting began, the issue between unionism and secession became direct, and neutrality was practically a dead letter.   The mask of the rebels was stripped off, and the people were no longer deceived by the schemes of the secessionists.   Throughout Kentucky, and particularly in Louisville, where the issue was most saliently presented, singular scenes were the result of the situation ; and from this time until the occupation of the state by the contending armies, Louisville was in a curious condition.   Rebel and Union recruiting stations were found in the same streets, and presenting the same appearance, save that the rebels dared not plant their flag, and displayed only that of Kentucky.   Squads of Union and rebel recruits daily passed each other on the streets *en route* to their camps, and saluted each other with groans, and hisses, and ridicule, but attempted no violence.   Day was made noisy with the huzzas of the rebels " for Jeff.

Davis and the Confederacy," and night made hideous by rebel songs from rebel throats that had not the lame excuse of being husky with liquor. Many of their songs were set to very beautiful airs, and often large crowds of enthusiastic young men would gather in the principal drinking saloons of the city and join in these choruses, producing a very beautiful melody, but uttering devilish poor sentiments. Frequently these songs were inspired by the appearance of some well-known Union man, around whom they would gather, like the witches in Macbeth, and at whom they sung their songs as if in defiance. These scenes and songs often led to dangerous encounters and riotous proceedings. The division of sentiment created by this state of affairs entered into families, and extended even to the congregations of churches. I remember one sad instance, in the family of Col. Henry Clay, son of the sage of Ashland, and the one who fell so gloriously at Buena Vista. In 1861, his two sons, Thomas and Henry Clay, were living at Louisville. One of them, Thomas, became fascinated with the manner and imbued with the ideas of Buckner, and followed him to the Confederacy, and, as it happened, to ruin and to the grave. Henry, the younger brother, a more thoughtful, quiet young man, less enthusiastic, but more persistent than Thomas, joined the Union army, and served, until his early death, on the staff of Gen. Richard W. Johnson. One of the most amusing instances of the effects produced by the prevailing sentiments occurred in one of the churches at Louisville, where, on the occasion of a prayer-meeting, a notorious secessionist and a prominent Union man had what was called at the time "a praying match." During

the prayer-meeting the minister asked the secession brother to pray, which he did, asking, among other things, the
" removal of our evil rulers."   He did not explain whom
he meant by " evil rulers," but the congregation knew;
so, not waiting to be called on, the Union brother requested the congregation to join him in prayer, and prayed for
"the rulers set over us, and the removal from his place
of power of Kentucky's traitorous governor."   This was
a positive defiance; the rebelliously-inclined brother felt
it his duty to reply, and did so in a regular secession
prayer, asking the blessing of heaven on " the Confederate government, rulers, and people, "and "confusion upon
the councils of the Northern abolitionists and vandals."
To close the bout and end the affray of words, the Unionist replied in a regular true blue Union prayer, asking
that God would bless and prosper the Union cause, smile
upon her arms, lead her soldiers to triumph, smite the
traitors, and bring back to their allegiance our misguided
brethren of the South; and capped the climax which he
had reached by giving out the hymn beginning

"Oh, conquer this rebellious will."

The secessionist did not reply, and thus the Unionist won
his first victory.   He was a graduate of West Point, but
I do not know that what he learned there aided him
much in his praying match.

The excitement of this conflict of ideas and passions
reached its culminating point at Louisville on the day
following the battle of Bull Run, and produced one of
the most remarkable scenes I have ever witnessed.   The
first telegraphic news of the battle, published on the
morning after the engagement, was of a highly favorable

character, and the Unionists of Louisville ate their break-
fasts and digested the good news of the first great victory
with the firm conviction that Mr. Seward was right, and
that the war would be over in ninety days, if not sooner.
That morning every thing was *couleur de rose* to even less
sanguine natures than Mr. Seward. About noon of the
same day the bad news began to arrive, but the people
knew nothing definite regarding the final result of the
battle until about three o'clock P.M., when the afternoon
editions of the papers made their appearance. Then the
news of the rebel victory spread like wildfire, and in half
an hour—at the time, it seemed as if it were instantaneous
—the whole city was a perfect pandemonium. The rebel
flag, which had until then shrunk from the light, flaunted
from buildings and dwellings, from carriage windows in
the hands of women, on omnibuses, and carts, and trucks,
and wagons in the hands of men wild with excitement.
Men on horseback, with the rebel flag flying, dashed
wildly through the principal streets, crying with husky
voices, "Hurrah for Jeff. Davis." The streets were alive
with drunken and noisy rebels, who hooted at Unionists,
cheered secessionists, embraced each other, and yelled
themselves hoarse in bravos for " Jafe Davis." For nearly two hours the rebels had full possession of the city,
and crowded about their ringleader, a notorious fellow
named John Tompkins, with every expression of their
delight. It was decided, and Tompkins announced his intention, to raise a flag-staff and display the rebel flag from
the roof of the Courier newspaper office, and to aid him
in this the rebels gathered around him. But it was destined that this feat should not be accomplished. One of

the policemen of the city, named Green, having received orders to suppress all noisy demonstrations such as Tompkins was guilty of in hallooing for Davis and the Confederacy, approached him and ordered him to desist. The only reply was a repetition of the offense. Green again repeated his order, explaining that these were his instructions, when Tompkins drew a pistol, and, retreating a few steps, fired at the policeman. Simultaneously Green had also retreated a few steps, drawing his pistol at the same time, and, in answer to the other's ineffective fire, shot the rioter directly through the heart, killing him instantly. Never was a riot so cheaply suppressed nor so instantaneously. In ten minutes after the death of the ringleader the rioters dispersed, rebel flags disappeared, the huzzas for Davis were hushed : not a rebel remained on the streets, not a flag was to be seen unfurled, not a huzza was to be heard, and Louisville slept sounder that night than she had slept for months.

The secessionists of Louisville did not, however, entirely desist from their efforts to aid the rebels, but on the 17th of August they called a meeting of sympathy with the South. At night, in pursuance of the call, they early mustered their strength at the court-house. Their leaders were on the stand, which was handsomely decorated with white or "peace" flags, awaiting the filling of the hall by their friends, and somewhat anxious at the appearance of numerous well-known Unionists, or "abolitionists," as they were then called by the rebel sympathizers. Every thing was in readiness to open the peace meeting, and James Trabue, the principal secession leader, had risen to call the assembly to order, when James

S. Speed, late United States Attorney General, quietly walked up the stand and approached the desk prepared for the chairman. He called the attention of the house by rapping on the desk with his cane, knocked aside with an air of contempt the "peace" flags on either side of him, and was about to speak, when he was interrupted by the clamor of the rebel leaders, who insisted that the house was theirs, and that the meeting was to be addressed by them. Amid the excitement, and above the clamor which ensued, was heard the stentorian voice of Rousseau, proposing Judge Speed as president of the meeting. He immediately put the question to a vote. A deafening "Ay!" drowned the "Noes" of the rebels, and, perfectly calm and cool, Mr. Speed reached forward, removed the white flags from the stand, and unfurled two small star-spangled banners in their stead. In an instant, as if by preconcerted arrangement, from different parts of the hall, large and small United States flags were unfurled, and ten minutes afterward the secessionists had left the hall, amid the groans of the loyal citizens. Judges Speed and Harlan, and Messrs. Wolfe, Rousseau, and others, followed in strong Union anti-neutral speeches, and the meeting adopted several very strong resolutions. Next to Rousseau's establishment of the Union recruiting camp opposite Louisville, this affair was the first determined step taken by the Unionists of Kentucky to keep the state in the Union.

Meantime Rousseau had quietly, but rapidly, filled up his two regiments as authorized, and they were sworn into the service. Fremont was then in want of troops in Missouri, and sent his aid, Richard Corwin, of Ohio, to inspect Rousseau's force, and, if found available for field service, to make application at Washington for it. An intimation came to Rousseau that he would be sent to Missouri (he was growing anxious to go to any department in which active work would afford him opportunities to win promotion and reputation), and he determined to invade Kentucky soil at least once before going, and so announced his intention of parading his corps through the streets of Louisville. A delegation of rebel and neutral citizens waited on him, and begged him to forbear his intention, representing that the indignant citizens would rise up in their anger and attack his soldiers.

"By Heaven!" exclaimed Rousseau, "the d—d scoundrels shall have enough of it, then, before I am done with them."

The march of the brigade through the city was undisturbed, and it returned to camp without having received any more deadly volley than a few curses from the neutrals and secessionists. One of the effects of the parade, and the announcement of the intention to send Rousseau to Missouri, was the presentation of an appeal to the President, signed by the principal of the Union men, protesting against the removal of Rousseau from the vicinity of the city. A copy of this protest was shown by a friend to Colonel Rousseau. When he read it he grew furiously enraged, cursing the protesting individuals as a set of marplots who had opposed him at every turn, and he immediately took steps to break up camp and be on the march to Missouri before the countermanding order could come. He was stopped in the midst of his preparations, however, and ordered by President Lincoln to remain in camp at "Camp Joe Holt," the name given to his encampment, in honor of the Secretary of War, Colonel Joseph Holt, now Judge Advocate General of the Army. It was a fortunate order, that, for the fair "City of the Falls."

Buckner had not been idle all this time, and recruiting for "Camp Boone," the rebel Kentucky encampment, had proceeded really under his directions, but ostensibly in opposition to his wishes; and a few thousand Kentuckians, and a large force of Tennesseeans and other Southern troops, had gathered upon the southern border of the state for the purpose of seizing Louisville and other places, and establishing a defensive line along the Ohio River. Had that project not been frustrated by the position and force of Rousseau, the fate of the Confederacy would not have been sealed as soon as it was. The line of the Ohio, occupied in force by the rebels, would have been very difficult to break. If the Ohio River had been blockaded by rebel guns, the Union forces along it would have been fed and moved with great difficulty.. Subsequently to the frustration of this project by Rousseau, Kentucky furnished ninety thousand men to the Union army, few or none of which would have been raised with the state under rebel occupation, and numbers of whom would have been conscripted into the rebel army. These would have been some of the results of the occupation of the Ohio, and serious disasters they would have proved to the Union cause. In the prosecution of this scheme, Buckner labored with a zeal that one could confidently expect from a man of his Cassius-like proportions. In the prosecution of the plan he went to Washington, represented himself as a Union man, and obtained from Generals Scott and McDowell much valuable information. When about to return to Kentucky he called upon General McDowell, and, in parting with him, placed both hands upon McDowell's shoulders, looked him steadily in the eye, and said,

"Mack, I am going back to Kentucky to raise troops for my country."

McDowell wished him "God speed" in the undertaking, and they parted. Buckner returned to Louisville, halted but a day, and hastened southward to the rebel "Camp Boone" to doff his garb of neutrality for the Confederate gray. A change can not be said to have been necessary, for, as the rebels practiced neutrality in Kentucky, it was *bona fide* rebellion, and wore the same outward garb. Three nights after the countermanding of the order to Rousseau to march to Missouri, Buckner invaded Kentucky and occupied Bowling Green. On the next day, September 17, 1861, he advanced with a large force upon Louisville, and Rousseau, the rejected, with the "Home Guards," which he had preserved from the defection which seized the State Guard, were the only defenders of the city to be found. On the night of September 17, 1861, Rousseau crossed the Ohio River, and marched through the uproarious streets of the excited and endangered city to meet the invader. With this little band he penetrated forty miles into the interior of the state, hourly expecting to meet the enemy, and intending to fight him whenever and wherever he did meet him. He made the passage of Rolling Fork River, and occupied the heights of Muldraugh's Hills, where Buckner was reported to be, but found the rebel had retired to Green River.

Ever since this memorable era, Kentucky has persisted in showing herself on every important occasion as belonging to the neuter gender of states, and her unenviable position on several questions of national interest within the last five or six years has all been owing to the influence of the same class of politicians as those who opposed action in 1861. A few independent, energetic men, with opinions of their own, and a spirit of progress consonant with that of the Union, like Rousseau, Cyrus H. Burnham, and one or two others, have hardly proven the leaven to the corrupt whole. Many of those who were neutral when the success of secession was doubtful, when the constitutional amendment was pending, would now like to present a different record; and one or two of this class have written me, since the publication of this sketch in "Harper's Magazine," to prove that they were not neutrals in 1861. I have not considered their claims worth notice. There are any number of men in Kentucky who would now like to have it appear that they stood with Rousseau in 1861, but it would be falsifying history to say so. I have written here the true story of Kentucky neutrality, and do not propose to alter it. The sponsor of that neutrality—the editor of the Louisville Journal—has corroborated this story as I tell it. On the evening of the 17th of June, 1862, exactly one year after having rejected Rousseau, and driven him to encamp his troops in another state, the Union men of Louisville welcomed him from the battle-field of Shiloh at a grand banquet, at which George D. Prentice, the editor of the Journal, thus narrated the trials and efforts of Rousseau, and condemned, as mistaken, himself and his neutral comrades who had opposed Rousseau:

"We have come together," he said, "to honor a man, a patriot, a hero, whom we can scarcely honor too much. A great debt is due to General Rousseau from our city, from our state, from our nation. At the hands of Louisville he deserves a civic wreath and a marble statue. He has stood between her and desolation. We all know what bitter hostilities on the one side, and what deep apprehensions and misgivings on the other, he had to contend against when he undertook the bold enterprise of raising a brigade to resist the rebellion. The best patriots among us doubted, and hesitated, and faltered, and attempted to divert him from his purpose, and he was even constrained by their appeals to go beyond the river, and erect upon the soil of another state the glorious standard around which he invoked Kentuckians to rally. Denounced, maligned, and cursed by all the rebels, he received, at best, but a cold, reluctant, and timid support from the masses of our loyal men. When he came, one day, from his encampment with two full and splendid regiments to pass a single hour in our city, the city of his home and his love, he marched his gleaming columns through our streets amid an almost deathless stillness, his enemies awed to silence by the appalling spectacle before them, and his friends scarcely deeming it prudent to give expression to the enthusiasm secretly swelling in their bosoms. It must have been with a keen sense of disappointment, if not of injustice and ingratitude, that he returned to the Indiana shore. But ere long there came to us all a night of mystery and terror. Suddenly the electric telegraph between our city and Nashville ceased to give forth its signs, and the railroad train, anxiously awaited for hours, came not. In every loyal soul there was a deep presentiment of impending calamity. It pervaded and burdened the atmosphere. Brave men gazed into each other's faces and whispered their fears. Then it was that all loyal eyes and hearts turned instantly to General Rousseau and his brigade. A signal apprised him of apprehended danger, and in an incredibly brief space of time, in less than two hours, he crossed the Ohio, and passed with his brigade so noiselessly through our streets, that even our citizens, living within thirty yards of his route, heard him not, and before midnight he was far on his way to meet the expected invaders. He took his position between Louisville and that rebel army which would have seized and despoiled her. He was her shield and her sword. He was her salvation. For this, among other things, we tender him our gratitude to-night; for this, we tender him our gratitude forever."

This episode of neutrality must always remain the most remarkable event of Rousseau's career. Very few lives find two such opportunities, and half the credit due Rousseau has been lost to him by the fact that it occurred amid a revolution which saw many more startling events. Only the Union people of the interior of Kentucky seemed to appreciate the magnitude of his service, and on every occasion expressed, in their strange way, their admiration of and gratitude to the man. The Army of the Ohio, under Sherman and Buell, was known to them only as "Rousseau's Army."   They never talked and hardly ever heard of Sherman, or Buell, or Thomas; and Rousseau could never make them clearly understand that he was not the supreme power and highest authority.   His popularity among the Union people of the state had a rather pleasing illustration in October, 1862, when he was on the march to Perryville.   At Maxville the mountaineers from the district gathered around his quarters in great numbers, and almost every family of the many which visited the general had with it an infant named after him, either "Lovell" or "Rousseau."   When the first infant was presented, instead of blessing it in the usual patriarchal style, the general picked out one from among a number of silver half dollars he had and gave it to the child's mother.   Several of the other infant Rousseaus received other half dollars, until the general began to suspect that the infants would be produced as long as the money lasted, and so he announced a suspension of specie payment.   The children, however, continued to make their appearance, until it became apparent that the name was never likely to die out among the mountaineers.   Rousseau used to tell with great glee how two blind and deaf brothers presented themselves at his quarters, and said that they "had walked five miles to *see* Rousseau and *hear* him talk."   The demonstrations of the poor mountaineers of Chaplin Hills, as the region was called, greatly affected the general, and, as a singular mode of expressing his gratification, he always insisted on calling the battle of Perryville, which he fought next day in the vicinity of Maxville, "the battle of Chaplin Hills."

Although Rousseau's military career was of the greatest credit to him, nothing of it reflects such honor on the soldier, or illustrates so nobly the character of the man, as did his conduct during the operations which I have sketched. Still, his military career won for him as great popularity with the army as his action in destroying neutrality had done with the people. His principal achievements were at Shiloh, Perryville, Stone River, the pursuit and defeat of Wheeler in Tennessee, the defense of Fortress Rosecrans, and in the admirably conducted and highly successful raid into Alabama. At Shiloh his post was subordinate, and he will not occupy the foreground of the pictures which history will paint of that field, though he won recognition from Sherman, McClernand, and Grant for his gallantry. At Perryville the glory is all his own, while no story of Stone River can be truthfully written that does not give him much of the credit for that very desperate "rough-and-tumble" fight, where, holding the reserve line, he sent word to Rosecrans that, "though the right wing was gone," he "would not budge a step—not a d—d inch, sir."

Without having the education, Rousseau had in him the military instinct which lights the fire and gives inspiration to others, and his every battle displays him in this light. During the engagement at Perryville he displayed great courage, and inspired his men with the same spirit. He laid no claim to tactical ability, and did not endeavor to manœuvre his troops, but by his presence with them kept them well together, and retained his organization during the whole day, although withstanding with a single division the repeated attacks of

Cheatham's, Buckner's, and Anderson's divisions of Bragg's army, under the latter's personal direction. Perhaps like a reckless general, but certainly like a brave man, he was always with the front line, and as he rode among the men encouraging them, they hailed him with enthusiastic cheers. At one time during the battle, seeing preparations making on the part of the rebels to repeat an attack on Harris's brigade, by which they had just been repulsed, Rousseau dashed up to the commanding officer of the Second Ohio, Major Anson McCook, who was on foot fighting his regiment, and was warning him of the approaching attack, when the men of the regiment, with shouts and hurrahs, gathered around him, hugging his legs and grasping his hands, throwing their caps in the air, and swearing to die with him. It was one of the most singular scenes ever witnessed on a battle-field, and was subsequently alluded to by rebel officers who had witnessed it, and who stated to our prisoners taken during the day that they frequently saw and recognized Rousseau riding up and down the line during the battle.

Rousseau was much predisposed, by reason of his mental organization, to excitability under fire, but it did not detract from his administrative power. He was as clearly administrative in danger as the more phlegmatic Thomas or Grant, but in a different way. Rousseau made very little, if any, use of his aids. If he had an order to give, he galloped across the field and gave it himself. If he had an advance to order, it was done by leading the troops in person. During this battle of Perryville, General McCook sent me to inform Rousseau, who was on the extreme left of the line, that his right was being turned and was falling back. Rousseau galloped to the endangered part of the line and rallied the troops in retreat, beating and cursing them into line, and actually breaking his sword over the head of one demoralized individual, who was thus brought to a stand. The enemy, however, continued to advance, and Rousseau was compelled to look around for farther assistance. Seeing Captain Charles O. Loomis's battery in position, in reserve, commanding a little valley into which the enemy had deployed, and through which they were rapidly advancing, he rode up to Captain Loomis and ordered him to open with canister. Loomis had not perceived the advancing enemy, and explained to Rousseau that he had been ordered into reserve by General McCook, and told to reserve his fire for close work.

"Close work!" exclaimed Rousseau; "what the devil do you call that, Captain Loomis?"

He pointed down the valley, and Loomis saw in an instant the advancing foe and his own danger. Loomis was a minute-man — one of the quickest-witted and brightest-eyed men I ever met — and in a second his six guns were pouring a destructive cross-fire into the rebel ranks that at once played havoc with the enemy and encouraged our own forces. The enemy thus advancing had flanked Lytle's brigade, and it was now falling back toward Loomis's position, but Rousseau's personal direction and appearance (Lytle had been left for dead on the field), and the opening guns of Loomis, soon reassured the men in retreat, and the line reformed. About the same time Sheridan's brigade was ordered in on the left by General Buell, and the enemy were speedily and bloodily repulsed.

His conduct in this engagement gained Rousseau his promotion to a major generalcy. The commission read, "promoted for distinguished gallantry," and was the first of the numerous promotions for gallantry issued during the war for the Union. His great popularity with the troops may be said to have dated from this day; and it grew still greater after the battle of Stone River, where, though commanding the reserves, he was among the first engaged. The love of the men became so intense that it broke out on every occasion. On the march, in camp, on parade, their admiration grew demonstrative, and cheers greeted him wherever he went. During the winter of 1862–'63, while the troops were in camp at Murfreesborough, great numbers of rabbits were frequently frightened from their burrows, when an entire regiment would start in pursuit with noisy yells. The demonstrations of admiration for Rousseau and these noisy pursuits of the rabbits became so frequent that it was a common remark, whenever the cheering of the soldiers was heard, that they were either after "Rousseau or a rabbit."

I have said that Rousseau was clearly administrative under all circumstances. He was once, and once only, known to betray any considerable nervousness under fire. It was during a brief engagement fought at Chehaw Station, when on his famous Alabama raid. He had sent forward Colonel Thomas Harrison, of the Eighth Indiana Cavalry (better known as the Thirty-ninth Mounted Infantry), to destroy a part of the railroad in his rear—the expedition then being on its return, having performed its principal purpose. Colonel Harrison unexpectedly became briskly engaged with the rebel forces under General James H. Clanton. Rousseau was some distance in the rear of the fight, and the extent of the engagement was only known to him by the amount of the firing and the number of wounded men brought to the rear. One of his aids — Captain Elkin — observed Rousseau's nervousness gradually increasing, as evinced by his twirling his long black mustache, and repeating aloud, but evidently communing with himself,

"I shouldn't have got into this affair. I'm very much afraid this isn't judicious."

Elkin penetrated through the swamps to Harrison's front, and returned with the information that the enemy were being driven, and that the result was not at all doubtful.

"There's no reason," he said, "to be uneasy about Harrison, general."

"Uneasy about Harrison!" exclaimed the general. "Tom Harrison can whip all the militia in Alabama. But what shall I do with my poor wounded boys? We are a thousand miles from home, and no way to carry them comfortably?"

He had to leave his wounded, and he took rather odd but effective means to have them well cared for. Having succeeded in capturing a company of Montgomery Cadets, the members of which were all young boys of less than seventeen years of age, he had them drawn up near his quarters, and released them unconditionally, with this suggestion:

"Boys," he said, "go home and tell your parents that

Rousseau does not war on women and children; and, mark you! do *you*. see that they don't make war on wounded prisoners."

The Cadets were modest enough to be glad to be considered and laughed at as boys on condition of their release; and on returning home showed their gratitude to Rousseau by taking as good care of his wounded as they were permitted to do.

When Sherman sent Rousseau on this raid to the rear of Hood's army (it was Joe Johnston's when Rousseau started), he did not anticipate his early return, nor expect him and his force to escape capture. When Rousseau reported to him on his return from the raid, Sherman was as much surprised as delighted. He made Rousseau detail the work of destruction which he had accomplished. After he had done so, Sherman said,

"That's well done, Rousseau, well done; but I didn't expect to see you back."

"Why not?" asked Rousseau, somewhat surprised.

"I expected you to tear up the road, but I thought they would gobble you."

"You are a pretty fellow," said Rousseau, laughingly, "to send me off on such a trip."

"You proposed it yourself," returned Sherman; "besides, I knew they wouldn't hurt you, and I thought you would pay for yourself."

On the occasion of the passage of Rolling Fork of Salt river there occurred an incident which is illustrative of the view which I have taken of the character of Rousseau as a natural-born leader. When giving the command to cross the river, which was then flood-high—it was a very cold morning besides—Rousseau rose in his saddle, and crying out to his men, "Follow me, boys! I expect no soldier to undergo any hardship that I will not share!" he sprang from his horse, entered the ford, and waded to the other shore. His men followed with cheers and bravos, and the brigade followed, soon disappearing on the wood-lined road which leads to the summit of Muldraugh's Hills.

I have not space here to enter as I could wish into the details of Rousseau's military career. He must always remain a representative of one of the peculiar phases of the late war, and every event I could give will in the future be valuable; but at this time it is impossible to allude farther to his military career. He left the army soon after the battle of Nashville (during which engagement he held the left position of Thomas's line at Fortress Rosecrans, near Murfreesborough), and returned to Louisville at the request of his friends, to contest with Robert Mallory, Esq., the latter's place in Congress. That congressional race was nothing more nor less than a crusade against the remnant of slavery left by the war in Kentucky, probably as a punishment for her attempted crime of neutrality. It was another brilliant triumph won by the exercise of the same decisive action which has always characterized him. The Convention which nominated Rousseau was, in political parlance, merely a "pocket convention," and its nominee found, on leaving the military field to examine the political course, that he had really no party to back him. He had to build up a party, and without hesitation he decided that it should be an avowedly abolition party in principle and purpose.

He began by announcing that he favored the adoption by the State of Kentucky of the constitutional amendment abolishing slavery, and denounced slavery as unjust, unwise, and impolitic — a curse and blight on the state. When he first made the speech in which he declared this, the people wildly stared at him, and when he had done they pronounced him insane. They were so completely blinded by their prejudices that they could or would not see the truth of his arguments, and at last he resorted to ridicule with better effect.

" I wish to say again," he said, on one occasion, " that slavery, thank God, is dead. Its own friends have destroyed it. They placed it at the foundation of Jeff Davis's government, and invited, nay, forced us to assail it. They forced the whole liberal world to make war upon it, and presented to us the alternative to destroy slavery or see our government perish. Our duty was a plain one, to kill slavery and rebellion with it, and let the government live. Both of these things are accomplished facts, and in the whole Christian world there remain but three slave states—*Cuba, Brazil, and Kentucky.*"

This climax, so ridiculous to every Kentuckian with any state pride in his soul, was hailed wherever heard with shouts of laughter; and Rousseau once remarked that it was a curious fact that the laughter generally began with the returned rebel soldiers, who possess less pro-slavery prejudices than the rebels who staid at home. Rousseau generally followed up this effective ridicule with what he called his " special argument against slavery." " We in Kentucky," he would say, " are in the habit of arguing the slavery question more from the economical than the moral stand-point;" and he would then go on to show how the institution had curtailed the prosperity of Kentucky and of the South. "But," he would add, "I wish to add a little argument of my own. I want to tell you why slavery will not pay. It is because we have a God in heaven, who has arranged the affairs of men in such a way that wrong and injustice won't pay, and don't pay. Has not the South lost more in the destruction of houses, and fences, and railroads, and crops, and other property, and expenditures for munitions of war, etc., in the last four years of a rebellion, carried on for the benefit of slavery, than it wrung out of the sweat of the slave in the forty years preceding? Add to this the half a million of her brave sons who died or were crippled in battle and in camp, half the entire arms-bearing population of the rebel states, and tell me if slavery was a paying institution to them? And do you think it can be restored now and not lead to a bloodier and fiercer war? And why is this? Simply because God in his wisdom has arranged the world so that in the long-run a system of wrong will not and can not pay."

After four weeks active canvassing of the district Rousseau was returned to Congress by a heavy majority, although the opposition pro-slavery party employed a former United States officer to make the race in order to split the Union or amendment vote. The scheme failed. Rousseau's personal popularity, and his positive, determined, and patriotic stand, carried him successfully through, and he was shortly after nominated for the Senate, which position he will doubtless attain. In these crusades against neutrality and slavery Rousseau has established a character for firmness and persistence which have made him a most popular leader and the first man of his state; and he is already accepted as the true successor in principles, purposes, and patriotism of the late great leader in Kentucky, Henry Clay.

The very close intimacy existing between Sherman and Rousseau is a fine illustration of the rule that opposite natures are often kindred spirits. Two natures in greater contrast can hardly be conceived. Rousseau has none of Sherman's nervousness of thought or action, while Sherman has nothing of the excitability of Rousseau under fire. Rousseau is personally a most conspicuous—perhaps *the* most conspicuous officer in the United States army, while Sherman is among the most commonplace in appearance. Yet their friendship, which began early in the war, is hardly the less remarkable than that existing between Grant and Sherman, and is much more demonstrative, because Rousseau and Sherman are of affectionate and demonstrative dispositions, while Grant is rather cold and formal. Sherman was very fond of quoting Rousseau's speech about him, delivered at the banquet to the latter at Louisville in 1862. Rousseau had then said of Sherman:

"Of all the men I ever saw, he is the most untiring, vigilant, and patient. No man that ever lived could surprise him. His enemies say he was surprised at Shiloh. I tell you no. He was not surprised, nor whipped, for he fights by the week. Devoid of ambition, incapable of envy, he is brave, gallant, and just. At Shiloh his old legion met him just as the battle was ended, and at the sight of him, placing their hats upon their bayonets, gave him three cheers. It was a touching and fitting compliment to the gallant chieftain. I am thankful for this occasion to do justice to a brave, honest, and knightly gentleman."

When Sherman first read this speech, immediately after the battle, when he was still laboring under the insanity charge, he jumped from his seat, ran around his quarters from tent to tent, reading the speech to all his staff, and swearing that there was " one sensible man in the country who understood him."

As may be rightly suspected from this article, Rousseau is rather a hero of mine. He has many of the most admirable qualities of man; and in long years of intercourse with him I saw a great deal to admire, and but little to condemn. I defy any man with an honest love of bold, albeit rugged honesty, to know the man and not to admire him. He was loyal, true, and affectionate to the back-bone. He stuck to his friends to the last, and only the firmer in adversity. The strong pressure of his mighty hand gave you no fear of what the clenched fist might do, but inspired confidence. He was, perhaps, too unsuspicious, and too hopeful and buoyant: these were the faults of his character, if faults it had, for knaves frequently imposed on him in the guise of honest poverty, and his hopeful nature sometimes led him to promise his friends more than he had the power, but not more than he had the disposition to perform.

Rousseau is fully six feet two, perhaps three inches high, and otherwise Herculean in build and strength. When mounted—he always rides great, ponderous, and invariably blooded horses—he displays to great advantage, and no more graceful and impressive figure can be conceived than Rousseau mounted. He was born a gentleman, and his elegant manners are as natural as his bravery and high sense of honor are intuitive.

L

CHAPTER VII.

PECULIARITIES OF VARIOUS GENERALS.

I WAS particularly fortunate during the war in coming in frequent contact with the four great characters who most deeply impressed themselves upon the public mind, and won the first positions in the history of the era. Sherman, Thomas, Grant, and Sheridan were the ablest, and in the end the most successful of our leaders, and their fame is now a part of that of the country. Hooker and Rousseau were also representative soldiers, and will be quoted by posterity as examples, and regarded, not less than the others, as characters illustrative of the time and its events. Of the many other generals whom I met, and of whom I have many interesting and pleasing reminiscences to relate, there are none so distinctly marked for lasting and permanent fame as the six whom I have sketched in detail. Still many of those of whom I now propose to speak will attain a place in future history and obtain a firm hold in the mind of posterity as characters worthy of emulation or remembrance, as have the others. Circumstances conspired to rob a few of those whom I knew of their just fame; temporary greatness was thrust upon some totally unworthy of such distinction, while most of the others were *mediocre*, and could only have come to the surface of society in the general upheaval of a great revolution like that through which this country

DON CARLOS BUELL.

lately had the good fortune to pass to greater security and a grander future. Those I have sketched in detail were endowed with the unmistakable trait of greatness; the majority of those whom I remember possessed peculiarities merely, and their reputations were local.

Yet some few of them did not lack in ability, or the industry, energy, and courage which creates opportunity and wins renown. One of those whom circumstances robbed of his just renown, and who is now generally looked upon as one of the greatest failures of the war, was to my mind one of our ablest soldiers, and, as a tactician, was the equal of Grant or Thomas, or any of their subordinates. General Don Carlos Buell was a perfect soldier—perfect in manner, bearing, coolness, courage, energy—physically and mentally a perfect soldier—but he failed. If he had a fault, it resulted from education, and from this fault came this failure. "A little learning is a dangerous thing," as Pope, Bulwer Lytton, and every other person who has attempted to dispense knowledge second-handed has discovered to his sorrow; but there is also such a thing as drinking too deep of the " Pierian Spring." To be a valedictorian is quite often to be an unfortunate; and more signal failures have emanated from the first section (Engineer) graduates of West Point, and the valedictorians of Yale and Hartford, than from less brilliant, less studious, but more practically educated classes of the same institutions. Not one of the valedictorians of West Point, from the time at which class-rank was first established—1820, I believe—has ever made a great success in practical life, and few of them have ever been famous outside of the army. They are learned and able undoubtedly, but they lack in practicability, and, when they come to wrestle with the world, find themselves ill adapted to the struggle. The Engineer Corps of the army into which the higher graduates of the Academy are placed has given us fewer successful soldiers than the Infantry, which is considered the lowest arm of the service. All of the engineers have, as generals, been visibly affected in their administration, strategy, and tactics by their education, and have preferred to depend more upon mud walls than living phalanges, and their strategic marches have been more correct in mathematical calculations than successful in execution. Benham, Stevens, Franklin, W. H. C. Whiting, McPherson, McClellan, Lee, and dozens of others I could name, have in the late war proven this to be true ; and Quincy A. Gilmore has proved about the only exception to the rule, doubtless from the fact that after his graduation he left the Engineer Corps for the Artillery.

Buell was not exactly a valedictorian, and was not in the Engineer Corps, but nevertheless he was one to whom all this I have said and exampled is applicable. He was not made impracticable, but too methodical by his pupilage. Not too much learning, but too much routine ruined him. He was not too much of a book-worm, but too much of a red tapist. His Alma Mater was not West Point, but that more pitiless school, the adjutant general's office. Thirteen years' constant service in that department of the army made him too systematic—smothered the fire in his heart, the impulsive in his nature, and, like Thomas, he taught himself "not to feel." It rendered him cool in danger, while not depriving him of his readiness in emergency, but it also unfortunately made him so systematic that it injured the originality of his conceptions. The adjutant general's office made him too much of a regular, so that when he came to command a great volunteer force he looked for and strove in vain to attain the perfectness in appointment, organization, drill, and all that routine duty to which he had been accustomed in the old army. Buell was a thoroughly educated soldier, as a strategist and tactician the equal of Grant; but he was too much of an organizer, and this, with a volunteer army to command, really detracted from his merit. Good organizers of large armies seldom succeed in handling them to signal advantage. Buell was too good an organizer. This mere routine duty absorbed too much of his mind; his mind became too much accustomed to dwell upon that specialty, and he gave it too much importance and consideration. So thoroughly had Buell's mind become imbued with the importance of giving to volunteer armies the precise organization of the regulars, that in taking leave of the army which he had formed from " Sherman's mob," he congratulated the soldiers who had saved us Shiloh, first, as more important in his eye than their victories, on their conversion " from raw levies into a powerful army, honored by common consent for its discipline and efficient organization, and for its *esprit de corps.*"

And yet this army thus congratulated was the weakest in organization of any great army that ever existed. It was not imperfect in its details; on the contrary, it was very admirable in that respect, but certainly no army was ever so weak in its corps commanders—McCook, Crittenden, and Gilbert. Circumstances took the organization out of Buell's hand. On the arrival of the army at Louisville in pursuit of Bragg, in September, 1862, General Halleck, then commander-in-chief, concluded that Buell ought to be removed. Halleck was one of those men who, instead of arguing himself from an array of facts into a correct position, would first conclude that affairs were in the condition that he wished or feared, and would then argue himself into the belief that they undoubtedly were so. He would wish his enemy to occupy a certain position, and actually bring himself to the belief that he had done so. Too good a lawyer ever to be a good soldier, he depended for success on tricks in war as he had on quibbles in the law. He concluded, in 1862, that Buell's army was demoralized through want of confidence in its commander, and decided upon his removal. The command was tendered to General George H. Thomas, who not only declined, but promptly urged the retention of General Buell. The other corps commanders then joined in this request, and Buell was retained. He was forced to hastily organize his army in order to continue the pursuit of Bragg, and, consolidating Nelson's army, decided upon three corps, with Nelson, McCook, and Crittenden in command, while General Thomas acted as second under Buell. This last arrangement was very faulty. Thomas was the best man in the army, and this arrangement virtually deprived the army of his services, and made him merely an inspector general. Before the campaign had opened, Nelson, who was a very superior soldier, was assassinated, and his place was supplied —it is really ridiculous to say so, however—by General

C. C. Gilbert. Never did a single army possess three such weak corps commanders as Alexander McDowell McCook, C. C. Gilbert, and Thomas L. Crittenden. They were doubtless brave and gallant—every soldier is supposed to be that; they doubtless did their duty to their full ability—every soldier does that, and expects no particular commendation for it; but these men were not capacitated by nature or education for the positions they held. Not one of them had any iron in his nature—neither were deep reasoners or positive characters. They were of that class of men who "intended to do well," but who, without any fixed and unswerving principle to guide them, vacillated and procrastinated until the great motive and the propitious time for action had passed, and left them the doers only of positive evil or negative good, which is just as bad. McCook was an overgrown school-boy, without dignity (Sherman, once alluding to him, called him "a juvenile"); Crittenden was a country lawyer with little legal and no military ability, and Gilbert a martinet, without an idea of discipline or system— the worst kind of a martinet. It would have been a miracle had Buell succeeded. His campaign was a failure when the circumstances of Nelson's death and Halleck's interference made Thomas the "fifth wheel to the coach," and McCook, Crittenden, and Gilbert the immediate directors of the corps forming the Army of the Ohio.

Buell was removed for the failure at Perryville, and actually court-martialed for that crime of McCook and Gilbert. The fact is that it was fought against Buell's express orders; and McCook, the corps commander directing it, boasted during the battle to Captain James S.

Stokes (formerly of the regular army, but at that time in command of the Chicago Board of Trade Battery) that he had General Buell's orders not to fight in his pocket, and added that if General Buell supposed that "Aleck McCook was coming in sight of the enemy without fighting him, he was much mistaken in his man." The fact is that Perryville was an unnecessary battle, and was fought only through the jealousy existing between our commanders. The great blessing of the late civil war in this country—I am not going to stop now to say how it was a great blessing, taking, as it eventually did, the form of a crusade against ignorance and slavery—a crusade for knowledge and liberty, in which all Christendom of this enlightened age should have joined with the same fervor that in a darker age it did in the crusade against the Crescent for the Tomb—this great blessing brought with it certain evils, and the basest of these was jealousy. This most degrading passion existed in our armies to a most surprising degree—to such an extent, indeed, that noble actions, instead of being held up as examples worthy of emulation, were often—in nine cases out of every ten—in which the actor survived, made the means of bringing him into ridicule among his immediate associates. Great men were injured in their prospects—brave men have been debarred from their just reward of promotion—ay, and even great campaigns retarded and ruined by the jealous interference of the envious and malicious. Important junctions of armies were prevented, needed re-enforcements held back, and many a brave man sacrificed by the jealousy and envy of commanders who would be great, but who could

not suffer to see others great.   Jealousy did more actual
damage to the cause during the war than did incompetency, and I don't think I can put the fact any more forcibly than by saying that.

Perryville was a battle growing out of jealousy, and
lost through jealousy.   The first movement made by our
troops, and the one that induced the attack of the rebels,
who would have been glad to lie still and avoid a conflict which could only interfere with their retreat, was
the result of General James S. Jackson's jealousy of General Rousseau, into whose line of battle circumstances
had placed one of the former's brigades.   Jackson went
to McCook and begged to be placed in position in another
part of the field, where he could fight his command un-
trammeled.   To gratify this desire, McCook moved him
nearly a mile to the front, and, as it happened, directly
upon the enemy, who attacked and surprised him.   Jackson was killed, and the brigade routed.   Despite the reverse, McCook was confident he could win the fight and
the glory unaided, and so jealous was he of Gilbert that
he would not ask for assistance, although Gilbert lay
with his whole corps within a stone's throw, looking
with interest on the desperate fight of Rousseau's division, which was all that was left of McCook's corps after
Jackson had been routed.   And Gilbert was such a martinet that he would not tender aid unasked, and so jealous of McCook that he looked upon his probable defeat
with positive pleasure.   And although Generals Steedman and Sheridan begged permission to go to Rousseau's
aid, Gilbert declined to give them permission, because
General McCook had not, and would not ask for assist-

ance. Alas! for the vanity of human calculations! While McCook and Gilbert thus indulged in criminal jealousy of each other, Rousseau, a subordinate of both, but a greater than either, stepped in and carried off the laurels by saving that portion of the army which their jealousy had endangered. For this failure of McCook's Buell was removed, and Rosecrans given the command. The latter improved the faulty organization only by returning Thomas to the immediate command of his corps. It was a fortunate thing that he did so, for this corps, under Thomas's immediate direction, at Stone River and Chickamauga, twice saved Rosecrans's army from total annihilation.

Had the military genius of Buell been developed in 1863 instead of 1861, that officer would have won a splendid reputation with the public, and a fine position in the army. In 1861 the people were clamorous for successes, even if bloody; in 1863 they were rapidly growing wiser, and demanded positive advantages for every drop of blood. Buell was one of the early developments sacrificed to the nation's ignorance of war. His policy would have been admired in 1864, but it ruined him in 1862. Then his policy was misrepresented, his character maligned, and even his loyalty impeached, and he was placed on trial before a court, one member of which, General Scheopff, was openly convicted of having declared that he "believed General Buell to be a traitor." There were other members of the same court who held similar opinions, but in the end the court failed to criminate Buell fully. He was acquitted, and ordered to duty. General Buell believed that Andrew Johnson, then Governor of Tennessee, and now President of the United States, was the principal instigator of this persecution of him, and always entertained toward that officer a very bitter and hostile feeling. Governor Johnson believed that Buell's usefulness in Tennessee had departed, was much opposed to his returning to command in that department, and when its command was again tendered Buell, he telegraphed to Washington to protest against the appointment. Before Buell could accept or decline the command, he received a notice that the order was changed, and that he would assume command of the Department of the Gulf, relieving General Banks. General Buell shortly after declined, also, to accept the latter appointment, no explanation being given. I was much interested in the study of Buell's character at the time, and wrote him asking his reasons. His reply to me touched upon several other points of his administration which I had inquired about in a previous letter, and there was but a single paragraph explaining his reasons for resigning. He stated that on receiving notice that he had been transferred from the Tennessee to the Gulf Department, he had made unofficial inquiries at Washington, and had discovered that the change had been ordered by President Lincoln immediately on receipt of the protest of Governor Johnson. On learning this, Buell resigned. Shortly after this he published a letter, giving as his grounds for resigning that the officers to whom he had been ordered to report (Sherman and Canby) were his juniors. I can not but have wished that he had put his motive for resigning on the higher grounds upon which he really acted, however unfounded may have been his prejudice against Governor Johnson; for, though it is doubtful if the latter acted from personal prejudices, certainly General Buell would have been justified in declining to serve a government which removed, transferred, and court-martialed him on the representation of a single person.

Numerous were the misrepresentations made of the supposed quarrel between Buell and Johnson, much to the damage of the former and disgust of the latter. Among the other stories told were two to the effect that Governor Johnson had forced General Buell to fortify Nashville, and secondly to garrison instead of evacuating the city. During the summer of 1862, Governor Johnson became convinced that it would have a good effect upon the rebel citizens of Nashville to fortify it, as evidence of the intention of the army to hold the place. In the absence of General Buell, the governor called upon Major Sidell, who was Buell's adjutant general stationed at Nashville, and, opening the subject, got excited in its elaboration, and delivered a stump speech of half an hour's duration. When he had retired, Sidell came to the conclusion that the governor had intended what he had said for General Buell's ear, and immediately wrote out a synopsis of the speech in a letter to the general, and forwarded it to him. The answer came back, "Consult with Governor Johnson, and commence the works." Major Sidell called upon the governor, and the two rode around the city, and at last decided upon the erection of a stockade fort on what was known as St. Cloud Hill. This was the commencement of that series of works which now so formidably environ Nashville, and which formed such an impregnable barrier to Hood's advance in 1864. The story of the evacuation, as popularly received, is a very gross exaggeration of Governor Johnson's would-be, but mistaken friends. When the army was moving through Nashville in September, 1862, in pursuit of Bragg, it certainly looked very much like an evacuation was about to take place, and many of the Union citizens became nervous over the prospect. Governor Johnson, accompanied by a single aid, waited upon General Buell, and found him in his quarters poring over a map. Governor Johnson at once opened his budget — remarked that the movement of the troops had created the fear on the part of the people that the intention was to abandon Nashville to the enemy, and if such was the purpose, the Union citizens should be informed, in order that they might be enabled to leave with the army. He therefore requested of General Buell to know his intention in that respect. General Buell laid aside his maps, and with that dignity and deliberation which characterized his every word and action, replied,

"Governor, according to all the rules of military art, I ought to evacuate this city, for its possession depends upon the result of the battle which is to be fought with Bragg in Kentucky, whither he is now advancing, and where I am pursuing him. To hold this city deprives me not only of a large force available in a battle, but also places me at the disadvantage of having to watch two important points, Louisville and Nashville, at once. If Bragg is attacked and defeated (and the force necessary to garrison this city can materially contribute to that result), I can reoccupy Nashville at any moment. If

Bragg attacks and defeats me, the force left here will be endangered, I shall be powerless to aid it, and it will eventually be sacrificed with the city. But the moral effect of holding Nashville will be very great upon my army and upon the people of the North, though it may prevent my attacking Bragg; and for that reason I have determined to hold it, and shall leave General Thomas in command, with his corps for its garrison."

To this speech Governor Johnson replied, expressing his gratification, and immediately retired. General Thomas was left in command, but on reaching Gallatin, and finding Bragg was still in advance of him, moving north upon Louisville, General Buell sent orders to General Thomas to leave General James S. Negley in command of the garrison, and to join him with the rest of his corps. It was to this movement that Governor Johnson objected, and on his representation General Thomas so far disobeyed Buell's orders as to leave General John M. Palmer and his division, as well as that of General Negley, to hold Nashville.

The speech of General Buell to Governor Johnson embraced his whole plan of the campaign, and he followed it out faithfully and successfully. He followed Bragg closely, but refused to fight him, covered Nashville and protected Louisville, and eventually forced Bragg to retreat from the state by way of the mountains of East Tennessee. Had he urged battle and been defeated, or even disabled, General Negley would have been forced to retreat, harassed at every step, to the Ohio River, at Paducah. As it was, Bragg accomplished nothing, and had Buell remained in command he would never have again advanced north of Chattanooga. Buell having driven Bragg from Kentucky, proposed to go by forced marches to Murfreesborough, Tennessee, drive Breckinridge from that point, and reoccupy the rich country of Middle Tennessee. But he was very unwisely superseded by Rosecrans, who delayed until Bragg had moved north to Murfreesborough, and had actually advanced to take Nashville. This delay necessitated the fighting of the battle of Stone River, and cost us ten thousand men.

In manners and habits, as well as in modesty and sternness, General Buell is not unlike Thomas, possessing the same dignity of deportment, and reservedness and imperturbability so characteristic of the latter officer. He possessed, too, the same regular habits of business, and is a model of reticence and secrecy. He is, if any thing, too cold in demonstration, and won in consequence, while in the army, a reputation for gruffness which he did not deserve. He smiled as seldom as Thomas. One morning, during a recess of the court which was examining into his conduct at Nashville in December, 1862, he grew unusually lively in a playful controversy with a young daughter of General Rousseau, and perpetrated several rather comical jokes. Miss Rousseau, utterly astonished at this unexpected liveliness on the general's part, expressed her surprise by exclaiming, "Why, General Buell, I never knew you to laugh aloud before."

"Ah! my child," replied the general, suddenly growing serious, "you never knew me when I felt free to laugh as now."

Although very small of stature, General Buell possesses almost Herculean strength, and frequently has been known to lift his wife, a lady of at least 140 pounds' weight, at arm's length, and stand her on a mantle-shelf nearly as high as himself. His frame, compactly built, is all muscle and sinew.

When Buell was relieved by Rosecrans, the army threw up its hat in delight, and the country re-echoed their bravos of approval. Never was joy so inappropriate—never was there a change of commanders so injudicious, and it required only a year of time, but, alas! many a human life, to prove how criminal it was. Politics nor war ever thrust upon the nation a more incompetent leader than William Starke Rosecrans. He had not one of the attributes of generalship. He was neither a strategist nor a tactician, and all he knew of the art of war were its tricks—the tricks that every Indian and all uncivilized nations most excel in. He inspired dread in his enemies only by his reputation for trickery, and was known throughout the camps of the foe as "that wily Dutchman, Rosecrans." He was eminently fitted by nature and education to be the provost-marshal and chief of spies to a great army like that which he commanded, but nothing more.

Nature unfitted him for the task of directing a great army by making him extremely nervous. His nervousness, unlike that of Sherman, was a weakness. His excitability rendered it not only impossible for him to execute, but it made him incoherent, and he could not direct others. I have known him, when merely directing an orderly to carry a dispatch from one point to another, grow so excited, vehement, and incoherent as to utterly confound the messenger. In great danger as in small

WILLIAM S. ROSECRANS.

things, this nervousness incapacitated him from the intelligible direction of his officers or effective execution of his plans. He possessed no control over himself, and consequently was not capable of directing others.

Rosecrans was not an impressive man. It was too apparent that all he did was for "effect," in the theatrical sense. He possessed very little dignity; and he dwindled terribly as you came to know him most intimately. He did not "wear well" even with the troops, who are the last of an army to give up their worship of a general. He was not long admired by his subordinate officers, and, though a great favorite with his soldiers, they never lavished upon him that intense devotion which they felt for Thomas, and which seldom found utterance in noisy demonstration. Rosecrans had a system by which to gain the affections of his men totally different from that of Thomas or Grant. It was, however, the false system of the demagogue. He never passed a regiment without having a pleasant word for the men. He chatted freely and even jocularly with them. He blamed the officers for every thing—the men for nothing. If a knapsack was put on carelessly, he told the guilty man's captain that he "didn't know how to strap on a knapsack." If a canteen was missing, he ridiculed the soldier who thought he could fight without water, and scolded his officer. All this pleased the men, without exactly offending the officer, and the whole army had a hearty laugh over every such scene, and felt an increased admiration for the general. But this admiration died out on the first apparent failure of the idol, and transferred itself to the successor, who had won their confidence by saving their former idol and themselves. Shortly after the retirement from Chickamauga to Chattanooga, and while the whole of his army was engaged in building the defenses of that place, Rosecrans, accompanied by Thomas, rode around the line to examine the works. It happened that this was also General Thomas's first public appearance after the battle of Chickamauga, and whenever the two made their appearance, the troops threw down their spades and picks, gathered in tumultuous and noisy crowds around the person of Thomas, grasped and kissed his hands and embraced his legs, to the total neglect of Rosecrans, and much to the latter's disgust and Thomas's confusion. The distinction was too marked to remain unnoticed, and Rosecrans saw in that demonstration his approaching downfall.

The immediate cause of Rosecrans's removal was his failure at Chickamauga. There were other offenses laid to his charge, but this was enough to condemn him; and he would have been relieved immediately after that event had it not been necessary, in Mr. Lincoln's opinion, to retain him in the position until after the Ohio election for governor. So little were the people understood, and so little was their deep earnestness appreciated, that there were wise counselors of the President who believed that the removal of Rosecrans at that time would strengthen Vallandigham, and perhaps secure his election over Brough. As soon as the election was over, however, Rosecrans was removed, and very properly too, for his entire campaign had been one series of great mistakes, which circumstances have served to hide from general observation. I am in some measure responsible for the false impressions prevailing about that campaign, for I was so placed—as correspondent for a leading paper of the country—that I could have given them publication, but the sin was one of omission only. A little circumstance prevented me at the time from telling the whole truth about the battle of Chickamauga, or even all I had proposed to tell. As it was, I was condemned, abused, and ridiculed by half the papers in the country for what little I did say, and for a few weeks I felt myself the best abused man in the country. It was not until Rosecrans, and McCook, and Crittenden were relieved that people began to understand that I was right, and I to feel that I had made a mistake in not giving the whole story in full. The circumstance which induced me to do otherwise was this: A week or two before the battle of Chickamauga, the Assistant Secretary of War, Charles A. Dana, arrived at Rosecrans's head-quarters, and he was received by the army as if he was a bird of evil omen. It was whispered at head-quarters that he had come as the spy of the War Department, and to find justification for Rosecrans's intended removal; the rumor spread to the camp; officers looked upon him with scowls, and the men ridiculed him by pretending to mistake him for a sutler, and by calling after him as he would ride by in the wake of Rosecrans, " Hey, old sutler! when are you going to open out?" Mr. Dana's position must have been very unpleasant to him, for he was evidently an object of suspicion in every body's eyes, and his mission "to ruin Rosecrans" was the talk of the whole camp. On the morning after the battle, when about leaving Chattanooga for New York, in order to write up an account of the battle for the Herald, I waited on General Rosecrans to obtain his approval to a dispatch to be forwarded by telegraph. The general, Garfield, Dana, and one or two aids, were at lunch. While General Garfield read and approved the dispatch, General Rosecrans asked me, among other questions, what I proposed to tell about the late battle. I answered, " The plain, unvarnished truth, I hope." Soon after I left, and Mr. Dana arose and followed me to the telegraph office. Here he very officiously told the telegraph operators to see that my dispatch went through without delay, and otherwise showed almost too plainly a disposition to serve me. Before I could leave the house and mount my horse to ride to the nearest railroad station, I heard two operators talking of collusion between myself and Mr. Dana, while a third told me very plainly "that it was evident that Mr. Dana and myself were both disposed to blame Rosecrans for the defeat." To have written what I had intended would have been to justify this suspicion, and hence much that I would liked to have said of the battle at that time in the Herald I was compelled to defer until the present time and the present book.

In the first place, I would have liked to have said then that the battle of Chickamauga was useless; that there was not the slightest necessity for fighting it, and, despite all that has been said, and written, and misrepresented to the contrary, to have shown that the troops could have been easily concentrated in Chattanooga without fighting a battle of any dimensions. The campaign was well managed until the occupation of Chattanooga, and the crossing of Lookout Mountain excited Rosecrans so that he lost his self-possession, when he made the gross mistake of sending his three corps in pursuit, by widely divergent lines, of a foe concentrated immediately in front of his centre. General Thomas made the discovery of this position of the enemy, and without consulting Rosecrans, who was some distance away, ordered McCook, already fifty miles distant on his way to Rome, to return immediately. For this Rosecrans blamed Thomas at first, but allowed himself to be argued into confirming the orders, which order really saved McCook, for another twenty-four hours' delay would have prevented him from reaching the main army. Nevertheless, having retreated west of Lookout Mountain, McCook was safe and could have pursued his way to Chattanooga, whither Thomas, and Crittenden too, could have fallen back had they not waited for McCook to recross the mountain and concentrate upon the west bank of the Chickamauga. Forty-eight valuable hours were lost by this movement, and made the battle of Chickamauga not only a necessity, but a failure. Had the proper plan been pursued, the campaign of Rosecrans would have ended with the successful siege and battles of Chattanooga, without their terrible precursor, Chickamauga.

The engagement itself was the worst managed battle of the war. The public blamed Rosecrans, and the President relieved him for leaving the field and retiring to Chattanooga, but it is not generally known that Rosecrans never saw the battle-field of Chickamauga; yet such is the fact; and he has to this day no knowledge of the roads or configuration of that field from personal examination. He did not actually see a gun fired on that field except when Longstreet broke McCook's corps and pushed through Rosecrans's quarters, which were in the rear of that part of the field.   On the first day his quarters were a mile to the right and rear of the line of battle, and two miles from the main fight, which Thomas conducted.   During this day's battle Rosecrans paced up and down his quarters, while his engineer sat near by with a map, a pencil, and a compass, endeavoring to locate on the map the line of the battle by its sounds! Never was any thing so ridiculous as this scene.   A countrywoman named Glenn, who resided at the house, was called into requisition as an aide, and, standing by the engineer's side, would, in reply to his questions, " guess" the locality of the firing as " about a mile fornenst John Kelly's house," or " nigh out about Reid's bridge somewhar." The firing could be distinctly heard, and as on one or two occasions the cannonading and musketry grew more rapid, I heard Rosecrans, rubbing his hands and fairly quivering with excitement, exclaim, "Ah! there goes Brannin!" or " That's Negley going in!" and really understanding no more about the actual situation than the poor woman who aided Garfield and St. Clair Morton to locate the line on the map.   Meantime, on the field, each corps commander fought "on his own hook," and thus Crittenden, who never, on the battle-field, had an opinion of his own, or ever assumed any responsibility that he could possibly avoid, failed to advance his corps when that of Thomas charged and drove the enemy.   Had he done so, all the force which Bragg, on that first day of the engagement, had on our side of the Chickamauga River must have inevitably been driven into that stream.   As

it was, the right flank of Thomas's advancing corps became exposed and turned, and he·was forced to ·retire
from the field he had won, the fruits of his victory frittered away by Crittenden's negativeness. All this was undoubtedly owing to Rosecrans's absence from the field.
The whole story of this terrible mistake was told that
night by General John M. Palmer in an incident which
illustrated it very handsomely. I had met him during
the day when his troops were somewhat scattered. During the night ensuing, I was sitting at the table of the
telegraph operators at Rosecrans's quarters, writing a dispatch, when General Palmer came in.

"Since I saw you this morning," he said, addressing
me, "I have got my troops together again. They are in
good spirits, and ready for another fight. I have no hesitation in saying to you"—at this moment he saw Assistant Secretary of War Dana at the other end of the table,
and would have liked to stop, but had gone too far, and
so he added, "and I have no hesitation in saying to *you*,
Mr. Dana, that this battle has been lost because we had
no supreme head to the army on the field to direct it."

Nothing was ever truer than this. All that was at
one time needed to have secured us a great victory was
to have had some one to tell Crittenden that it was his
manifest duty to charge with Thomas. The next day
was too late; Longstreet was then across the river;
McCook was routed ; he, Crittenden, and Rosecrans
were in Chattanooga (the latter had already telegraphed
to Washington that his army was totally defeated and
routed); and all that Thomas could hope to do with his
remnant of the army was to cover the retreat. This he

was enabled to do by the timely appearance of the reserve corps and its two very able leaders, Granger and
Steedman.

Granger was the character, Steedman the remarkable
man of these two, and both such men as Thomas needed
in his emergency. They brought with them the reserve
corps of twenty-five thousand men—fifteen thousand of
them enlisted men, the other ten thousand were Steedman and Granger themselves. They were each men in
whom their troops had implicit confidence, and this
doubled their strength, or rather was their strength, for
no army can be said to have any strength if it has not
confidence in its leaders.

Gordon Granger is a rude, rough, and tough soldier,
and the confidence of his men was inspired not so much
by their knowledge of his ability as of admiration of
his bravery. His ability as a director is not great, but
he is a good leader of men. Granger is a man without any sense of fear — is more thoroughly indifferent
to the dangers of battle than any man I ever remember to have met. He was not the coolest man I have
seen on a battle-field; on the contrary, he was what
might be called fidgety, in order to avoid saying that he
was excitable, which would not be true ; but so totally
and absolutely fearless that it was not merely apparent,
but remarkable, and called forth frequent allusion from
his fellow-officers, and the constant admiration of his
men. This quality of his nature constituted him a leader, as inspiring the confidence of his men, and this confidence formed the discipline and the morale of his command. Granger ought to have been an artillerist rather

GORDON GRANGER.

than an infantry-man, for he was devoted to the artillery, and the greatest fault of his character as a leader was this predilection for artillery. Not unfrequently Granger would abandon the direction of a corps to command a battery. At Chickamauga he left Steedman to lead his corps while he mounted a battery on General Woods's front, and opened on the enemy a fire which had the effect of calling forth a reply which made Thomas's quarters too hot to be comfortable even for that old salamander. During the first day of the battles of Chattanooga, in November, 1863, Granger devoted himself in the same way to the big guns in Fort Wood, Grant's head-quarters, and so disturbed Grant by his repeated firing of the monsters that the latter had to order him to the front, where his troops had carried a position. The ruling passion was too strong in Granger to be exorcised by a hint, and he had hardly been on the front line five minutes when he had a battery mounted, and was firing away at the rebels at a shorter range.

Granger was a man equally courageous morally as physically, and pursued an object, or criticised a subject or person without the slightest regard to others' opinions. He never shirked a responsibility—in fact, would rather act without authority than not, as giving zest to the undertaking. He was free in his criticisms as Hooker, but ruder. He had as little policy in such things as " Fighting Joe," but nothing of the sarcastic bitterness of that officer. Granger was almost gruff, not only in his criticisms, but in his language, and never disliked a man without showing it. When the army occupied East Tennessee, after the expulsion of Longstreet from the vicinity of Knoxville, Sherman left Granger in command at Loudon with but little food for his troops, and almost no provender for his animals. Granger complained of his wants to Grant, who referred the matter to Sherman. The latter declared that there was plenty of all kinds of supplies in East Tennessee, and in indorsing the papers, advised Granger to live off the country. "Living off the country" was a favorite idea with Sherman, but Granger saw greater difficulty in it, and nearly starved in trying to do so. Shortly after this Grant went to the Potomac, and Sherman succeeded him in command of the Military Division of the Mississippi. While making an inspection of his command in the ensuing spring, Sherman one day arrived at Loudon, Granger's head-quarters. On jumping off the cars at that place, Sherman saw Granger in front of his quarters, and, going up to him, began, in that quick, nervous manner in which Sherman always speaks,

"I say, Granger, I wish you would give me and my staff something to eat—only a mouthful—only a mouthful, and a cup of coffee. Haven't had any thing to eat since daylight."

"See you starved first," muttered Granger *sotto voce*, but still loud enough to be heard. "Why don't you 'live off the country?'"

He did, however, give Sherman his rations—of the plainest materials he could gather—"Lincoln platform" (hard bread) and rye coffee, but could not avoid the temptation to repeatedly apologize for the plain fare by the remark,

"You see, general, we have to 'live off the country.'"

Although a great admirer of Rosecrans, Granger was not more particular in his language to him than to Sherman. After Thomas had fallen back to Rossville, after the battle of Chickamauga, he sent General Granger to Chattanooga to represent the situation to Rosecrans, and obtain his order to retire upon Chattanooga. Granger found Rosecrans, and had very little difficulty in arguing him into adopting Thomas's ideas. He sat down at a table, and, with Granger looking over his shoulder, began to write the order to Thomas to fall back. Instead of making it a brief command, Rosecrans went on to detail how the retreat must be conducted, how the troops should be marshaled, this division here and another there, who should be in the van and who in the rear, and was adding that great fires must be built all along the line before the retreat began, in order to deceive the enemy into the belief that they were going to stay there (a favorite *trick* of the wily Rosecrans), when Granger interrupted him—

"Oh, that's all nonsense, general! Send Thomas an order to retire. He knows what he's about as well as you do."

Rosecrans silently obeyed, tore up the order, and wrote another, which proved a model of brevity, and fully as satisfactory to Thomas.

This independence in speech rather interfered with Granger's character for gallantry—sadly so on one occasion, in the estimation of a charming Miss Saunders, of Nashville, step-daughter of Governor Aaron V. Brown, and a niece of the rebel General Gideon Pillow. Miss Saunders was particularly proud of her uncle Gideon, and never lost an opportunity of sounding his praise. On one occasion she was indulging in this praise of Pillow to Granger, and among other things remarked that her uncle "would have held a very high rank in the Confederate army had it not been for the personal enmity existing between him and Jeff Davis. Very unexpectedly, the ungallant and over-candid Granger replied,

"General Pillow never amounted to much."

The brow of the charming young lady contracted, and her eyes flashed fire as she exclaimed,

"General Granger, how dare you speak so of my uncle?"

"Oh," answered Granger, "you can't fool me with 'painted mules.'" (Granger had been a quarter-master, and in his early days had frequently been imposed upon by traders in repaired condemned animals.) "I knew Gid Pillow in Mexico, and he always was an old fool."

The disgust of the niece can be better imagined than described, and the ungallant and rough Granger was forever after banished from her presence.

Like most similarly candid men, Granger was a firm, warm, and constant friend. I had quite a quarrel with him during the battle of Mission Ridge for having alluded to a story told me by Senator Nesmith, of Oregon, of his comical adventures in escaping from capture at Chickamauga, and his retreat to civilization. I could not for some time understand Granger's wrath, until he told me that Senator Nesmith was a particular and intimate friend of his, and he should not be abused in his presence. It was not until I had explained that Nesmith had himself told me the story, and that it was highly creditable to his nerve and courage, though comical in the extreme, that Granger at last became mollified.

General Granger was fond of the young men associated with him at head-quarters as members of his staff, and particularly so of Captain Russell, his adjutant general. During the battle of Chickamauga, he sent Captain Russell to some part of the line to carry an order to General Steedman. While riding along a ridge over which he had to pass, Russell became exposed to the rebel fire, and fell pierced by several balls. His horse was wounded in the hip, and, riderless, came back to where Granger was then engaged in fighting, firing and almost loading a battery which he had placed in position, and upon which the enemy were at the time charging. The horse singled Granger out in the crowd and excitement, ran up to him, fondled about him with his head, and did every thing that a dumb brute could do to attract attention. At first, Granger, busy at the guns, did not notice the horse, until the animal grew troublesome. His own horse and that of Captain Russell were very much alike, and, mistaking the animal for his own, Granger called to his orderly to take him away. The orderly explained that it was not his horse, and Granger then saw that it was Russell's, and noticed that it had been wounded. The truth flashed across his mind at once, and he sent several of his body-guard in search of the body of his adjutant, the faithful horse guiding them to where his master had fallen. Granger forgot "his ruling passion," the artillery —forgot to send another aid with the order which Russell had, of course, failed to deliver, and when the orderlies returned with the dead body of the captain, Granger gave himself up to his grief. At last his great sorrow vented itself in an exclamation addressed to General Thomas—

"By G—d, general, he was the best soldier I ever knew!"

After this, the fountain of his tears seemed to dry up. He ordered the body to be cared for, returned to his artillery, and became again the rough soldier of the moment before.

"Old Steady," as the soldiers affectionately called General James B. Steedman, possessed, perhaps, not greater, but certainly more available talents than Gordon Granger. He was more practical, of equally effective presence, equal daring morally, and greater daring mentally. Gordon Granger delights in responsibilities. Steedman dares to assume responsibilities which are at times appalling, and does so with so much cool impudence as silences you in astonishment, and such sublime nerve and boldness as hushes you in admiration. He defies argument by the preposterousness of his plans, and silences opposition by the daring with which he executes them. He hesitates at nothing. The magnitude of an undertaking has a charm for him, and he accomplishes great things in the most unexpected of ways. He is never so great as when struggling against great obstacles, or fighting against great odds. He is a positive and decided man; not merely opinionated and obstinate, but firm, unflinching, and resolute. Clear-headed and cool-headed—a man of uncommonly strong common sense—he always knows his own mind and always follows it. No man was ever less in want of advice, or ever treated it with such con-

JAMES B. STEEDMAN.

tempt. "Never, under any circumstances, take any body's advice, nor refuse any body's information," is an accepted motto with Steedman. He did not adopt it from actual experience, but received it intuitively, and is constituted, not educated, to depend upon and decide for himself. Experience, education, and natural shrewdness have taught him to instinctively divine the true in principle and character, and he seldom fails to correctly analyze men and motives. The same long experience, thorough education, and natural shrewdness have made him a splendid administrative officer, full of resources and ingenuity, which, added to the boldness, or perhaps it is best described by calling it the impudence, with which he acts, gives assured success to all his plans.

These traits of extravagance in the formation and boldness in the execution of his plans find many illustrations in Steedman's public career. Before the war one of the great men among Ohio local politicians and a leading spirit of the Democrats, he was the ruler of all the Democratic Conventions of his state from 1850 to 1860, and was noted for the ingenuity with which he pulled the political wires of his party. And not the least remarkable fact in connection with this matter is, that he attained this controlling position through his election as Superintendent of Public Works, an office which had previously been of minor importance and little patronage, but which Steedman made, by his positiveness and boldness, of such influence and power as to make its occupant a— in fact, *the* power in the party. And by his audacity and strong will, exercised with wonderful success over men, he retained, and still retains, this power to this day.

His bolder confederates used to declare that he was destroying the party by the irregularity and impossibility
of his schemes, and thus endeavor to impair his influence;
but as, after each election, the party under his leadership
came out ahead, faith in his boldness of manœuvre was
restored, and his ambitious comrades, who wished to be
also his rivals, would, like the more obedient of the party, rally again to his support and fight under his leadership. His boldness was really nothing more than the
clear defining of the principle fought for, and in this lay
the secret of success. It is related of Steedman that on
one occasion he concocted a curious scheme for reconcil-
ing the discordant elements which threatened the unity
of a State Convention of the party called to meet at Co-
lumbus. He went to the proprietor of the hotel at which
the delegation usually boarded, and told him that when
certain men whom he named, and who were the leaders
of the two factions, arrived in town and called for rooms,
they were to be told that the house was full, but that
"probably Mr. Steedman might accommodate them in
his room," which Steedman had taken care should be
the largest in the house. The trick succeeded, and the
leaders of the rival factions found themselves, much to
their surprise, domiciled together in Steedman's room,
and so intent on watching each other that neither faction
could hold its proposed caucus. The evening before the
Convention, having succeeded in getting the leaders of
the two factions closeted in his room, Steedman exposed
to each the private schemes of the other, and thus dis-
armed both. By the plentiful use of argument and the
judicious use of ridicule, he reconciled the oil and water

(not by *lie* however), and at last got them to agree on his platform and his candidate. I am not certain that he was not himself the candidate selected. The joke was too good to keep, and the hotel proprietor exposed it to the leaders, who went home declaring that they had one satisfaction, and that was, that "Jim Steedman had to sleep on the floor during the whole of the Convention, while they slept in his beds."

Sleeping on a carpeted floor was not a particularly severe hardship for the sinewey Steedman, for when under great mental or nervous excitement he can not sleep at all. At the Cincinnati Convention of 1856, in which he was the leading Ohio wire-puller, he went for four days and nights without closing his eyes, and three fourths of the time he was on his feet on the cold stone floor of the Burnett House, "manipulating" the politicians. He can neither eat nor drink under great excitement. At the battle of Chickamauga he ate nothing for two days, and though he carried a canteen of whisky through the entire battle, he forgot all about it until after the retreat to Rossville, when a wounded soldier in the hospital asked for a drink, and Steedman gave him his canteen.

Steedman was a Douglas Democrat of very strong proclivities, and very much astonished his friends, when the war was about beginning, by arguing in his paper, the Toledo Herald and Times, the propriety of permitting the Southern states "to go out," *i. e.*, to peaceably secede. Such a doctrine from a Douglas Democrat was astonishing, and the article created much comment. Without saying that the states ought to be allowed to depart, he argued that secession was its own punishment; that the

seceded states could not hold together if allowed to secede; and that a few years only would elapse before they
would be begging their way back into the Union; and
that, while it would cost a river of blood to keep them
in, a war would not more effectually settle the question
of secession than if allowed to fall of its own weight.
Steedman's friends declared him crazy, but he only
laughed at them, and in the next issue of his paper finished his argument, or rather gave the other side of the
question. Claiming that the first conclusion was correct,
and that the course suggested would be equally effective
with war, he then went on to show that it was not the one
which a great people could pursue; that peaceable secession was a doctrine we ought not to admit merely for the
sake of the humanitarian argument of "no bloodshed,"
and that nothing was left for the loyal people but the other
bitter alternative of war. That alternative the people of
the North, he declared, would unanimously accept in the
spirit of right and justice, and that it became the people
to prepare for the blood-letting which was to ensue. The
first of these articles eventually found its way into Congress at a time when Steedman's confirmation as brigadier general was pending, and being construed into "Cop-
perheadism," retarded that confirmation for nearly two
years, Mr. Ashley, who had defeated Steedman for Congress, holding it over his head as a balance of power to
keep the general from running against him for that position. At the next election, instead of agreeing to abandon the field to Ashley, and thus secure his confirmation,
Steedman took the very opposite grounds, and announced
his intention, since he was not likely to be confirmed a

brigadier general, of running against Mr. Ashley. This had the desired effect, and Ashley hastened, by his recommendation and influence, to secure Steedman's confirmation in the Senate, and shortly after, also, that of major general, to which Steedman was nominated after the battle of Chickamauga.

Steedman's admiration of Douglas amounted almost to idolatry, and to such excess that Douglas's *political* enemies were held by Steedman to be his *personal* foes, and more than one of them was treated so by him. When Steedman was public printer at Washington, Isaac Cook, postmaster of Chicago, and a former Douglas Democrat, but who had, in order to retain his position, sided with Buchanan in his famous quarrel with Douglas, came into his office complaining that Douglas had abused him for his defection. In relating what had taken place, and in what manner Douglas had denounced him, Cook remarked to Steedman that he had just met Douglas in the Capitol, and was prepared, in case the "Little Giant" spoke to him, to "give him a good caning." The picture of Stephen A. Douglas being caned by "Ike" Cook was too much for Steedman. Clearing a table which stood between him and Cook at a bound, he seized the astonished postmaster by the collar, and with a furious oath exclaimed,

"You cane Douglas! You strike Stephen A. Douglas, who made you all you are! Get out of this office, or I'll kick you out!"

Cook began to expostulate, when the infuriated Steedman carried out his threat, and Cook made a hasty and inelegant retreat.

Next day President Buchanan sent for Steedman, and lectured him regarding his treatment of Cook. Steedman had by this time began to look at the comic side of the affair, and listened patiently and good-humoredly to the President's lecture, until Mr. Buchanan alluded to Douglas contemptuously as "the little traitor." Steedman's blood boiled with fury, but by a great effort he controlled his passion, and, rising, said, with a voice of measured calmness,

"Mr. President, I have been a warm friend of Stephen A. Douglas for many years. I supported him in the convention which nominated you for the Presidency because I believed him to be incomparably the ablest and the best man for the position. *I think so still.* Good-morning, sir."

A few hours after, Steedman received a note from the Postmaster General:

"Sir,—I am directed by the President to inform you that in future Mr. Cornelius Wendell will do the printing of this department."

This was followed by a general withdrawal of government patronage where it was possible, and thus Steedman lost a great deal of his business in consequence of his candor.

I have intimated in the sketch of General Thomas that the famous charge of the reserve corps at Chickamauga was made at Steedman's suggestion. The idea of advancing at that time was a most preposterous one—it looked simply suicidal—and I would have been less surprised if the army had made arrangements to surrender than I was to see Steedman's corps charging and carrying the ridge against Longstreet's corps, which had a few

hours before scattered a larger force than that of Steedman's at a single blow. The charge was not less of a
surprise to the enemy, and the fact that it was unexpected and unaccountable under the circumstances had much
to do with its success, since it puzzled and confused
both Longstreet and Bragg so much as to convince them
that Thomas had a large reserve force, and to cause a
long and highly important delay and cessation of hostilities.

During this famous charge of Steedman's occurred an
incident which at once illustrates the boldness and extravagance of the man. The fighting was very heavy,
the ridge which Longstreet held very high and difficult,
and at one time Steedman saw a portion of his line wavering. Before he could ride forward to their position,
this wavering brigade broke and began to retire, following a flag in the hands of a color-bearer, who had taken
the lead in retreating. Meeting the retiring brigade,
Steedman grasped the flag from the bearer and waved it
above his head. All the line saw the action, but only a
part of it heard his stentorian voice as he cried,

"Run away, boys—run away like cowards; but the
flag can't go with you."

Not the words, but the advancing flag had the desired
effect, and these men returned to the charge, and, led by
the broad-shouldered, broad-breasted old soldier, they
carried the hill before them.

Before going into this battle, Steedman became strangely impressed with the idea that he was to lose his right
leg, and, though no believer in presentiments, so forcibly
and frequently did the thought occur to his mind, that

he confided his feelings to some of his staff and friends. Among others to whom he mentioned it was Gordon Granger, who laughed at the idea, and jocosely asked Steedman what he could do for him in case he was wounded or killed.

"Yes," said Steedman to his inquiry, "you can do me a great favor, and I beg that you will attend to it."

"What is it?" asked Granger.   "I swear to do it."

"See that my name is spelled right in the newspapers. The printers always spell it Stead."

And with this request Steedman rode into the battle. An hour or two after it had begun, his horse was shot under him, and another was brought for him. He mounted him, but the right stirrup-leather becoming twisted, he raised the stirrup with his foot, lifting his leg at the same time, in order to reach down and catch hold of the leather and take the twist out of it, when a musket-ball struck the strap, and, cutting it in two, passed between his leg and the saddle.

"By George!" exclaimed Steedman, "I'm all right!" and the troublesome presentiment passed away from his mind, for he was now firmly convinced that the bullet which had cut the leather was the one which he had had intimations to fear.

It is not generally known, I believe, that Granger and Steedman got to the battle-field of Chickamauga against orders.   Rosecrans had assigned to the reserve corps the duty of guarding Rossville Gap, a very important position ; but when the straggling troops of McCook began to pour into Chattanooga by this gap, Granger began looking about for Rosecrans, in the hope of getting orders to advance to Thomas's aid. While Granger was looking for orders, Steedman marched forward, and it was thus that he happened to reach Thomas's position before Granger did. Steedman has acted without orders in this way on more than one important occasion. He fought the battle of Carnifex Ferry, Western Virginia, without either orders or assistance, and defeated Floyd's brigade with a single regiment. He was ordered to hold Chattanooga when Hood marched against Nashville; but, finding no very formidable force near him, and being cut off from communication with Thomas at Nashville, Steedman left a small force of negro troops in Chattanooga, and started with a large force of white and negro volunteers for Nashville. Hood's cavalry advance cut the railroad and precipitated his trains into Mill Creek, a small stream a few miles from Nashville, but he fought his way through on foot to the city, and appeared with his ten thousand men before General Thomas's headquarters. To Thomas's look of inquiry, and perhaps of censure, Steedman replied,

"General, I was cut off from communication, and have come here in hopes I may get leave to re-enforce Nashville, and take a hand in the battle."

He got the order and the opportunity. In his report of his participation in the battle, he states that he made the movement by General Thomas's order, but does not explain how he obtained it.

Steedman had great faith in negro troops. One of his most daring efforts was that of leading a thousand negroes in a charge at Dalton, Georgia, upon Wheeler's cavalry, twenty-five hundred strong, defeating them, and capturing the place. His main force at the battle of Nashville was two brigades of negro troops, and their conduct was highly commended by him. He made much character and great personal popularity, while in command of the Department of Georgia, by his efforts in alleviating the condition of the freedmen. An incident illustrative of his policy with the freedmen, and his ideas of justice as applied to them, is told of him while stationed at Augusta, Georgia.

A railroad contractor came to him one day and asked for a military force to compel the negroes to work in repairing the line from Savannah to Augusta.

"They won't work, general," said the contractor.

"How much do you pay them?" asked the general.

"Ten dollars per month," was the answer.

"The devil!" exclaimed Steedman. "Give 'em thirty, and see whether they'll work then. I never gave a man less than eighty-seven and a half cents a day in my life. I think I could get a brigade at that price here. You try it; and, I say," he added, "if I hear of your offering less, I'll *try* you."

The contractor tried the plan, and found he had no use for a military guard, and no work for half the applicants who swarmed about his office.

Steedman in appearance is like a hale, hearty farmer, with stout, burly form, largely made, and of great physical power and endurance. He weighs over two hundred pounds, and is one of the strongest men in the country. He is as frank as he is bold, and as honest as impudent.

When General Rosecrans retired to Chattanooga during the battle of Chickamauga, thus abandoning his army, he committed the grand mistake of his military career. He soon found this to be so, and soon felt and knew that his unfortunate retreat had left him utterly defenseless. He feared at first to condemn any one, and endeavored to make friends with all. He could not condemn McCook and Crittenden, for in running away from the battle-field they had only followed his example, and to condemn them for this was to condemn himself. Some victim was necessary as an explanation of his defeat and retreat, and Generals Thomas J. Wood and James S. Negley were selected, the latter before and Wood after the removal of Rosecrans. Negley was a volunteer officer, who had incurred the enmity of Brannin, Davis, Baldy Smith, and one or two regular officers of inferior rank, and he was sacrificed by Rosecrans in order to obtain the support of what was known as the "regular clique" of the army, and which embraced these and other regular officers. Wood was not relieved by Rosecrans as Negley was, nor did Rosecrans venture to publicly censure him until after his own removal, when, very much to every body's surprise, Rosecrans condemned Wood in his official report for having caused the disaster to the army. The fact is that Rosecrans was not entitled to make a report of the battle of Chickamauga, for he did not see it, was not present, and, as written, his report, after its description of the general topography of North Alabama and Georgia, is merely a lame apology for his own strange conduct.

The two men thus made the scapegoats of Rosecrans were men of more than ordinary abilities, and it is a great pity that the reputation of such men should ever

N

be placed in the hands of such generals as Rosecrans. General Negley, though not educated for the army, was one of the best-read officers in military matters that we had in the volunteer service, and possessed a natural adaptation for, and many qualities as a leader. He was a man of quick perception and decided judgment, intuitive talents which "stood him in hand" on more than one occasion, as, for instance, at Stone River, where he replied to Breckenridge's assault of his troops by a counter-charge which, made with great force and rapidity, turned the fortunes of the day, and won an advantage which decided Bragg to abandon the field of which he was still master. Bragg relieved Breckenridge from his command for his defeat by Negley.

Among the most important services rendered by General Negley, or by any other general officer of the army, were the operations embracing the reconnoissance and battle at Dug Gap, Georgia, on September 11, 1863. He commanded the advance of the centre column of Rosecrans's army in crossing Lookout Mountain. The three columns had been widely separated—fifty miles intervening between the right wing and centre, and about thirty between the centre and left wing. Knowing this, Bragg had concentrated his forces in front of the centre, abandoning Chattanooga in such a way as to indicate he was in full retreat. Rosecrans ordered him to be pursued, and General Negley, debouching from Stevens's Gap of Lookout Mountain, was ordered to take Lafayette, Georgia. General Negley was advised and had reported that Bragg was concentrating his forces at that very point, but the report was discredited by General Rosecrans, and Negley was ordered forward. He advanced cautiously on the morning of September 11, in command of his own and Baird's divisions, and, as he anticipated, soon encountered the enemy. He drove them for some time, but soon found that he had Bragg's whole army in his front and on his flanks. It was subsequently dis-covered that Bragg had issued positive and peremptory orders to Generals Hindman, Hill, Buckner, and Polk, to attack and destroy Negley, promising himself the easy capture of the other columns in detail. But Negley was too shrewd to be caught thus; although his trains and those of Baird encumbered the road in his rear, which the enemy soon threatened by moving on his flanks, he succeeded in saving every wagon and in slowly retiring on Stevens's Gap, where he could afford to battle with thrice his numbers. This engagement, which lasted all the day, was the first convincing proof which Rosecrans had of the presence of Bragg, and the first premonition of danger. It induced him to gather his scattered col-umns together. General Negley's discretion and valor on this occasion were not only alike commended by Generals Rosecrans and Thomas, but by General Bragg, who, in his anger at their failure to destroy him, arrested Hindman and Polk, and preferred charges against them. These charges, which attributed Negley's escape from this danger to delay on the part of the rebel officers arrested, were never sustained, and they were returned to duty. The fact was that Negley had outwitted them, and had forewarned Rosecrans in time to save the army.

When the battle of Chickamauga began, General Neg-ley's division was on the move, marching to the sound of the artillery, and it reached the field just in time to push forward on the right and fill up a gap created by the dispersion of General Van Cleve's division. In the desperate fight which ensued, the rebel General Preston Smith was killed, and the enemy driven in confusion. On the second day of the battle General Negley's division was not so fortunate. One brigade was sent to the extreme left, another was placed in the centre, and the third held in reserve. Later in the day the general himself was taken from the command of the division and ordered to the command of a number of batteries which were concentrated on a hill on a new line to which it was proposed to retire, and which were intended to cover the retrograde movement. Before this manœuvre could be executed, however, the right wing and centre of the army were broken, and the troops fell back in confusion. The enemy charged upon the guns of General Negley in great force, and, moving upon the flanks, greatly threatened their capture. By great exertions the general succeeded in carrying them from the field without the aid of any infantry supports, and thus saved about fifty guns from capture.

On retiring to Rossville, he found himself, in the absence of Rosecrans, McCook, and Crittenden at Chattanooga, the senior officer in that part of the field, and he immediately began the work of reorganizing the troops of the several divisions gathered indiscriminately there. He succeeded in reorganizing a large number of men, and, selecting a strong position at Rossville Gap, endeavored to open communication with General Thomas. This was found impracticable, however. During the night

General Thomas retired to this position, and, forming a junction with General Negley, ordered him to post the forces along the line selected by him, and prepared to give the enemy a warm reception on the next morning. Bragg was too wise to attack, and contented himself with merely reconnoitering the position. On the succeeding day the troops were retired to Chattanooga, and preparations were made for the siege which followed. During this siege General Negley was relieved from duty by General Rosecrans in such a manner and so unjustly that he was induced to demand an examination into his official conduct. This was granted; a court of inquiry was convened and an investigation made, resulting in General Negley's acquittal. The official record of the court states in conclusion " that General Negley exhibited throughout the day (the second day of the battle) and the following night great activity and zeal in the discharge of his duties, and the court do not find in the evidence before them any ground for censure." General Negley, on the conclusion of the trial, was ordered to report to the Adjutant General at Washington, and did so, but soon after resigned. He is now engaged in the cultivation of his farm near Pittsburg, Pennsylvania.

Negley is one of the most accomplished horticulturists in the country, and when in the field of war his leisure hours were devoted to the study of various fruits, flowers, and shrubs in which the Southern fields and woods abounded. Many a march, long, tedious, exhausting, has been rendered delightful to his staff by his interesting descriptive illustrations of the hidden beauties and virtues of fragrant flowers and repulsive weeds. I have known him to spend hours in explaining the properties of shrubs and wild-flowers which grew about his bivouac or head-quarters, and he would, when on the march, frequently spring from his saddle to pluck a sensitive plant, that he might "point a moral" in showing how soon it, like life or fame, withered at the touch of death or disgrace. He was a remarkably well-made man—something of the robust, sinewy frame of Steedman and Buell. His grasp was like a vice. He was as tough as he was strong, and as elastic as enduring. He was an exceedingly prompt and active man, and his division of the Army of the Cumberland was by far its best in drill, appointments, and in its commissariat. Negley's troops used to boast that while he commanded they had never, under any circumstances, wanted for food or clothing, and they used frequently to call him "Commissary General Negley."

General Thomas J. Wood might in some slight respects be compared to Negley, but they appear to better effect when drawn in contrast. Negley was considered a martinet among volunteers, Wood a martinet among regulars. I do not mean martinet in the sense which a few brainless officers have given the title by their illustrations of it, but in its proper sense, as indicating a thorough and efficient disciplinarian. Both Negley and Wood made their men soldiers through discipline, and there were no better soldiers in the army. Their fate, too, was similar. The advancement of each was slow and labored, and their friends began to fear that their promotion was to be of that ungenerous, posthumous order which was too frequent, and which always looked to me like giving a handsome tomb-stone to a man unjustly treated all his life.

General Wood was a captious officer, but a decided, brave, and energetic one. History, which is rapidly beginning to be just, and which will grow harsher every day, and more just with all her harshness, will say that it was highly proper that the appointment of General Wood as major general should read as it did—"vice Crittenden, resigned." The place which that clever gentleman, but very poor soldier, Thomas L. Crittenden, filled, was properly Tom Wood's years before he got it, for he really filled it. Always under the command of Crittenden, he was ever at his right hand and as his right hand, and furnished him with all the military brains, and formed for him all the military character he ever had. It may be impolite to say this now, but it is anticipating history but a short time. This is a decree which must be submitted to eventually, and why not now?

When the army of Rosecrans was drawing itself up in front of Murfreesborough, Tennessee, the very day before the battle of December 31, 1862, Crittenden's wing was on the left, and Tom Wood's division held its advance. On approaching the rebel position, Wood, of course, came to a halt, and, reconnoitering the position, reported to Crittenden that the enemy were intrenched in his immediate front. Crittenden went forward to Wood's position and satisfied himself of the presence of the enemy in force, and approved the halt. A short time after he received a communication from General Rosecrans stating that General David S. Stanley, who, with his cavalry corps, had gone to Murfreesborough, reported that the

enemy had evacuated, and he therefore ordered Crittenden to cross Stone River and occupy the town. Crittenden showed the order to Wood, and told him that he
must advance and occupy the town. Wood argued that
Rosecrans's information, to his own and to Crittenden's
knowledge, was incorrect, and that, of course, it would
not do to implicitly obey the order. Crittenden thought
that its terms were positive, and no course was left him
but to obey it. Wood urged Crittenden to report the
circumstances, announce to Rosecrans that the movement
was delayed an hour in order to report those facts, and
stand ready to obey it if then repeated. It was some
time before Wood could make Crittenden understand
that this was the proper proceeding under the circumstances. He rode back to Rosecrans and reported the
facts, when that officer, examining for himself, approved
of the course pursued, and taught Crittenden that positive orders were not always to be implicitly obeyed.

In three years of active warfare Tom Wood won honor
from every action, from Shiloh to Nashville. The disasters of his corps were not disasters for him. He came
out of the crucibles refined and sparkling with renewed
glory. Whether proving, as he did at Shiloh, that he
had made by his discipline veterans out of men who had
never seen a battle—whether stemming the adverse current of battle at Chickamauga—whether scaling with ir-
resistible power the heights of Mission Ridge, and carrying at the point of the bayonet the strongly-manned position, which looked strong enough to hold itself—whether
repulsing the charge at Franklin, or making it at Nashville, he stands forth prominent as one of the coolest, self-

OLIVER O. HOWARD.

possessed, and gallant spirits of the day. I was glad to see him at the close of the war joining hands with his noble friend Rousseau for the redemption of Kentucky from slavery, and uniting with that band of progressive spirits to whom she will in a few years acknowledge that she owes her prosperity and welfare.

Among the many original characters whom I met, and who had been developed by the war, and by no means the least remarkable of them, was Major General Oliver Otis Howard. In many respects he was not unlike General George H. Thomas, possessing the same quiet, dignified, and reserved demeanor, the same methodical turn of mind, and the same earnest, industrious habits: but Howard was Thomas with the addition of several peculiarities, not to say eccentricities. He had none of General Thomas's cold-bloodedness, and though, like him, a statue in dignity of demeanor, Howard, unlike Thomas, had blood in him that often flowed warm with sympathy, and pulses that sometimes beat quicker with excitement. General Thomas guided himself in his course through life by his immediate surroundings, adapting himself, without sycophancy, however, to present circumstances without regard to past consistency, and was in power and favor at all times, because content to obey as long as he remained a subordinate. Howard began life with certain aims in view, and sailed a straight course, remaining always constant to his principles, and consequently finding himself, like all men with either firm principles or advanced ideas, at times unpopular. He had little of General Thomas's practicability, and General Thomas had little of Howard's faith in the strength and final triumph •

of great principles.   One trusted in the physical strength, the other in the innate power of the principles of a great cause.   Thomas believed the late war the triumph of good soldiers over their inferiors—the triumph of num-bers, skill, and strength; Howard will tell you, with a flush of feeling and a slight touch of the extravagance of an enthusiast, that it was the triumph of right over wrong.   Thomas thinks, with Napoleon, that God sides with the force that has the most cannon; Howard be-lieves, with Bryant, that "the eternal years of God" are truths; and with the Psalmist, that

"Great is truth, and mighty above all things."

The faith of Howard in the principles which he advo-cated was sublime.   I knew of but one other who began the war with loftier purposes of universal good, purer motives of right, justice, and liberty, or truer ideas of the nature of the struggle as a crusade against slavery and ignorance, and he was not a general—only a major of infantry, though a brilliant "first section" graduate at West Point, but worthy ten times over of greater rank than the army could grant.   Nothing could have been more beautiful than the firm faith which William H. Si-dell felt from the first in the final triumph of the right, not merely in restoring the country to its former glory, unity, and strength, but in restoring and rejuvenating it, purified of that which was at once its weakness and its shame.   It is somewhat of a digression to run off from Howard in this manner to speak of Major Sidell, but every reader who knew the man will think it pardonable. Sidell was a man of firm convictions, and hence a man of great influence.   It used to seem to me that he was intended for the single purpose of making up other people's minds, and deciding for his acquaintances what was right and what wrong. He possessed a singularly effective, epigrammatical style of conversation, and his generally very original ideas were always expressed with great force and vigor. When he got hold of a great idea, he would talk it at you without cessation, repeating it as frequently as he found a hearer, and persist with something of the manner of those religious preachers who pride themselves on "preaching in season and out of season" until conviction followed. His ideas possessed not only value, but his language had a stamp as coinage has, and both ideas and language passed current. His ideas, oft repeated, thoroughly inculcated, found wide circulation in the army with which he served, and it was often amusing to hear his language repeated in places where they were least expected, and by persons who were never suspected of possessing minds capable of retaining grand ideas, or hearts true enough to comprehend great principles. His ideas were traceable in the language of the soldiers, relieved and often illustrated by the happy use of their familiar, commonplace "slang." They got strangely mixed up in the orders of commanding generals with whom he served, and I have even detected Sidell's undeniable stamp in one of the Executive documents.

The great charm of the man was the effective style in which he advocated the firm convictions of his mind, and expressed the deep sympathies of his nature; and no man could rise from a conversation on the topics to which his mind naturally reverted, whenever he found a willing listener, without feeling the better for it, and with a better opinion of humanity in general. If he had a fault, it was that he conceived too much. His was

" A vigorous, various, versatile mind,"

which grasped a subject as if to struggle with it, and pursued an idea "to the death." It was, however, only his convictions in regard to great principles that 'he inculcated and forced upon others. He originated so much that he executed too little, and never gave practical effect to two or three of his mechanical inventions which have made fortunes for more practical and more shallow men. Sidell was in some respects the only counterpart I ever met to Sherman, and the parallel between them only held good with regard to their head work. They conceived equally, but Sherman executed most.

General Howard possessed these same attributes of firm, honest conviction, and the same fixedness of principles which distinguished Sidell. His moral honesty won him more admiration than his speeches or his abilities as a soldier; for, though energetic and persevering in his administration as a commander, and generally successful in his military efforts, his reputation in the army was more that of the Christian gentleman than of the great soldier. It was through the constant observation of his Christian duties that he won the title of the "Havelock of the war" and the reputation of an exemplar. He was strictly temperate, never imbibing intoxicating drinks, never profane, and always religious. There was not a great excess of religion in the army, particularly among the general officers, and Howard therefore became a prominent example, the more particularly as religion was looked upon by a great majority of the men only to be ridiculed. There was very little of religious feeling among the men of the army, save among those in the hospital.. The hospital was the church of the camp, and there was little religious fervor among our veterans which did not date from the hospital. The soldier in the hospital was another being from the soldier in camp. He abandoned his bad habits when he lost his health or received his wound, and grew serious as he grew sick. The lion of the camp was invariably the lamb of the hospital. The almost universal habit of swearing in camp was abandoned in the hospital; profanity gave place to prayer, and the sick veteran became meek, talked in soft tones, and never failed to thank you for the smallest kindnesses where before he had laughed at them. I have often seen the convalescents gather in the sunshine to sing familiar hymns, and generally the wildest in camp were the most earnest in these religious exercises.

When Howard took command of the Army of the Tennessee, an old officer remarked that there was at last one chaplain in it. That particular army had not paid much attention to religion, believing, like Sherman, that crackers and meat were more necessary; and at first the men displayed but little respect for the "intruder from the Potomac," as much, indeed, from the fact that he came from the Potomac army as that he was what the men called " nothing but a parson." A very short time after taking command of this army, Howard gave orders that the batteries of his command, then in position besieging Atlanta, should not fire on the enemy on the Sabbath, unless it became absolutely necessary. The enemy soon heard of this order, and generally busied themselves on the Sabbath in casemating their guns and otherwise strengthening their works in Howard's front, exposing themselves with impunity, satisfied that Howard's men would keep the Sabbath holy, though doing so under compulsion. The soldiers did not like this forced silence, declaring that "it wasn't Grant's nor Sherman's way, nor Black Jack's (Logan) neither;" and one of the general officers went so far as to say that "a man who neglected his duty because it happened to be Sunday was doubtless a Christian, but not much of a soldier." The troops soon learned, however, that Howard was also a soldier; and when, a year afterward, he was relieved of the command by General Logan, he had won the love and admiration of his men.

General Howard would have liked to have been thought the representative man of the Army of the Tennessee, but there were no points of resemblance between him and the real representative man of that army. The Western soldiers were of a peculiar race, and under Grant the Army of the Tennessee, the representative army of the West, was drilled, marched, and fought into a peculiar type of an army. Sherman took command of it subsequently, and gave it many peculiarities, not all of which were creditable; but neither Grant nor Sherman were its representatives. Howard endeavored to reform the army morally and in its discipline, which even under Grant had been bad, and under Sherman very lax indeed, but failed to impart to it as a body any of the qualities which shone so prominently in his character. The real

JOHN A. LOGAN.

representative man of that remarkable army was General John A. Logan, of Illinois.

"Black Jack Logan," as he was facetiously called by his soldiers, in consequence of his dark complexion, is the very opposite in appearance and manner of Howard. Logan is a man of Sheridan's short and stumpy style of figure. Sheridan used to be called by the card-playing soldiers the "Jack of Clubs," and Logan was known as the "Jack of Spades." Logan is, too, the same daring, enthusiastic, and vigorous fighter that Sheridan is. He will always be prominent among the Marshal Neys of the war for the Union, and belongs to that representative class of fighting generals of which Sheridan, Hancock, Rousseau, and Hooker are the most distinguished graduates. A man of great daring, and full of dash and vim, Logan was, like the others, great only as a leader, and made no pretensions to generalship. He had the habit of decision to perfection, and went at every thing apparently without previous thought. He is a man who, possessing all that vigor and boldness of heart which great physical strength and health gives, united with a naturally warm, enthusiastic, and daring temperament, engaged heart and soul in every task that allured or interested him, and never abandoned it as a failure. A man of action, he was untiring, and, did he more definitely lay out his plans in life, would win a front place among the great men of the age. Not that he is vacillating, nor yet indecisive, but simply because he is not thoughtful, far-seeing, and politic, but impulsive. He is, indeed, too passionate to ever be politic.

With little prudence in planning, Logan had the daring to act, and his decision was shown in frequent emergencies. During the battle of Hope Church, Georgia, the rebels made a sudden charge upon a battery posted in Logan's line, and, before being repulsed, had secured two of the guns, which they attempted to carry off with them. Logan was busy in another part of the field, but, seeing the rebels retiring unpursued with the trophies of their charge, he dashed up to one of the regiments which had repulsed them, and exclaiming to his men, " Bring back those guns, you d—d rascals," led them in a charge for their recovery. The men followed him without regard to formation, and overtook and defeated the rebels before they could reach their lines, and secured the captured artillery.

On another occasion, when new to the service, a portion of Logan's regiment mutinied, and, stacking arms, refused to do duty. The adjutant informed Colonel Logan of the difficulty, and he, on hearing it, exclaimed, " Stacked arms! the devil they have!" Then, pausing a second as he considered the emergency, he continued, " Well, adjutant, I'll give them enough of stacking arms!" Accordingly, he formed the remaining four companies in line with loaded muskets, and stood them over the malcontents, whom he compelled to stack and unstack arms for twelve hours.

Logan's readiness to act was not always acceptable to his immediate commanders, because perhaps in some instances his activity was a reproach to less decisive men. Indecision and too great precaution in others was revolting to him; and I think I never saw a more thoroughly disgusted man than Logan was on the occasion of the failure before Resaca, Georgia, on May 9, 1864, consequent on the refusal of McPherson to assault the town. Not only was Logan's offer to accomplish the desired object declined as impracticable, but the campaign was robbed of its promised fruits by that refusal, and not only Logan, but the whole country had reason to be disgusted. Logan took no pains to conceal his chagrin and disgust. The facts of the unfortunate affair were about these:

The Army of the Tennessee, at the time forming the right wing of Sherman's Grand Army, had, on the morning of May 9, debouched through the narrow defile of Snake Creek Gap, and appeared before Resaca, McPherson having positive orders to occupy the place. The movement through the Gap had turned Joe Johnston's position at Dalton, placed the Army of the Tennessee in his rear, and, if Resaca had been taken, would have closed the direct route to Atlanta, and forced the rebels to retreat by circuitous and almost impracticable roads, and at the probable cost of all his trains and heavy guns. There was no good reason, had Resaca been carried, why Johnston should not have been seriously damaged, and perhaps his army dispersed; and there is no good reason why Resaca was not taken on this occasion. The force defending it was the small garrison of a ten-gun fort and sixteen hundred dismounted cavalry under the rebel General Canty, who were engaged in patroling and observing the Oostanaula River. Johnston could not, on May 9, have concentrated two thousand men at Resaca for its defense. General McPherson had not less than thirty thousand men in front of the position, and not a mile distant from the fort. Unfortunately, General Granville M.

Dodge, commanding the Sixteenth Corps, and a man of even less decision than McPherson, happened on that morning to be in advance, and Logan was in reserve. On approaching Resaca, and after occupying a low ridge of hills commanding the town and the river in its front, General Dodge halted his command and began to reconnoitre. The delay in the advance brought McPherson and Logan to the front, and from a prominent knob of the range of hills which had been carried by Dodge, they examined the town and calculated in their own minds the chances of carrying the position. Dodge finally reported the passage of the river and the capture of the fort as impracticable, and declared it as his belief that a large force was then in the town. Logan rather warmly and hastily disputed this, and declared that he could carry the fort and town with his corps. General McPherson revolved the matter over in his mind, and as the woman who hesitates is lost, so with the commander who in an emergency stops to calculate, he lost the opportunity. While he was hesitating and doubting between the arguments of Dodge and the assertions and declarations of Logan—for Logan is not the man to offer arguments when the opportunity for demonstration is at hand—time was consumed, and finally, much to the disgust of every body who had come out to fight, McPherson ordered the whole army back to Snake Creek Gap, and employed a large part of it all the ensuing night in throwing up works to defend a defile which was apparently strong enough to defend itself.

The next day Sherman began moving the rest of the army through Snake Creek Gap, and at the same time Johnston evacuated Dalton, and began marching on Resaca. At night on that or the next day, May 11th, while General Logan and staff and myself were at supper, General John M. Palmer and others on the march stopped at Logan's tent, and were asked to take a cup of coffee. While we were eating, the conversation turned on the situation, and I remarked that evidently "Joe Johnston had been caught sleeping." Logan and Palmer both in a breath answered that it wasn't at all certain that Johnston was napping, but that, on the contrary, it was very improbable that we could do more than strike his rear guard at Resaca. This turned out, in the end, to be the case. The whole of Sherman's army was not ready to advance until the 12th of May, when it moved forward, Logan this time in advance, and occupied, after considerable hard fighting with Johnston's rear division, the very same position which McPherson had previously held on the 9th, and from which, even with Resaca uncaptured, Johnston would have had great difficulty in dislodging him. But now, three days behind time, Sherman, and Thomas, and Logan, and a number of others who had gathered on the bald knob to which I have before alluded as overlooking Resaca, had the melancholy pleasure of witnessing Joe Johnston's army filing through the town and taking up positions defending it, and covering the bridges and fords of the Oostanaula.

When he had first secured this position, Logan ordered one of his batteries, commanded by Captain De Gress, to take position on the knob I have mentioned, and open upon the bridge and fort. The order was obeyed with alacrity. Courage is a sort of magnet which attracts its like; it surrounded Logan with men of his own stamp, among whom were Major Charles J. Stolbrand and Captain Francis De Gress, and it was not long before these two had the battery posted and ready to open at Logan's command. I was at the time on this knob, and anticipated seeing some handsome artillery practice and a great scattering among the rebels, very plainly visible below, crossing the river and moving about in the fort, not much over a mile distant. But it was destined that the scattering should be among our own forces supporting De Gress's battery and lying along the ridge, and particularly was there to be "much scattering" on my part. I had noticed, as had others, the peculiar appearance of the hill on which the battery was posted and on which I stood, but had not suspected why the change had been wrought. The trees, with the exception of a single tall, straight oak left standing in the centre and on the very summit of the knob, had been carefully felled, and the tops thrown down the sides and slope of the hill, forming a sort of abatis, and making the approach to the summit rather difficult. Several persons had made inquiries and suggestions as to the purpose of the rebels in clearing the hill and forming the abatis around it, but it was not until De Gress had opened fire on Resaca that the mystery was solved. Then it suddenly flashed on the minds of all simultaneously with the flash of the first rebel gun in the fort in Resaca. The first round of De Gress came very near being his last, for the ten guns in the rebel fort beyond the river opened simultaneously on him, and every shot fell among the guns and troops supporting them. It was then discovered that the hill on which De Gress had posted his guns had been cleared by the rebels and one tree left standing as a target for artillery practice. For at least a year the gunners in the fort in Resaca had been practicing by firing at this tree, and they had the range of the hill to such accuracy that every shot fell in our midst. The first broadside sent me to cover, and I hastily dropped behind a huge oak stump left standing, and which afforded ample protection. Here I could see the rebels at their guns, watch De Gress and Stolbrand at theirs, and, by turning half around, see the troops which lay near me supporting the battery. The first shells thrown by the rebels had wounded several of these, and their cries of pain, as they were carried to the rear, could be plainly heard, and did not in any great measure add to my comfort, or increase my confidence in the invulnerability of my position, and I began to conclude it was not bomb proof. Meantime the rebels were firing vigorously, and after two or three shots De Gress was silenced—not that his guns were disabled, but that the men could not work them. The place was literally too hot to allow of a man exposing himself, and all but Logan, Stolbrand, and De Gress sought cover, and clung as closely as possible to the ground. These three, however, stood their ground, very foolishly I thought at the time, and how they escaped being struck I can not conceive. The fire of the rebels was singularly accurate, and from the cries of our wounded it was apparent that it was also very effective. I had been lying behind the stump whose protection I had sought for twenty minutes, looking with interest at the firing of the rebels, when a shell from one of their guns struck directly in front of the stump, entered and plowed up the ground for a distance

O

of ten feet, sending the soil high in the air like spray, and then, striking the stump, bounded high above it, and fell about five feet behind me with a heavy *thug!* The soil which had been thrown up by it descended about me, and, as I crouched low, making myself as small as possible, and wishing myself even smaller, literally buried me alive. I thought every piece of the soil which struck me was going through me. At last, when the shell descended near me, my demoralization was complete. Fearing that it would explode, I sprang up from my recumbent position and ran with all my speed to the left of the line. As I did so I came to the abatis of timber, heaped at least four feet high. I never stopped to consider, but, without hesitation, made a tremendous leap, and cleared the obstructions at a bound, amid the loud laughter of a whole brigade, which, looking on, actually rose up to laugh at and applaud my hasty retreat. When I reached a place of safety out of range of the rebels, and beyond reach of the particular shell which I had so much dreaded, I found that the confounded thing had not exploded. I was too much demoralized, however, to contemplate going back while the rebels held the range of that hill, and so sat down, carefully getting behind another stump, to receive the congratulations of the colonel and adjutant of one of the supporting regiments on the gymnastic abilities which I had just displayed.

It was not until sundown and after the cessation of the firing that I ventured to return to the hill. Here Logan and Stolbrand still remained, and Sherman, Thomas, and others had also come up. While the others consulted together Logan sat aside, leaning against *my* stump, and

JOHN W. GEARY.

looking exceedingly glum and disgusted. When I approached him he looked up and laughed, evidently at the recollection of my demoralization and flight. I sat down beside him and said,

" Well, general, you see I was right last night. Some body was asleep."

" Yes," said he, in answer, "but you was mistaken in the person. It was not Joe Johnston who was napping."

There was good reason to be morose over this affair. The failure of McPherson on the 9th of May made the campaign of Atlanta a necessity. Had Logan, instead of Dodge, been in advance of McPherson's army on the 9th of May, there would have been no Hope Church affair, no Kenesaw Mountain sacrifice, no battles on the Chattahoochee, or before Atlanta, or at Jonesborough, for the campaign would have been ended, and Atlanta captured at Resaca in the dispersion of Joe Johnston's army.

Something of this same ability in execution which was developed in Logan and the others to whom I have alluded characterized General John W. Geary, of Pennsylvania, and few officers labored more zealously or more effectively than he did. His adventurous disposition, developed early in life, and leading him to a remarkably varied career, could not be other than the result of a bold and daring nature, which led him early to seek activity when he might have chosen a more passive but less glorious life. His enthusiastic ardor for military life rendered him in his youth an adept in all military matters, and led him naturally into the military service of the country. He was built, too, for a soldier, possessing a rare *physique*, his tall, burly figure reminding one of

Rousseau or Steedman. His adventurous career began in Mexico, where, as colonel of the Second Pennsylvania, he served with distinction under Scott, from Vera Cruz to the capital, suffering wounds at Chepultepec and at the assault of the city of Mexico. After the war, sighing, like Hooker, for the excitements of California, he went to San Francisco, and was soon after appointed postmaster, and subsequently elected mayor. President Pierce appointed him Governor of Kansas, but Buchanan decapitated him on account of his adherence to the person and principles of Douglas. He early entered the war for the Union as Colonel of the Twenty-eighth Pennsylvania Infantry, and fought through each grade to the position of major general, winning a bright reputation as a bold and unflinching fighter.

The most remarkable of Geary's exploits was the famous " midnight battle of Wauhatchie," a sort of companion picture to Joe Hooker's " battle above the clouds." It took place, too, at the foot of the mountain on which Hooker fought, and was, in a measure, preliminary to that struggle. It was fought for position, but a position of vital importance to both the rebels and Union forces, and consequently it was fought for with great desperation. The movement which brought it about was the first of those looking to the relief of the starving army at Chattanooga, and the purpose was to occupy a position which would cover a road by which provisions could be brought from the railroad terminus at Bridgeport. The occupation of this position was absolutely necessary, and Geary was fully impressed with the importance of quickly seizing and desperately holding on to it. By the success of the movement the route to Bridgeport would be shortened by many miles; on its being thus shortened depended the provisioning of Chattanooga; on this contingency depended the holding of that position, and on the retention of that position the safety of the army and its immense and valuable material.

Geary seized the position with great alacrity, and much to the astonishment of the rebel Longstreet, who watched him from the summit of Lookout Mountain. From his position on "Signal Rock"—an overarching rock on the western side of the mountain—Longstreet had before his eyes the whole country as on a map, and when, in the dusk of evening, the camp-fires of Geary and Howard's troops located the positions which Hooker had seized and was fortifying, the importance of the success attained flashed upon Longstreet's mind in an instant, and he saw, in the seizure of Wauhatchie by Geary, the virtual relief of the besieged garrison of Chattanooga. He at once communicated with Bragg, and on explaining the altered situation to that officer, the latter at once directed Longstreet to attack Geary and Howard, and drive them back at all hazards. Longstreet returned to his position on "Signal Rock," and soon had his troops in readiness to descend from their position on the mountain, and assault Geary at Wauhatchie. From his position on "Signal Rock" Longstreet directed the assault by signals, and to this circumstance, singularly enough, he owed his defeat. Geary's force was totally inadequate to contend with the superior forces of the enemy. General Schurz, who was sent by Hooker to re-enforce him, never reached the position, and but from the fact that Geary's signal-officers could read the rebel signals, he must have been over-whelmed and driven from the position. For some months previous to this battle our signal-officers had been in possession of the rebel signal code, and hence the flaming torches of Longstreet's signal-officers on "Signal Rock" revealed to Geary every order given to the rebel troops advancing against him. He was thus made aware of Longstreet's plan of attack, was enabled to anticipate and meet every movement of the rebels, and, thus forewarned, so to employ his small force by concentration in the crit-ical part of the field at the critical moment of attack as to repulse every assault which was made, either by counter-charges or rapid flank movements. After re-peatedly throwing themselves against Geary's force in vain, the rebels at length drew off discomfited. During the whole battle the flaming torch of Longstreet flashed orders that showed, after each repulse, his increased des-peration, and finally, much to Geary's gratification, he saw it signal the recall. All the while the figure of Longstreet on "Signal Rock," standing out boldly against the dark sky, was plainly visible, and, as Geary once re-marked, forcibly reminded him of a picture which he had once seen of Satan on the mountain pointing out the riches of the world to the Tempted, save that only the figure of the Tempter was visible.

CHAPTER VIII.

SOME PECULIARITIES OF OUR VETERANS.

EVERY leader of our armies has had his story written —has carved it out with his sword, and impressed himself on the time.

But who shall write the history of our soldiers?

Who shall dare attempt to tell the story or portray the characteristics of our veterans?

The nation, in its hour of distress, found leaders worthy to lead in any cause. No better marshals followed the great Napoleon. We shall leave to posterity the task of comparing our greatest general, Grant, with Napoleon; but the present generation may be bold enough to defy any ardent admirer of the "Little Corporal" to find among his marshals the equal of Grant, who rather resembles in his characteristics, and, it is said, in his features too, the conqueror of Napoleon. We developed, indeed, counterparts for all the great generals of modern warfare. The tenacious Thomas has the colossal proportions of mind and body of Kleber, the clearness in danger of Massena, and, though ponderous and unwieldy in his movements, is not more so than was Macdonald. Halleck, like Marmont, "understands the theory of war perfectly," and we might say of him, as Soult once said of Marmont, and in the same sarcastic sense, that "History will tell what he

did with his knowledge." His biographer's description
of Mack, wherein he says, "Although able in the war
office, he was wholly deficient in the qualities of a commander in the field," is a perfect description of Halleck,
and adding the paragraph about Mack's popularity with
the soldiers it applies equally well to McClellan. The
"first strategist of Europe," Soult, was not one whit the
superior in conception of Sherman, and not his equal in
mobility and energy. Sherman has all the vigor and
acuteness which characterized Frederick the Great, and
is at heart his equal as a military despot. Hooker has
all the ardor, and Howard all the enthusiasm of Gustavus, and were capable of as great things. Steedman has
all the roughness, nonchalance, and impudence of Suwa-
roff. McPherson was a Moreau, alike young, indecisive,
and unfortunate. True, we have developed many Grou-
chys, who can not command above a few thousand men,
and several Berthiers, who can not even calculate a day's
march correctly; but we have also given opportunity to
one or two Neys in Sheridan and Rousseau, and several
Murats in Hancock, Logan, and Gordon Granger.

But not less worthy of the cause have been the men
who fought in the ranks of our armies, and still more
worthy to be compared to the best armies of Europe than
are our generals to be paralleled with the great leaders of
Europe. The superiors of our veterans never witnessed
battle. They form, as combined in armies, a study not
less enticing and interesting than that of the characters
of their leaders.

One of the many fallacies which have been dissipated
by our late warlike experience is the idea which once

prevailed that an uneducated man made as good, if not a better soldier than the educated man. When the late war began, it was an assertion made as positively as frequently. It was believed, particularly by the regular officers, that the persons of the former class more readily and completely adapted themselves to the discipline of the camps—more readily became the pliant and obedient tools that regular soldiers are too often made. It is to the veteran volunteers of the late war for the Union that we are indebted for the explosion of this fallacy. The proofs of its falsity are not less interesting than conclusive.

Every reader familiar with the history of modern warfare in Europe must have noticed, in watching the events of the late rebellion in this country, the very great difference between the practice of war as carried on in Europe and by ourselves. The rules have been the same; the theory of war is too firmly and philosophically established to be changed. It can not be said that we originated a single new rule, but our application of those long established has been unlike any other practice known to history. The extent of the field of operations, the peculiar configuration of the country, and the extended line of coast and inland frontier which each party to the contest had to guard, conspired to this end, and caused to be originated such peculiarities of warfare as long and arduous raids by entire armies, flank marches of an extent and boldness never before conceived, the construction of many leagues of fortified lines, and the execution of strategic marches of great originality and brilliancy, while there have been effected at the same time, owing to changes and improvements in the arms, several innovations in minor tactics not less curious than important. The contending parties fought dozens of battles, each of which would have been decisive of a war between any two of the great powers of Europe. There the limits of the field of operations are restricted by the presence of armed neutral powers on each frontier. Here the line of frontier extended across a whole continent. No necessities exist there, as here, for large numbers of large armies. The most important and extensive modern European wars witnessed the prosecution of only one important operation at a time, while in this country we have carried on several campaigns simultaneously, and fought pitched battles whose tactical as well as strategic success depended on the result of operations five hundred miles distant. Bragg won the victory of Chickamauga only by the aid of re-enforcements sent him from Richmond; the besieged army of Rosecrans at Chattanooga was saved from dispersion only by the timely re-enforcements sent him, under Hooker, from Washington; while Schofield, with twenty thousand men, after fighting at Nashville, Tennessee, in the middle of winter, was operating in North Carolina, opening communications with Sherman, a fortnight subsequently. In Europe, concentration is forced on each party by the configuration and confined area of the seat of war. In this country the opposite effect has naturally been the result of the opposite circumstances, and the finest display of generalship which we have had was shown by Grant in the consummate skill with which, in the latter year of the war, he concentrated our two greatest armies, and employed his cavalry against the vital point of the rebellion, while with the fractional organizations he kept the enemy employed in the far West. Generally speaking, any two European powers at war are represented each by a single army, which are brought together upon a field of battle to decide at a blow the question in dispute, and thus the European generals are afforded better chances for the display of tactical abilities. In Europe, cavalry plays an important part on every battle-field, while in this country its assistance has seldom been asked in actual battle, though a no less effective application has been made of it in destroying communications. Except in the battle of General Sheridan, and in some instances where accident has brought cavalry into battle, our troopers were never legitimately employed. The art of marching as practiced in Europe was also varied here, and the European system of supplying an army is very different from our own. Their lines of march are decided by the necessities for providing cantonments in the numerous villages of the country, while on this continent marches are retarded, if not controlled, by the necessity of carrying tents for camps. The parallel which is here merely outlined might be pursued by one better fitted for the task to a highly suggestive and interesting conclusion.

In the same sense, and in still better defined contrast, the armies of America and of Europe have differed in their *personnel*. The armies of the principal powers of Europe are composed of men forced to arms by necessity in time of peace, and conscriptions in time of war; not, like the people of our own country, volunteering when the crisis demanded, with a clear sense of the danger before them, and for the stern purpose of vindicating the flag, and forcing obedience to the laws of the country. The European soldiers are conscripted for life, become confirmed in the habits of the camp, and are subjected to a system of discipline which tends to the ultimate purpose of rendering them mere pliant tools in the hands of a leader; while those of the United States, separated from the outer world only by the lax discipline necessary to the government of a camp, are open to every influence that books, that letters, and, to a certain extent, that society can lend. The highest aim of the European system is to sink individuality, and to teach the recruit that he is but the fraction of a great machine, to the proper working of which his perfectness in drill and discipline is absolutely necessary. In the United States volunteer army this same system was only partially enforced, and individuality was lost only on the battle-field, and then only so far as was necessary to *morale* did the man sink into the soldier. The private who in camp disagreed and disputed with his captain on questions of politics or science was not necessarily disobedient and demoralized on the battle-field. No late opportunity for a comparison between the prowess of our own and any European army has been presented, though the reader will have very little difficulty in convincing himself that the discipline of our troops in the South was better than that of the English in the Crimea or the French in Italy; while the "outrages of the Northern soldiers," at which England murmured in her partiality for the rebels, were not certainly as horrible as those committed by her own troops in India.

This same difference was visible in the *personnel* of our

own and the rebel armies, and it resulted from the same cause, and that cause was education. The Union army was superior in prowess to that of the South because superior in discipline, and it was superior in discipline because superior in education. The Union army was recruited from a people confirmed in habits of industry, and inured to hard and severe manual and mental labor. That of the rebels was recruited from among men reared in the comparative idleness of agricultural life, and not habituated to severe toil, or conscripted from that hardier class of "poor whites" whose spirits had been broken by long existence in a state of ignorance and of slavery not less abject because indirectly enforced and unsuspectedly endured. Neither fraction of the rebel army, as a class, was the equal either in refinement, education, or habits of the men of the North, nor were both combined in an army organization equal in discipline, or the courage and effectiveness which results from it, to that which sprang to the nation's aid in 1861. Although the camp morality of both armies might have been better, there can be no doubt in any unprejudiced mind that the moral sentiment of the soldiers of the North was much more refined and correct than that of the organized forces of the South. Not only was their discipline better, not only were they under superior control in battle and in camp, but when, at times, relieved of the restrictions which are thrown around camps, their thoughts naturally turned less to dissipation and excesses than those of the Southern soldiers. The military despotism at the South was much more severely enforced by the rebel armies than it was by our own, though looked upon as that of an enemy. The excesses which at times existed in both armies were of Southern parentage. Sherman's "bummers" were legitimate descendants of Morgan's raiders and Stuart's cavalry, and at no time during the period in which they were "let loose" in Georgia and South Carolina could they excel Wheeler's cavalry in the art of plundering and destroying. The destruction of Atlanta and Columbia by our army under Sherman occurred nearly two years after the burning of Chambersburg by the rebels under Ewell.

The superiority of our veterans over those of the rebel armies was evinced not only in the grand result of the war, but in all its details. Their superior endurance was acknowledged by their enemies on dozens of fields, and their superior discipline was generally confessed. Northern men are by nature no braver than Southern men, and the superiority of the Northern army was not the result of natural gifts, but of cultivation. The Northern people are the superiors of the Southern classes, first, in education, and, secondly, in habits and physique. Their endurance was the result of the latter advantage; their superiority in discipline and *morale* was naturally the consequence of the former. Though something of the spirit, endurance, patience, and thorough discipline of our armies was to be attributed to the consciousness of the justice of the cause for which they fought, the general superiority of our veterans over the rebel soldiers was, without dispute, the result of the superior general education received by the Northern masses.

And, *par parenthesis*, while on this subject of education, let me stop to say, even though I break the continuity of the argument, that I think, if there is a single duty which the North, as the conqueror, owes to the South as the conquered, it is the granting to her people —ay, even enforcing upon them, the great educational advantages with which the North is so bountifully blessed. The first plank in the reconstruction platform of the *people*—not the mere politicians, for so much virtue can not be expected of them—should provide for the education of the Southern masses, white as well as black. All the reconstruction schemes which have been advanced are calculated for speedy operation, and political power, not the social improvement and prosperity of the people, is aimed at. Universal suffrage, as a remedy, is chimerical, and one which can not enter into the practical solution of the question. Negro suffrage is an experiment as dangerous to the country as it can possibly be advantageous to the negro. I would gladly see the present generation of adult negroes allowed by the states to vote in all local elections, for his vote is really all the protection he has against the injustice of an elective judiciary, each member of which naturally enough decides in all suits against the negro without a vote, to curry favor and popularity with the white man with a vote. But in the event of a general election for presidency, the giving of the right of suffrage to the negroes would be practically equivalent to throwing the power of the government again into the hands of the three hundred thousand slaveholders who formerly ruled the country, and who, still remaining the capitalists of the South, through the influence of their capital would rule the vote of the negroes and laborers. A generation for reconstruction is short enough, and the only true means for the permanent re-construction of the people is through education.

The great strength of the rebellion lay in the ignorance of the Southern masses. The "poor whites" of the South are among the most ignorant people on the face of God's earth. The slaveholders purposely kept them in igno-rance—kept them from books, and schools, and news-papers more carefully, more persistently than they did their slaves. They surrounded their section and their people with a Chinese wall of prejudice, against which all arrays of fact, argument, appeal, threw themselves in vain. Through this ignorance, the "poor whites" of the South were ruled even more despotically than the slaves; and through this ignorance the slaveholders of the South were enabled to commit the greatest of wrongs against hu-manity. They engendered prejudices between the "poor whites" and the negroes, never losing an opportunity of fostering the hatred and enmity which they were soon enabled to create. A perfect system prevailed all over the South, and the "poor whites" were placed in every position, socially, politically, and otherwise, in which they could be made offensive to the slaves. The harsh over-seer was always a "poor white," and, if possible, he was selected from among the "Yankee" emigrants; the sher-iff who tied the slave to the whipping-post, and the con-stable who laid on the lash, were always elected from the "poor whites;" and the men who, with bloodhounds, hunted the runaway negro through marsh and wood, were hired from among the "poor white" neighbors. In their ignorance, these two factions of the same laboring class of the South were made to believe that their interests were antagonistic instead of identical, and that the slaveholders were the mutual enemies of each. Andrew Johnson, in laboring for years in Tennessee to create a feeling of antagonism between the " poor whites" and the rich slaveholders, was touching at one root of the evil, but not the root. The war has thrown open the field to the laborers of the North, and if the people of the country seek to restore harmony, to obliterate all sectional feelings, to make the union of the States really one and indivisible, they must aid in the work of educating the Southern people, black and white, into understanding their former condition and false positions toward each other. A few good men, like General Wager Swayne (who understands this great question thoroughly, who is a charming enthusiast on the subject, and who ought to be at the head of an Educational Bureau instead of a subordinate in the Freedmen's Bureau), and General Davis Tillson, and one or two others, are doing much good by encouraging education among the negroes. But the sympathy of the country should not be entirely absorbed by the blacks. There are four millions of " poor whites" in the South who need education fully as much as do the negroes, and, deceived, betrayed, and ruined by their leaders, they deserve sympathy and aid fully as much. One inalienable right which should not be denied even to traitors—and if there had been education at the South there would have been no treason—is the right to educate himself; and since the Constitution provides that there shall be no attainder of blood for treason, the North owes it to the rising generation of these deceived people to educate them into a proper appreciation of the liberty which our veterans have won for them in defeating and conquering their fathers. Oh, how grand and sublime would appear the record in history that the Great Republic, after putting down the most monstrous rebellion the world ever saw, imposed upon the conquered only the tax for their own education, and erected no prisons save those of the school-house and the church!

In returning to the subject of the effect of education on armies, I have even a better illustration of the idea I have advanced than those already given. When the war first broke out, it will be remembered that the organization of the troops, brigades, and even divisions were formed of regiments coming from a single state, and we were thus rapidly falling into an error which, had it not been wisely corrected, would have left us, at the close of the war, with an army distracted by the same contemptible jealousies, resulting from state or sectional pride, which were among the minor causes of the rebellion. But, though that error was corrected by the commingling of regiments from different states in the same brigade organization, we did commit the error of forming two grand armies, each composed of troops exclusively from the Eastern and Western States. The Army of the Potomac was the representative army of the Northeastern States, being composed almost exclusively of Eastern men. The Army of the Tennessee was composed of men from the West, and, as it existed under General Grant, was properly the representative army of the West. The same army was *dovetailed* with that of the Cumberland, and placed under General Sherman, and at the time of its dissolution was not so clearly a representative army, Sherman having impressed his own manner on his men, and made them a peculiar and not exactly proper type of the Western soldier. The contrast between the men of these two armies of the East and West, in *physique*, habits, discipline, and *morale*, was so apparent that it is difficult to conceive that they did not belong to different nationalities. Any comparison which would assert the superiority of either army in endurance, courage, or fighting qualities would be invidious and untrue, for the men of both sections fought with equal effect and won equal honor; but it is undeniable that the Potomac Army was by far the best disciplined army we ever had in the field. The Potomac Army rivaled the regulars in evolutions, while Sherman's Western boys, with their careless, free, easy gait, would outmarch a battalion of the hardiest of the old regulars. The Potomac men did not march as well as Sherman's troops; they had less of the elastic spring of Western men, were perhaps too exact, and disposed to be too stiff and prim, but they marched with a precision equal to the regulars of any army. McClellan taught the Potomac Army the pure discipline of the old regulars, and it would have required but little more of such teaching to make them all that is expected of such troops; but Sherman, forcible a tutor as he is, could never hope to transform them into " bummers." General McClellan would have failed, as General Buell did, in making regulars of the Western volunteers; and I very much doubt if any of the old army officers who remained constantly in the service, and who had become confirmed in the ideas of the Academy, could have succeeded in making effectives of the Western men in the short time that Grant and Sherman did. The success of Grant appears to have been much influenced by his absorption, during his long residence in the West, of the elements of the Western character, and the toning down of the West Point precision in his education. The same may be said of Sherman. No army of the country was under better control, or committed fewer excesses, than the Army of the East, as the Potomac force should have properly been called. No army committed so many useless excesses as did that of General Sherman, and in none was the discipline so lax, yet no army could be more implicitly trusted in the emergencies of battle than Sherman's Army of the West. The Potomac Army wore kid gloves off duty, and had the air of an exquisite on parade, but this exquisite was a proficient in the warlike arts, was always ready to fight, and did not hesitate to accept battle with courage and confidence equal to that of its rougher ally of the West. The Army of the West cared nothing for appearances, wore a slouched hat and a loose blouse, and had the air of careless ease and indifference which we often see in the pioneer. The Western veteran had more care for his rifle than his uniform, paid more attention to his cartridge-box than his carriage, and heartily despised drill and parade. The Western troops lacked culture, they had less respect for "the proprieties" than the Eastern troops, and the relations of officer and man were maintained by them with less of the strictness that is due to proper discipline than among Eastern troops. The Eastern men were very particular regarding their dress, and displayed their badges and medals with commendable pride. They devoted many hours to the adornment of their camps, and nothing could have been more beautiful and picturesque than many of their old camps in the Southern pine country. The decorations were generally made with the evergreens which abound in the South, but often mechanical contrivances operated by the wind produced picturesque and curious effects. They indulged in gymnastic and ball exercises to a great extent, and were very fond of horse-racing and the higher order of games at cards. The amusements of the Western troops were of a ruder character. Cock-fighting and card-playing were the chief recreations. Every man was armed with a pack of cards, and each company boasted a fighting-cock, while every brigade had its fast horse. The Western soldier had a clearer appreciation of the practical than the picturesque, and their camps were seldom or never decorated as were those of the Eastern men. Practice with the pistol was a frequent amusement in the Western Army. Cats and dogs seemed to be necessaries of camp life. "Company" and "head-quarter" cows were a common article of pets, and the evidences of care, kindness, and affection shown for them by their self-constituted proprietors were often very amusing. In the Western Army fighting-cocks were favorite pets, and they were almost as numerous as the men themselves. During the campaign in the Carolinas General Sherman gave one of his attendants permission to occupy a wagon with his spoils, chiefly consisting of fighting chickens. He was very much astonished to find, in a few days, that the one wagon had increased to a dozen, other followers having also employed a wagon or two to carry their spoils. The general immediately ordered them to be burned, and executed the order with a remorseless hand until he came to the wagon he had originally permitted. He was about to burn this too, as it had been the bad example which was plead in excuse for the others, when he was appealed to to spare that, as "it contained all the head-quarter fighting-cocks." Sherman occasionally enjoyed the sport himself, and the appeal saved the wagon and chickens. Card-playing was common among the veterans from both the East and West, but the style of games played varied according to the education of the men. Among the Eastern troops, " Whist" and " Euchre" were the favorite games; among the Western men, " Poker" and "Seven up," invariably for money, were popular. Gambling was the great vice of the veterans, as jealousy was the great crime of their generals. Immediately after the appearance of the pay-master, the troops of both armies invariably indulged in cards as persistently and as regularly as the generals did in bickering after a battle.

Here the contrast ends and the comparison begins. The Eastern and Western men had many peculiarities in common, and the cause of the existing differences, education, produced the similarities. The fighting qualities of each were the same. Both armies went into battle with the same resolute air of men of business, and, under the same leaders, each displayed equal endurance. Grant was instrumental in showing the equality existing in this respect, and at the same time he smothered a painful feeling which at one time existed in the West, based on the ill success of the Potomac Army under former leaders, and finding expression in the idea that the Eastern troops did not fight as well as the Western men. This feeling

at one time threatened to become a serious sectional difficulty, when General Grant took immediate control over
the Potomac Army, and infused his spirit of persistence
into it. The discipline of the Potomac Army men amid
the continually recurring disasters of the first three years
of the war, their firmness under defeat or questionable
success, was always admirable, and it only required the
tutorship of Grant to prove their endurance, and make
them the admiration of the whole country. That army
always confronted the best of the rebel armies at the key-
point of the field. It fought more battles than any other
two armies in the field. Grant added the only lesson it
needed to make its education perfect, and taught it, as
he had taught the Army of the Tennessee, how to display its endurance by showing it how to fight its battles
through.

The same cause, education, which produces this marked distinction, may also be observed as tracing a difference between either of these classes in our army and a
third class—a mere fraction, however—representing the
Southern element. In the Union army there have been
from the first a number of Southern Unionists, generally
mountaineers and refugees from the East Tennessee regions, who, according to all statistics and observation,
were uneducated and ignorant, and whose lax discipline
has more than once caused slurs to be cast upon the
army. In camp they were unclean, on the march they
were great stragglers, and in battle untrustworthy and
ineffective. Only the very strict discipline of one or two
regular officers assigned to their command redeemed the
character of a few of these regiments from this general

reputation. The men of this class were not superior to the rebel soldiers in any respect.

It is not to be inferred, from any argument used to · show that an educated man makes a better soldier than an uneducated one, that discipline was neither demanded nor enforced in our army of educated soldiers. The thorough discipline of the Union army made it invincible. Its superiority to that of the rebels was the result only of the higher discipline which they were capable, through education, of receiving, and which was thoroughly enforced. From the very moment that the Bull Run · defeat violently dissipated the fallacies which we entertained of a brief and bloodless struggle, and taught the country that a long and terrible war was before it, the army, with a dogged perseverance of which our mercurial people did not believe themselves capable, went directly to work to discipline itself. The ineffectives were rooted out by the surgeons, and sent home or to the hospital. Regiments were reduced in numbers, but increased in efficiency. What was lost in numerical strength was more than gained in the effectiveness which resulted from the stricter discipline which was instituted. Incompetent officers of the line were forced to give place to their betters. This soon extended to higher ranks, and bad generals were supplanted by better. There was little system in our first choice of generals. We blundered on until the right man was found at last, and through him the proper subordinates were chosen. At first the blunders were serious, and men with false ideas of the crisis were thrust forward by circumstances, to be discovered at fearful cost and after long delay. With

portions of the army discipline was allowed to degenerate into mere drill, and devotion to the cause became di-
vided with devotion to a popular leader; while in other
parts of the country the forces, though thoroughly drill-.
ed, felt no admiration or love for their leader, or were
never taught that confidence in their commanders which
is at the root of all discipline. It was the fault of the
Western armies that too little attention was paid to the
moral sentiments of the men, and that in the Eastern
Army the thoroughly-taught sentiment of devotion to the
cause was permitted to partially degenerate into love of
the leader. Circumstances, however, soon corrected these
great evils, and through much tribulation, numerous dis-
heartenings, and many defeats, the men slowly became
veterans.

A thorough system of discipline was necessary not
only to the organization and *morale,* but to the courage
of our army, as it is of any large body of men. Men in
battle are not individually courageous. Courage amid
the horrors and under the conflicting emotions of the
battle-field is as much derived from discipline as from
nature. The fact that this war affords more numerous
instances of personal heroism displayed in battle than
any other which can be recalled, does not disprove the
rule. On the contrary, it corroborates the assertion; for
if we closely inquire into the characters of those who
have distinguished themselves by heroic deeds and individual prowess, we shall find that they have invariably
been men confirmed in steady habits, and veterans of
thorough discipline. Courage is derived from the electric touch of shoulder to shoulder of men in the line.

As long as the current is perfect, extending through the line and concentrating in the person of the commander, whose mind directs all, and in whom all have perfect confidence, the line can not be defeated. It may be driven, may be broken, but the men are invincible. Break the current, and at once the *morale*, the discipline, and the courage break with it, and men that were a moment before invincible fly to the rear, not overcome by fright and terror, but with the dogged, stubborn, and gruff manner of disheartened men. A broken column in disordered flight is one of the most wonderful studies which can be conceived. The actuality is the very reverse of what the imagination would conceive. "Panic-stricken men," who will "fly" fifteen and twenty miles from a battlefield, proceed to execute that manœuvre in a manner as systematic as if they had been taught it. They "fly"— they run from the field—only until beyond the immediate reach of stray bullets. The flight is disordered. The men scatter for safety apparently with the same instinct that actuates quails to separate in rising from a field before the hunter. When beyond the reach of the enemy's guns, they are so scattered that it is almost impossible to rally them as they were formerly organized, and it is next to impossible to induce a demoralized man to fight with any other than his own regiment. When they are beyond the reach of the enemy's guns they generally halt, look back, and examine into matters. They will look about them, inquire for their regiments, talk of the danger from which they have escaped, and in a perfectly intelligible manner, until a stray bullet falling about them gives assurance that the enemy is advancing, when, without a word, they resume their retreat for a few hundred yards farther, deaf alike to the threats and entreaties of any officer who does not happen to be their immediate commander. Yet these men who are thus broken in one battle will fight with desperate courage in the next, and, retaining their organization, go through the engagement with great credit. Often circumstances, such as the former location of a camp near the battle-field, previous positions in the reserve line, the existence of rifle-pits, and various other localities which serve as a rallying-point, enable broken troops to re-form and again go into action. Men often rally on the part of an intrenched line which they formerly held; and one of the best uses to which rifle-pits have ever been put by offensive armies is that of forming a rallying-line when attacking troops fail or are broken. It is a use known only to the practice, and is not recognized by the theory of war.

Men under thorough discipline lose in a great measure their individuality. A regiment becomes as a single man, moved by a single impulse. The men individually are but fractions, each being able to perform their part of the task only by the aid of the others. These fractions are curious beings under fire. They perform deeds which it would be morally impossible for an individual without similar surroundings to accomplish. Thousands of our veterans will tell you that in going into battle they have never imagined nor felt that they were going to be shot; they have never felt as if in danger themselves, but that their fears are for the comrades with whom they march shoulder to shoulder. They become painfully indifferent in regard to themselves, and appear to have none of those apprehensions with which they were so terrified when they were raw recruits. They swear as usual, with perhaps a little more emphasis, laugh at the comic features which prevail under all circumstances of battle, talk freely and sensibly, and do not betray any more, nor as much excitement as every one has witnessed in crowds at political and other gatherings. I have seen men in the "second line"—the reserves—playing cards while the first were receiving a charge, and the spent shots were dropping in their midst.   While the hardest fighting was going on at Chattanooga, November 25th, 1863, I saw three soldiers sitting near the guns of Callender's battery engaged, while under fire, in making entries in their diaries. This is a sight seen only in the ranks of the United States armies. During the battle of Murfreesborough, Tennessee, the rebels, in making a charge upon General Negley's division, frightened from the fields and woods a large number of rabbits, quails, and wild turkeys, driving them toward the Union lines. The birds appeared too frightened to fly, and, following the example of the rabbits, hopped and jumped over the field, escaping from the advancing rebels. They fled, of course, toward the rear, passing through and over our front line, and approached the reserve troops, who, without any reference to the fact that the rebel balls were now falling like great drops of rain among them, laid down their guns and went to capturing wild fowls. While still engaged in this employment, laughable even under the serious circumstances, the first line of our troops was broken, and the rebel soldiers charged upon the second. The veteran soldiers abandoned the chase of the wild-fowl, and, falling hastily

into line, thrice repulsed the advancing enemy. One of
the men who had captured a wild turkey carried it to
Lieutenant Kennedy, of General Negley's staff, and sold
it to him. Kennedy tied the bird to his saddle, intending to have it for supper that night, but was surprised to
find that a stray bullet had cut the strings by which the
turkey had been suspended, and robbed him of a meal.

No greater contrast can be conceived than the difference in the effect produced on soldiers when delivering
and receiving an assault. In receiving an attack they
are never quiet, although cool, composed, and self-possessed. Put them behind breast-works to receive an assault, and the preparations of the enemy for the attack
creates among those awaiting it an anxiety which devel-
ops into mental excitement, which finds vent in words,
noisy disputes, etc. Going to the assault, the same men
are different beings. The silence which prevails becomes
painful. A command given at one end of the line can
be distinctly heard at the other. The men become serious, and are disposed to be gruff. They converse but
little, and then in under-tones. They begin to understand what is to be done, that they are to do it, and,
without for a moment fearing to test the questions of defeat or victory, they carefully weigh in their own minds
the chances, not of life, but of success.

The most remarkable illustration of this peculiarity of
veteran troops which I can recall occurred during Sherman's battle at Chattanooga. Leaving a fortified line,
the Union troops of Colonel Loomis and Generals Ma-
thias, Corse, and Raum were required to cross a small
valley and assault a rebel fort located on a steep hill,

three hundred feet high, and of very rugged ascent. When the troops selected moved out in the line of reserves and marched down into the valley, the rebels, having full view of the column, grew excited and noisy. The orders of their officers were shouted, and were plainly heard in our lines, and, though it was impossible for the assaulting column to prepare for its work under an hour's time, the rebels evinced every indication of excitement, rushing hither and thither, and growing noisier every moment. The Union troops, on the contrary, prepared for the work slowly and quietly, with an unusually serious and composed air. They glanced up ever and anon at the steep hill before them, and many doubtless compared the mountain to the Walnut Hills of Vicksburg, where they met their first repulse. The assault was made in as serious a manner as the preparations. There was no breath wasted in loud cries. The men twice assaulted with desperate courage, were badly repulsed by a flanking force, and driven in confusion across the valley to their line of reserves, but, as they came back, passing through General Sherman's field-quarters, they looked as defiantly as ever, admitting no more than "that they had failed *this* time." There was no panic, no despair. They saw they had failed from sheer inability, not a want of effort or disposition to accomplish their task. They retreated, but not rushing wildly far to the rear. The powerful aided the weak, the strong bore off the wounded, and each came back as he had advanced, cool, composed, and serious.

The veteran when in camp had no curiosity. His indifference to matters going on around him was positively appalling to a stranger or a raw recruit. They would often be in camp for a month without knowing or caring what regiment was encamped next to them. A raw recruit of two months' standing was better authority on all *on dits* of camp, the location of other regiments, the names of their officers, and similar general information, than a veteran of three years' standing. The veteran laughed at the knowledge of the raw recruit, wondered where the utility of that information was, boasted of superior practical knowledge, and good-naturedly taught the raw recruit the more useful lessons of how to march easily, sleep well, provide himself with little luxuries, and how to take care of himself generally. The veteran had curious modes of making himself comfortable, which the raw recruit learned only from practice. Camp the veteran in a forest over night, and he would sleep under his shelter-tent raised high and made commodious, and on a soft bed of dry leaves. Encamp him for a month in the same forest, and he would live in a log house, sleep on good clean straw, dine off a wooden table, drink from glassware made from the empty ale or porter bottles from the sutler's tent, comb his whiskers before a framed looking-glass on a pine-board mantle-shelf, and look with the air of a millionaire through a foot and a half square window-frame on the camped world around him. The rebels used to call our men, when working on forts, rifle-pits, etc., "beavers in blue." The veteran was a regular beaver when building his house. He would buy, beg, or steal from the quarter-master (a species of theft recognized by the camp code of morals as entirely justifiable) the only tool he needed, an axe. With this he would cut, hew,

P 2

dig, drive—any thing you like, in fact. With his axe he would cut the logs for his cabin—miniature logs, two inches in diameter—trim them to the proper length, and drive the necessary piles. With his axe he would cut the brushwood or the evergreen, and thatch his roof. With his axe he would dig a mud-hole in which to make his plaster for filling the crevices of the logs, and thus shut out the cold. Doors, chimneys, benches, chairs, tables, all the furniture of his commodious house, he would make with the same instrument. When all was finished, he would sit comfortably down on his cot and laugh at the superficial knowledge of the raw recruit who had been shivering in his shelter-tent, looking on in amazement at the magical labors of the "beavers in blue."

If Napoleon could revisit the "glimpses of the moon," he would doubtless laugh—perhaps his nephew really does laugh at the idea of our calling the victors of this short-lived rebellion "veterans"—or with that sternness with which he once reproved his marine secretary, Truget, for propagating "the dangerous opinion that a soldier could be trained to all his duties in six months," the first Napoleon would ask us, with a look of imperial scorn, to show him in our boasted army a *corps* like the eighteen thousand troops of the French Monarchy that under his discipline became the Old Guard, which "died, but never surrendered." Julius Cæsar would doubtless smile at our presumption, and point to the old veteran legions of his armies with which he overran Europe, and into which no recruit was admitted until after eight years' service and discipline in other ranks, and ask us for veterans like his. Our soldiers were not, perhaps, the veterans for Napoleon or Cæsar, nor for such purpose as those of Napoleon or Cæsar, but they were such veterans as perished with Leonidas at Thermopylæ, and won victory in following Arnold Von Wilkenried in the mountain passes of Switzerland. Nothing can be sublimer than the patient heroism displayed by the veterans of the "War for the Union;" and when Time shall have hallowed, as it will, the yet familiar scenes of that struggle, tinting the story with a hue of romance, rounding the irregularities in the characters of the leaders, and toning down the rude points in the characters of the men, forgetting their excesses and remembering only their devotion and daring, the heroes and veterans who fought for the unity of the land will loom up as sacred in our eyes as are those who, in ages past, fought for its independence and liberty.

INDEX.

THE END.

Valuable & Interesting Books

Kinglake's Crimean War. The Invasion of the Crimea : its Origin, and an Account of its Progress down to the Death of Lord Raglan. By ALEXANDER WILLIAM KINGLAKE. With Maps and Plans. 2 vols. Vol. I. Maps. 12mo, Cloth, $2 00.

Abbott's Napoleon Bonaparte. The History of Napoleon Bonaparte. By JOHN S. C. ABBOTT. With Maps, Woodcuts, and Portraits on Steel. 2 vols., 8vo, Cloth, $10 00.

Szabad's Modern War. Modern War: its Theory and Practice. Illustrated from Celebrated Campaigns and Battles. With Maps and Diagrams. By EMERIO SZABAD, Captain U.S.A. 12mo, Cloth, $1 50.

Noyes's the Bivouac and Battle-field. The Bivouac and Battle-field; or, Campaign Sketches in Virginia and Maryland. By Captain GEORGE F. NOYES. 12mo, Cloth, $1 50.

Russell's American Diary. My Diary North and South. By WILLIAM HOWARD RUSSELL, LL.D. 8vo, Cloth, $1 00.

General Scott's Infantry Tactics ; or, Rules for the Exercise and Manoeuvres of the United States Infantry. Published by Authority. 3 vols., 24mo, Cloth, $3 00.

Butterfield's Camp and Outpost Duty. Camp and Outpost Duty for Infantry. With Standing Orders, Extracts from the Revised Regulations for the Army, Rules for Health, Maxims for Soldiers, and Duties of Officers. By Major-General DANIEL BUTTERFIELD, U.S.A. 18mo, Cloth, 60 cents. (Suited for the Pocket.)

Alison's Life of Marlborough. Military Life of John, Duke of Marlborough. With Maps. 12mo, Cloth, $1 75.

Story of the Peninsular War. By General CHARLES W. VANE, Marquis of Londonderry, &c. New Edition, revised, with considerable Additions. 12mo, Cloth, $1 50.

Carleton's Buena Vista. The Battle of Buena Vista, with the Operations of the "Army of Occupation" for One Month. By Captain CARLETON. 12mo, Cloth, $1 25.

Alison's History of Europe. First Series.—From the Commencement of the French Revolution, in 1789, to the Restoration of the Bourbons in 1815. [In addition to the Notes on Chapter LXXVI., which correct the errors of the original work concerning the United States, a copious Analytical Index has been appended to this American Edition.] SECOND SERIES.—From the Fall of Napoleon, in 1815, to the Accession of Louis Napoleon, in 1852. A New Series. 8 vols., 8vo, Cloth, $16 00.

Motley's Dutch Republic. The Rise of the Dutch Republic. A History. By JOHN LOTHROP MOTLEY, LL.D., D.C.L. With a Portrait of William of Orange. 3 vols., 8vo, Cloth, $9 00.

Motley's United Netherlands. History of the United Netherlands: from the Death of William the Silent to the Synod of Dort. With a full View of the English-Dutch Struggle against Spain, and of the Origin and Destruction of the Spanish Armada. By JOHN LOTHROP MOTLEY, LL.D., D.C.L., Author of "The Rise of the Dutch Republic." 2 vols., 8vo, Cloth, $6 00.

Hildreth's History of the United States. First Series.—From the First Settlement of the Country to the Adoption of the Federal Constitution. SECOND SERIES.—From the Adoption of the Federal Constitution to the End of the Sixteenth Congress. By RICHARD HILDRETH. 6 vols., 8vo, Cloth, $18 00.

It is a work of real historical value, the result of accurate criticism, written in a liberal spirit, and from first to last deeply interesting.—*Athenæum.*

The style is excellent, clear, vivid, eloquent; and the industry with which original sources have been investigated, and through which new light has been shed over perplexed incidents and characters, entitles Mr. Motley to a high rank in the literature of an age peculiarly rich in history.—*North British Review.*

It abounds in new information, and, as a first work, commands a very cordial recognition, not merely of the promise it gives, but of the extent and importance of the labor actually performed on it.—*London Examiner.*

Mr. Motley's "History" is a work of which any country might be proud.—*Press* (London).

Mr. Motley's History will be a standard book of reference in historical literature.—*London Literary Gazette.*

Mr. Motley has searched the whole range of historical documents necessary to the composition of his work.—*London Leader.*

This is really a great work. It belongs to the class of books in which we range our Grotes, Milmans, Merivales, and Macaulays, as the glories of English literature in the department of history. * * * Mr. Motley's gifts as a historical writer are among the highest and rarest.—*Nonconformist* (London).

Mr. Motley's volumes will well repay perusal. * * * For his learning, his liberal tone, and his generous enthusiasm, we heartily commend him, and bid him good speed for the remainer of his interesting and heroic narrative.—*Saturday Review.*

The story is a noble one, and is worthily treated. * * * Mr. Motley has had the patience to unravel, with unfailing perseverance, the thousand intricate plots of the adversaries of the Prince of Orange; but the details and the literal extracts which he has derived from original documents, and transferred to his pages, give a truthful color and a picturesque effect, which are especially charming.—*London Daily News.*

M. Lothrop Motley dans son magnifique tableau de la formation de notre République.—G. GROEN VAN PRINSTERER.

Our accomplished countryman, Mr. J. Lothrop Motley, who, during the last five years, for the better prosecution of his labors, has established his residence in the neighborhood of the scenes of his narrative. No one acquainted with the fine powers of mind possessed by this scholar, and the earnestness with which he has devoted himself to the task, can doubt that he will do full justice to his important but difficult subject.—W. H. PRESCOTT.

The production of such a work as this astonishes, while it gratifies the pride of the American reader.—*N. Y. Observer.*

The "Rise of the Dutch Republic" at once, and by acclamation, takes its place by the "Decline and Fall of the Roman Empire," as a work which, whether for research, substance, or style, will never be superseded.—*N. Y. Albion.*

A work upon which all who read the English language may congratulate themselves.—*New Yorker Handels Zeitung.*

Mr. Motley's place is now (alluding to this book) with Hallam and Lord Mahon, Alison and Macaulay in the Old Country, and with Washington Irving, Prescott, and Bancroft in this.—*N. Y. Times.*

THE authority, in the English tongue, for the history of the period and people to which it refers.—*N. Y. Courier and Enquirer.*

This work at once places the author on the list of American historians which has been so signally illustrated by the names of Irving, Prescott, Bancroft, and Hildreth.—*Boston Times.*

The work is a noble one, and a most desirable acquisition to our historical literature.—*Mobile Advertiser.*

Such a work is an honor to its author, to his country, and to the age in which it was written.—*Ohio Farmer.*

Published by *HARPER & BROTHERS,*

Franklin Square, New York.

Carlyle's Frederick.

HISTORY OF FRIEDRICH II., called Frederick the Great. By THOMAS CARLYLE, *Author of a "History of the French Revolution," "Oliver Cromwell," &c. With Portraits and Maps. Complete in Six Volumes.* 12*mo, Cloth,* $2 00 *per Volume.*

Mr. Carlyle is about the only living writer whose opinions are of value even when it is impossible to agree with them. No one is more fond than he of paradox, but few men's paradoxes hint at so important truths. No one with a more autocratic dogmatism sets up strong men as heroes, or condemns the hapless possessors of pot-bellies to infamy; but then his judgments, even when they can not be confirmed, always enforce some weighty principle which we were in danger of forgetting. And if it sometimes happens that neither the hero nor the principles commend themselves, still the thoroughness of the execution, and the fire with which all his writings are instinct, never fail to make a great work.—*London Review.*

He writes history just as no man but Carlyle can write it, and for this reason his history will be widely held in great admiration. We should never turn to this so much for a history of Frederick as for Carlyle: he gives us himself emphatically, amusingly, unquestionably, in these pages; yet he picks up facts to illustrate the life of his hero and his times that no other man would have thought of touching, and to the thinking mind these facts are full of the bone and sinew of history.—*Evening Post.*

History, in the true sense, he does not and can not write, for he looks on mankind as a herd without volition and without moral force; but such vivid pictures of events, such living conceptions of character, we find nowhere else in prose. The figures of most historians seem like dolls stuffed with bran, whose whole substance runs out through any hole that criticism may tear in them; but Carlyle's are so real that, if you prick them, they bleed.—*North American Review.*

When Carlyle writes a book we only look into it to see Carlyle, not the subject of which he writes. He stands up among authors like a knarled and sturdy oak, full of all sorts of fantastic shapes, ridiculous oddities that denote a superabundance of vigor in his growth—a vigor that will not be confined by the laws of ordinary life. Frederick, as seen through the eyes of Carlyle, will and does possess the attributes of a god that never existed among men. This book will seize the big-eared world, and compel it to listen.—*Boston Post.*

Probably the History of Frederick will forever remain one of the finest pieces of literary painting, as well as one of the most marvelous attempts at special pleading, extant in our own or any language.—*London Spectator.*

The *redacteur* can not adequately convey, in the short space allotted him, a conception of the masterly thought, the comely diction, the astute philosophy, which manifest themselves on every page of this last product of Carlyle's scholarly researches and gifted intellect. There are some publications submitted to his examination which, because of their incorporate, inherent power, can not receive from his pen a satisfactory mentioning of. "Frederick the Great" is one of them. Let the reviewer be never so succinct and comprehensive in the expression of his critical opinions, he can simply marvel in silence at the graphic details (as in the book now under our thumbing) of plots and campaigns, in cabinet council or on field of battle, which captivate his attention, and then do what we most sincerely desire in this respect—enjoin upon every reader an earnest perusal of the same. And this is the best, nay, *all*, that he can do.—*Home Journal.*

Carlyle is, indeed, quaint and odd; but he is no less earnest, and true, and noble, and grand. He is the one specimen of his kind, we really believe, of philosophers, historians, and poets. Of course we find his peculiarities all through the great work, and equally of course we find it profoundly interesting in matter and piquant in style.—*Episcopal Recorder.*

Mr. Carlyle has at last completed his graven image, and sets it up for the admiration of the world. The Smelfunguses and Dryasdusts, whom Carlyle delights to ridicule, have been great helps to him in gathering up the details of a life which at best was unamiable, if not brutal; stern and unlovely, if not repulsive—the life of a man whose love for war in the field was carried into the closet, and penetrated the gentler seclusion of the family circle. Mr. Carlyle, with that amazing fancy for hero-worship in which he excels, would force us to believe his paragon all that he paints him; and there is certainly power in the picture. The old records have been most thoroughly sifted by Carlyle, who seems to have eliminated every grain of wheat from bushels of chaff.—*Examiner and Chronicle.*

The reader is out of patience with him in almost every page, yet reads him through to the end, and closes the book still wishing for more. He is a man of tremendous prejudices and partialities. Frederick is one of his heroes. Carlyle, however, has reasons always to give for his likes and dislikes, and one is sure to be interested in the argument, whether he accepts the conclusion or not.—*Christian Times and Witness.*

Published by HARPER & BROTHERS, New York.

HARPER & BROTHERS *will send the above work by mail, postage prepaid, to any part of the United States, on receipt of the price.*

9 783337 219017